Down the Lane

Down the Lane

By Paul Lafferty

Printed in the United States of America

ISBN 978-0-9939950-9-5

Cover Image by Sushipumpum via Flickr

Chapter I

Twilight

I feel terrible. Truly, deeply, sincerely, genuinely, mind-bendingly terrible. It's like I have every symptom of a hangover amplified for a stadium crowd. And, as awful as it is, it has actually become my routine. I'm on Day 28 of what seems like a never-ending series of shifts because we're down to two DJs at Twilight.

And every strip club needs a DJ on duty from the time its doors open until they close again. As if that wasn't enough work, I still have to fill in as a doorman and am also expected to help run the club. I've been doing doubles on Mondays, Wednesdays, Fridays and Saturdays, along with night shifts the other days of the week. I'm supposed to be off Tuesdays, but it hasn't been possible for a while.

Of course, that never stopped me from going out after work. One of the many things this job has taught me is that the harder you work, the greater your desire to burn off energy afterward.

So, last night, I closed the bar and went straight to the Beerhouse (missing last call there is never an issue) and then to the hotel next door to lose 700 bucks playing cards. I usually stay in the game until about noon or whenever I would run out of cash, but around 5 this morning, I remembered that on top of all the other shit, I had to open the bar early with Vince, my boss, to interview a replacement DJ. So, I left the game early and tried to make it home for a little nap – just enough sleep to make me feel like shit when I woke up.

I have a pretty decent basement apartment in a quiet neighborhood. There are cops on either side of us, so it leads to a few dirty looks when some of the guys show up.

The house is owned by Max, the head bartender at Heart's Desire and one of my drinking buddies. He's an all-around good guy. He can drink with anyone but is smart enough to not get involved in too much else.

I've been living here for almost two years and have never had a major argument with the guy. Just about everyone else I know in the business has kids, lives in some shit hole or still is at home with their parents. Max is much easier for me to relate to.

Max and I had worked together at Heart's for years; until I decided to leave to run another club.

That was a decision I'm now starting to regret. It has its upside, though. The girls jump ship all the time, so all I have to do is pick up the phone and ask him who Max has working. That allows me to avoid seeing anyone I don't want to see. My on-again, off-again girlfriend, Jenny, works there, and it's just easier to pick up the phone and find out if she's there. If things are good with us, I'll stop by. If they're not, then I'll skip going in.

Max gets the same privileges at my club, Twilight. After a marriage and divorce in the span of six months, it seemed that he was banging every chick in both places, so he had to be careful.

I stumble upstairs and smell coffee. Max is one of those guys who can crash at 3 a.m. and still be up by 9. I am not. His coffee smells great but tastes like shit. So, I reach in the fridge for a Coke and some orange juice.

Max nods and gives me a look. "What?" I ask him.

"Nothing ..." he says, lighting a cigarette.

Between the coffee and the cigarettes, I think I'm going to be sick.

"... just that Tuesday is your day off, and you're usually not up before five in the afternoon ..."

That was true. I would usually make it home from Monday's drinking sometime on Tuesday, and sleep until dinnertime. I would get up, pay some bills, eat and go back to bed. What the hell, it worked for me.

"... and you came home alone."

He was right on both counts. More and more often these days, I just wanted to come home and crash. Did I sample the girls? Of course I did. Who wouldn't? But lately it just seemed less and less fun, and I preferred waking up alone.

"Yeah, well," I started, "I knew I had to go in today, so I tried to get some sleep." Max usually didn't ask too many questions. "Why are you asking?" I wanted to get the emphasis off me. "What did I do now?"

"Nothing," he said, with a pause. "But Jenny was pissed you never showed, and Chris and Stevie were looking for you."

Chris and Stevie had been my close friends since childhood. We had gone through pretty much everything together, but lately they've been hanging with the Burnt, a local motorcycle club. Most of their guys are from around here, so there's usually not a problem – they are strong supporters of the old adage about not shitting where you eat.

Hanging with the club hasn't changed Chris too much, but it's turned Stevie into a real dick.

Jimmy, the president of the local chapter, is an OK guy. We're on friendly terms. It seems to piss Stevie off that I can talk to Jimmy and he can't. Stevie's just a prospect for the club, and they do what they're told. He's not allowed to speak to Jimmy unless Jimmy speaks to him first. And, even if that does happen, Stevie knew that he couldn't say much more than "yes, sir."

A little while back, when I thought I might want to join Burnt, Jimmy laughed at me and said: "Well, well, well, the teacher wants to join. Won't work guy. You've got too big a mouth and you're too smart for these idiots. Finish your teaching degree and get the fuck out of this shit."

Because of that conversation, my nickname became Doc — and it became the name I used when I wrestled. How getting my teaching degree turned me into Doc, I don't know. But Jimmy did say these guys weren't too sharp.

Even so, if they were looking for me, it was something I would have to deal with. "Couldn't have been important," I told him. "Everybody knows where to find me on a Monday." My Monday routine hadn't changed in years: Work the day shift, watch some wrestling, hit the bars and then play cards at the Imperial Hotel.

"Yeah, well, Stevie is becoming a real dick," Max added, as though I wasn't just thinking that. "Gianni wants me to ban him from the bar." Gianni was Max's friend, and he owned Heart's. A lot of guys hated him, considered him a cheap douche bag, but he was always OK with me. After all the shit I pulled when I was working there and after I walked out on him when he needed me, I'm surprised he never tried to ban me. I think it had less to do with my sparkling personality than it had to do with the fact that he didn't want to deal with guys like Stevie. Once guys like him became full members of a gang, they were damn near impossible to get rid of. Hanging out with them but trying to stay out of their business was a balancing act I sometimes couldn't pull off.

That's when I knew where this line of questioning was headed. "Can you talk to him?" Max asked. What a way to start my day. Hey, roomie, he was essentially asking me, you know those two nut jobs you're always with? Can you tell them to knock it off with the bullshit?

"Yeah, I'll try," I told him, hoping he realized what an imposition it was. "But this whole biker thing is making talking to either one a fuckin' pain in the ass."

I just left the table to get ready for work when the doorbell rang. I never answered the door. I usually didn't want to talk to anyone. When Herbie got up to answer it, I could hear friendly conversation. "Hey, Vince is here," he let me know with a shout.

Vince Bruno was my boss. At 6-foot-5 and 325 pounds, all Vince usually had to do was stand up and guys would shut the fuck up. A major Division 1 football star, he was drafted by the New Orleans Saints, but blew his knee out in his first season. I know what you're thinking: Yeah, sure, lots of guys tell stories like that. But Vince has a rookie football card to prove it.

"Ready to go, fuckhead?" I'd been working with him for almost six months and he had never called me by my first name. "I wanted to make sure you made it in," he said, answering a question that wasn't asked but hung in the air like stink. We all knew that if I blew off the shift, he would have to get on the stick (what we DJs call a microphone). Over the years, he had done everything there was to do in a club but refused to DJ. I guess he was a little self-conscious, believe it or not.

"Yeah" I coughed out, "let's go."

We both walked out to Vince's car — a 1992 Corvette, black and always in immaculate condition. "Wipe your feet before you get in." Messing up the Corvette probably wasn't a smart idea. I got in and pulled out a smoke from behind my ear. He looked at me, took it and tossed it out the window. I grabbed another and lit it before he could grab it. He snatched it, took a drag and cuffed me in the ear. "No smoking in the 'Vette, idiot, now listen." There was no preamble with Vince. He always got right to the point. "Stevie and Chris showed up last night, and I wound up tossing Stevie out."

Great, I thought, just what I needed. Two bulls that were going to piss everywhere to prove who is in charge.

"I'm only telling you this because I know they're your friends ..."

"Well" I started, trying to choose my words carefully, "Stevie can be a dick."

"He's a fucking idiot," Vince answered. "And now he's hanging out with those guys from Burnt — that doesn't mean shit to me." Vince seemed to fear no one, which is pretty easy when you're his size. "Why the fuck are you hanging out with these guys anyway?" he asked.

"I've known them since I was a kid." I answered with the verbal equivalent of a shrug.

"Well, if you get drawn into their shit and get arrested with them, you can kiss the teaching deal goodbye."

He was right. I was teaching English as a second language part time at Brock University in St. Catharines. Although I tried my best to blend in, I still got stares parking my Honda 750 in the staff lot. It was back in the days when BlackBerries were still new and expensive, and mine seemed to go off every 10 minutes some days. One of the older profs actually had the nerve to comment that only drug dealers carried "those things." So, after a while, I put it on vibrate. Not long after, I saw the old prof had gotten himself one, the fuckin' hypocrite.

Vince could tell I was lost in thought, so he punched me in the shoulder. "Talk around the office is that Arnie wants you to run the new club." Ah, yes, the elusive new club; allegedly the reason I had been hired away from Heart's Desire. When I found myself putting in time at Twilight instead of the new club, I was told these things didn't happen overnight. Once Vince saw I could handle any position in the club and rarely turned down an extra shift, I was promoted into management. The money was good and came with a promise it would only get better. Like I haven't heard that shit before.

Vince was still talking: "It's only a matter of time before one of your buddies asks you to sell coke for them, or slaps one of the broads around."

Now I was getting annoyed. "What am I supposed to do?" While I was making an honest effort to sound justifiably pissed off, I could tell that it came out more like the bleating of a petulant child. "Just stop hanging out with guys I've known since kindergarten?"

"That's not what I said," he started in on me. "Just put a little distance between you and them. Do you really need to go out every night? When's the last time you got home before noon after a night out? You look like a fuckin' zombie, man. When's the last time you hit the gym?"

I couldn't argue with him there. I was getting run down. I tried spending more time on the teaching, but that easy money at the club was hard to turn down. Sometimes it was long and tedious, but it was always lucrative. Even with all the fucking around I did, I always had money. If I was going jump out of this lifestyle, it would have to be soon.

We pulled into the club and I couldn't believe there were actually people in cars waiting in the parking lot. We're right next door to another strip club, the legendary, maybe even notorious, Sunrise. For all my partying and going out, I never dealt too much with those guys. It was owned by this old Polish guy and his sons. The sons were idiots, but that can happen when you grow up rich.

Between these two places a lot of money changed hands and I wanted my piece. The problem was that I was becoming less choosy all the time about how I made it. I realized that I had to start thinking of an escape plan.

Vince pulled up to his usual spot, second one in on the left, and started putting the roof up. "Look" he started again, a little friendlier this time, "you're a good guy, and I know how much fun this place can be. But it gets old real fast, and one wrong move and it's all fucked up for you. Arnie asked me who should run the new place, and I said you. Billy and Pete almost shit their pants." He laughed at his own comment.

Billy and Pete were the other two managers and they were not big fans of mine. Billy weighed in at about 400 pounds and always looked like he was just one greasy meal away from a heart attack. Pete was a tough guy, but not all that bright.

"Arnie isn't going to trust you with a new club if he thinks you're out partying all the time," Vince told me with an air of genuine concern.

But did I even want to run another club? The people around me obviously assumed I did, and I guess I kind of gave them that idea, but I wasn't sure.

"Think about what I said, Ian," he advised. "I'll back you on running the club, but if you fuck me, Stevie and Chris will be the least of your problems." That was the first time he ever called me by my first name.

Opening the bar in the morning usually took about 20 minutes. I've got to turn on all the TVs, the DJ equipment, unlock the doors, check the bathrooms and get the sign-in book. Every single girl now has to sign in and I'm supposed to check their ID. Since it's daytime, and usually always the same girls, I'm not as strict as I am at night. Most of the girls working daytime are a little older, although there are a few younger ones that work during the day for their own reasons. I learned a long time ago not to ask why, because the answer is usually one you don't want to hear. You must have heard the stereotype about the girl dancing because she's working her way through college. I haven't met one yet who actually finished. Most of these girls are so fucked up that going back to school never works out for them. They can't handle being told what to do. Their answer to everything is a $50 tip or a blow job. Maybe that works when you get pulled over late at night, but it usually doesn't get you a degree. After a few years in the business, I could count on one hand the girls I would consider friends away from the bar. It's even stopped me from fucking some. In the beginning I did every one of them I could, but I quickly learned that the few minutes of sex aren't worth the hours of bullshit you put up with later. Besides, this is still a small town. Being seen with one of these girls won't exactly move me up the social ladder.

One benefit of the job is that the buffet is up and running when I get there. We actually have a good kitchen, and a plate of food usually helps after a night of drinking. The idea of a buffet attracting customers is a little old and outdated. Strip clubs have always had a $5 breakfast, or steak or a buffet. These days, it brings in more losers than good customers. They basically come in for cheap food. My first rule here? You need to buy a drink. I don't care if it's a coffee or water, but you're getting a drink. Besides, everything costs as much as a beer, so it doesn't matter what you order. Enforcing that rule got rid of a lot of the bums and guys I didn't think should be in the place anyway. Next time you bitch about getting a $5 water? Yeah, that was me. You don't want to drink booze? Well, you're going to pay for it anyway.

Man, this is just what I needed, I thought to myself. The buffet has lasagna, fettuccine, some salad, a few odds and ends and some bread. I get a huge piece of lasagna smothered with sauce and a Coke. Fuck, I realized, I drink more Coke than most people do coffee. I haven't been up an hour, and this is already my third can.

I usually grab the phone and put it on the table, so I don't have to get up to answer it. Daytime has the phone ringing all day. Are you guys open? Is Sonya there? Did you guys find a wallet? What time is Millie on? Mainly it's pimps or old guys looking for their favorite girl. It's a fucking hassle and sometimes I just let the machine pick it up, which usually leads to Vince threatening to smash me in the head with the phone. Strangely the phone is quiet today, which means I can eat in peace.

The table directly in front of the DJ booth is tacitly reserved for the DJs and managers. It's where we sit during our breaks, to eat or just see what's going on in the club. It's almost dead center of the bar, so you can view the entire club, the exits and the entrance. It also allows us to see who's going in and out of the change room. Most of the excitement is back there. Think Saturday night in the club is wild? Try hanging out in the back with 75 naked girls.

Vince sits with me and puts down huge plate of food, coffee, and water. "So, professor, why aren't you teaching full-time anyway?" I guess calling me by my first name isn't going to be a regular thing.

Vince was one of the few guys in this business that I knew had an actual degree, although he admitted to me that he very rarely went to class. "Well," I began to answer, "I've got a B.A., which allows me to teach this English program, but I can't teach full-time until I finish my teaching degree. There's a program in Buffalo that gets you a master's degree and your teaching degree at the same time."

Vince didn't speak but gave me a look that indicated he needed some more explanation.

"And even with my B.A., I still need a science and math credit, which I never got."

"How the fuck did you get so far in school without math or science?" he asked.

"It was before everything was on computers, so I dodged and weaved my way around it. I always thought I would teach French, so I didn't worry about the other shit."

"So, go back and get those credits" he replied.

I started to laugh. "When?" I asked him. "I haven't had a day off in almost a month."

He thought about what I had just said but kept eating. "If I get you the time off, would you go back? Take one credit a term, then you can ease your way back in."

That actually wasn't a bad idea. Go back, start slowly, it could work. "You would have to hire a DJ right away," I answered, "and everyone who comes in here either sucks or gets fired for some other reason."

"There's a guy coming in today," he mumbled while swallowing the last bit of his lasagna. "So just hire the guy and train him. How hard can it be? Cody is going to be out of jail soon, so there will be three of you."

I had forgotten about Cody. He'd been in jail for a while and was due out soon. He'd worked here forever — and honestly wasn't all that great — but he'd promoted himself like a god and convinced the owner that he was indispensable. He might suck, but he would be back. I just might be able to pull this off. How fuckin long could it take?

While I was thinking about that and finishing my food, I realized it was time to start the show. As soon as a customer walks in, the owner wants a girl onstage. I understand his point. No girl dancing and guys are going to walk out. But it always leads to the same arguments. No girl wants to go first. They say things like: Why am I going on for just one guy? I haven't eaten yet! Why am I first? That bitch stole my song! So, I made a system. The same four or five girls always went on first, so they knew when they were up. Even that led to a whole new set of bullshit. They'd pick three-minute songs, go on a minute into the song or hide in the bathroom and pretend they didn't hear me. I'd worked most of it out after a while, so there was a minimum of headaches. I tried to bump them if I saw they had customers for private dances, but there were a few that just whined about everything. I would make sure that they would go on first, so I didn't have to deal with them later. You have to understand that this was a gig where they made $500 a day, but every one of them complained that they were always broke, and they just seemed intent on sharing their misery every chance they got.

Before long, the DJ applicant showed up. I was praying he wasn't an idiot.

"Hey," he opened with, "I'm Sean."

So far, so good. He didn't seem like a complete moron. He gave me a resume, but it didn't really tell me much. It just listed a whole bunch of clubs around Ottawa. "So," I asked, "any strip clubs?"

He just stood there. That's not a good sign.

"Well?" I asked again.

"No, just dance clubs," he answered.

"So why are you applying?" I asked.

"Well I hang out at Sunrise a lot," he offered dully. "Some of the girls there said you guys were always hiring."

Great. Just fucking great. No experience, and he's a guy who hangs around the clubs. "Listen," I started, "hanging out in these places and working here are two different things."

"I know ..." he tried to answer before I cut him off.

"I don't think you do. Do you have any idea how many guys I've fired? This is not like working in a regular club. It's fucked up all the time, and the DJ has to run the show. It's all on you, man. The girls fuck with you, the customers fuck with you, everyone fucks with you. It's not just throwing on the music. You actually have a show to run."

He had no answer, he just stood there. My little speech is usually enough to scare guys off all by itself. Maybe this one was trainable. Maybe I just really needed to give him a break. "Look," I told him, "let's give it a shot. But if you can't hack it, you're gone. Just sit back and listen to me so you can get a feel."

I let him hang out in the booth so he could see what was actually required. Three-song sets, I explained. On the first song, they just kind of walk around. On the second song, the audience gets to see a bit, and by the end of the third song, the girls should be completely naked. Sounds simple, right? It's not.

I put the first girl up and told the kid that the girls pay him directly. "You and you alone are responsible for your own money, and almost every one of them will try to stiff you one way or another. Talk a little in between songs, but not too much. You're not the show, the naked chick is." I also told him that I usually give the dancers an extra minute in between their second and third songs.

While I'm demonstrating that, Tara has decided to use her extra time to talk to one of her regular customers, wasting half the song until I finally scream at her to "get the fuck onstage!" through the booth doors.

Our next little princess storms off stage and demands to know why I'm not playing Number 7. When I tell her I am, she storms offstage to check the player, seeing, of course, Number 7. She offers no apologies, just sneers at me and jumps back onstage.

"See what I'm talking about?" I yell over the music. "And this is just the day shift. Wait 'til the night shift when you have 75 of these idiots screaming at you."

It was make-or-break time. I tell him to take the stick. He doesn't refuse, but he's clearly not happy about it. "Hey look, you're gonna suck," I tell him. "But if I think you can pull it off, then maybe it will work.

I figured I might as well sit in the middle of the bar and hear how this guy sounded. Marisa, the day waitress saw me sit down and brought me an Export. She had the hottest ass in the bar, could fight better than most guys I know, and could drink with the best of them. I tried a few times, but she wasn't interested so we became drinking buddies.

Late one night, Arnie offered her a thousand bucks just to get onstage and drop her pants. She flat out refused. When I asked her why a couple of days later, she shook her head. "As soon as these guys see my cheeks, I'll be just another broad in the bar. This way, I don't take my clothes off and I keep them guessing." Smart girl, although I have to admit, I'd still like to see that ass.

Man, that beer went down easy. Marisa knows her floor and brings me another as I'm just looking up to wave for another. "So, what do ya think? This guy got what it takes to hang with us?" Without hesitation, she offers, "Fuck no, he sucks."

I almost choke to death on my beer laughing. "Everyone sucks when they start," I offer in his defense.

"He won't cut it, he's too soft," she laughs and walks away.

He's not that bad, I think to myself. I could work with this guy. As I'm trying to decide what to do about the kid, Cody our DJ savior walks in, orders a tequila and a beer, and plops down at my table. "When did you get out?" I ask him.

He downs his shot and guzzles half the beer. "Just now," he starts a rapid-fire succession of half-finished thoughts. "Had the cops drop me off here. Who's the new guy? He sucks. Even you weren't that bad."

He turns and orders us two beers and two scotches because he knows I don't do tequila. "Me," he continues, shouting now, "I was always good!"

"Well," I reply, "I wasn't around in the 50s, so I'll just have to take your word for it."

After telling me to go fuck myself, he gets us both another beer and a shot. Fuck, it's 30 minutes after noon and I'm already drunk.

"Got anything?" Cody asks.

I knew what he meant. "Yeah, in my locker. Let's go."

As soon as he sees my coke, Cody breaks out two lines bigger than I had ever imagined, let alone seen.

"Well, fuck this guy," he says to nobody in particular and apropos of nothing. Then he pours another line of coke, just for himself. "I'm back," he says. "And I talked Arnie into hiring the kid back."

Fuck me, I thought. That's not good news.

Chapter 2

DJ Meeting

"Anyway," Cody spat out, "Arnie wants to see all of us as soon as Tyler gets here."

Fucking Cody obvious by now that he had planned this whole fucking thing, and it left me at a loss. "So," I had to ask, "when we're you going to tell me about this meeting?"

He waved for two more beers and shrugged, "I'm telling you now."

"If you're telling me now, you fucking idiot, it's obvious it's been in the works for a while," I shouted at him.

He just looked the other way. Cody was trying to justify his bullshit, as usual. "Look, you weren't hired as a DJ ..." he began.

Here we go again. These guys all thought they were stars, and they pulled the same lame old excuses out of the book any time they didn't get their way. Even now, I can hear the list of excuses in my head: "You need me," "people drink here because of me," "I'm the show," "I'm the only one that these girls listen to." I should have them all printed on a T-shirt.

But the truth was, not many guys could put up with this kind of work without snapping. Cody was getting old and fucked up for the game, but Tyler was the definitive example of a strip club DJ – always high, taking money, fucking the wrong broad. For some reason, Arnie liked Tyler and kept bringing him back.

No matter what, every conversation with one of these guys ended the same way; they'd always say I couldn't understand because I wasn't "really" a DJ. That might have been true in the beginning, but by the time Cody was pulling this shit, I had clocked enough time on the stick to be considered decent at it.

Frustrated, I couldn't hold it in any longer. I stood up and flipped the table over. The sound of the empties and the two full bottles tumbling onto Cody echoed loudly through the bar.

Vince, the boss, stormed out of the office and stared at the two of us, giving us both the old what-the-fuck look.

Everyone else in the club backed away, figuring things had just started between Cody and me.

Cody simply looked at Vince and said: "Fuck, your boy never could drink."

Vince just kept on staring, because he knew it had to be more than that.

I got up from the table and wondered how I should handle the situation. Then I remembered the new guy in the booth. It must have been quite a show for him. I went to the booth, figuring that the little scene would have chased this guy out. Just before I made it to the booth, Vince grabbed me by the arm. "What the fuck is the matter with you? You're acting like an asshole," he said.

"I'm acting like an asshole?" I shot back angrily. "When were you gonna tell me that Tyler was coming back?"

He just stood there for a minute. Either he didn't know what I was talking about or he was playing me. "Who told you that?" he replied.

"That's what Cody just said," I explained. "Fuck this place." I grabbed my cigarettes and jacket and started for the door. Vince stood in front of it and blocked my way. There was no way I was getting around him.

I took a breath and stepped back. "Why the fuck" I started, "would they bring him back? Just to fire him again? To throw him in my face? How many times have you guys fired him?" I was already starting to not give a shit about my own argument. It didn't matter.

Vince looked at Cody. "That piece of shit," he said. "You know it's Cody. He wants his little buddy to party with. I swear those two have some fucking bromance going on with each other."

That made me laugh a bit. Although I had no use for Tyler, Cody thought the world of him. Cody had been married four times, and I always thought that was part of the reason he was so fucked up and needy. I partied a bit with Cody, but I kept my private life out of here. Back at the other club, everyone pretty much got along. But this fucking place was filled with petty little jealousies, office politics and in-fighting.

It didn't help that I just didn't like Tyler. I'd worked with his wife years ago, at another club and he always came in acting like an asshole. After showing up way too high one night, he broke a bottle and threatened to shove it up my ass. He still had a little scar on his neck where the bottle hit him when I tried to shove it up his ass.

We waited for Arnie to show up to have this fucking meeting. Tyler walked into the booth like he owned the place and tried to bully his way on to the mic. I stood in front of the new guy and told Tyler "you haven't been hired back yet."

Tyler grinned and put out his hand, which I ignored. "nice to see you're still an asshole, Doc" he replied.

"Hey," I shot back, "your neck healed up nicely."

Tyler backed up and tried to look around me. "Who's the new guy?" he asked.

"Hopefully your replacement," I shot back.

"You know he's going to bring me back," the piece of shit grinned at me.

"And you know you're just gonna fuck it up and get fired again." I looked at the new guy and told him "look, we're going to this meeting, so just stay on the stick for a while."

The look on his face indicated that he didn't seem too sure about what was going on. I tried to assure him. "We'll all be down the hall. If something goes wrong, the office extension is 178."

He didn't reply, but it was clear that he wasn't too sure about this place. It's daytime, nothing would happen, I assured him.

Arnie finally showed up. Fucking guy weighed about 335 pounds, and always looked like he was on the verge of a heart attack. He was the definitive image of a strip club owner. He dressed like a pimp, wanted to be a mobster, and still shared an apartment with his mom. Those dinner conversations must have been great. "So, what happened at work today, son?" Mom would ask.

"Oh, not much," he could answer. "We thought one of the girls was having a seizure, but she was just choking on a condom." Not exactly pleasant dinner conversation.

Arnie stuck his head in the DJ booth window and told us to make our way into the office. The booth provided a great view of the floor and the stages, so you could see what was going on, but it also left you blindsided by anyone coming through the side door or the office. All the time, I'd be shocked by someone suddenly in the window yelling at me. I got used to listening for the side door to close so at least I knew I was about to get screamed at. If Vince knew I was in a bad mood, he would walk by the window pretending to be Cary Granite from the Flintstones. That always made me laugh.

Matt, another DJ who was scheduled to work that day, hadn't shown up yet, but that didn't matter. He only wanted a shift or so a week. Never really got to know him, but he seemed OK, and actually pulled a shift or two while Cody was in jail and I was losing my mind.

The two idiots walked ahead of me and I hung behind with Vince. Just before we made our way down the hall to Arnie's office, Vince grabbed my arm again, looked at me and tugged the skin under his eye. This was always his way of saying, look out, who know what the fuck is going to happen.

You had to cross through the kitchen to get to Arnie's office. Millie ran the kitchen. She was almost 20 years older than me and still had the hottest body in the whole club. She had called me out of the blue one night to come over. Ever since then, it was probably two nights a week. We'd take care of it, she'd make me something to eat and then kick me out.

But this whole friends-with-benefits, a late-night ass call shit never worked for me. Somebody would start caring a little too much or get a little too territorial.

We'd taken the next step a few weeks later and went out for dinner. Nothing had changed yet, she kept her mouth shut. But I couldn't help thinking it was going to blow up in my face.

When I walked in, she addressed me just like one of the guys, nothing special. She was definitely keeping it cool. But as I was the last to walk by, she asked me to help move something for her. As I reached down, she whispered: "My place, tonight. Don't come too late."

Yep, this was absolutely going to blow up later.

Arnie had a big circular desk that he sat behind, making him look kind of like Jabba the Hut. As usual, there were two girls hanging around. He looked at the girls and told them to beat it. Cody and Tyler sat across from him, Vince and I sat to his left.

Arnie looked at Cody and asked: "So, douche bag, make any new friends in Thorold?" Thorold, just down the road from the Twilight, housed the local jail. Any time you were given that was less than two years, you did your time in Thorold.

"Yeah, well," Cody replied, "they pretty much left me alone. Actually, there was this one guy ..."

"Yeah, anyway," Arnie interrupted, "let's get this done." He didn't give a shit about Cody's bit, it was just another chance to needle someone, prove he was the boss. "So, here's how it goes" Jabba Arnie started, "Cody gets his shifts back. Monday, Tuesday, Thursday and Friday night. Tyler takes Wednesday, both shifts. He also takes Saturday night. That fucking new guy, he gets Sunday day, Tuesday day, and Friday day."

What was this shit? I thought to myself. After holding this whole place together, I was getting the scraps. But I knew better than to complain. If I did, he would have taken all my shifts away. As a concession, Arnie told me I could take door shifts if money was tight. Great. I could go back to acting like an idiot in a bow tie for 50 bucks a night. “Is that it?” I asked as I got up, “I gotta go back to the booth and look after the new guy.”

“Fuck him,” Arnie spat out. “If he can’t handle it, we’ll get rid of him. Cody will train him. You take the rest of the day off. I’ve got something for you and Vince to do tomorrow.”

I walked out of the office, but Tyler felt he had to catch up to me and start in. “Schedule sounds good. Thanks for holding it together for us.”

That was too much. I spun around, separated Tyler from the others by turning my back on them, and gave my least favorite DJ a three-punch combo, one of the few things I remembered from karate class. The first left hit him in the eye, the right hit him in the chest, and the last left hit him square in the balls. He went down like a house of cards. I dropped down and put my knee on his throat. By now, normally, one of the others should have jumped in, but no one stopped me. It was Arnie’s little fucking game, to see how much I would put up with. I couldn’t hit Arnie, so this was the next best thing. “You’re going to fuck this up,” I said, “and one way or another, you’ll be gone. If you come near me again, I’ll fucking kill you.”

I thought Millie would run, but she just stood there and watched. Tyler had always tried with her, but never got anywhere. Without thinking, I stood up and said, “I’ll see you tonight” to her and left.

Now Tyler was back on his feet, screaming at me, with Cody holding him back. “I’ll fucking kill you!” he started to scream. I turned back to face him but thought better of it. I had already gotten away with enough.

Millie just stared and smiled.

I made my way back to the DJ booth. Vince gave me a minute to calm down before he walked in.

“Quite the display” Vince started. “What the fuck was I supposed to do?” I asked. “Put up with that shit? Fuck this, I don't need it." I started emptying my locker. "I've done everything I could to fit in, and I get fucked over by those two."

Vince just stared. "But now they know they can only push you so far. Now they'll back off."

I just kept putting my shit in a bag. Vince grabbed the bag and threw all my shit back into my locker. "Look, go to the bar, have a few. Then go home. Arnie needs us to go to Toronto tomorrow."

I couldn't believe that. "After that, he wants a favor?" I asked. "You fucking guys operate in your own little world."

As time passed, I would have no idea how right I was.

Vince grabbed my smokes, lit one, and shoved a 50 in my pocket. "He needs us to do security for his lawyer's kid's bar mitzvah. She's turning 13 I guess."

"When it's a girl, it's a bat mitzvah."

Vince just stared and cuffed me in the back of the head. "Shut the fuck up and go have a drink. Take the new guy with you. Tell him his schedule."

I turned to the new guy and said: "C'mon, time for a drink."

He looked back and forth at Vince and I and said: "It's just after 12."

Vince stared in disbelief. "What are you? A fuckin' Mormon? Go have a drink."

We both made our way to the bar. Marisa came over immediately. "Two scotches and two Exports, beautiful."

The new guy looked up and said: "I don't really drink either of those."

"Did I ask what the fuck you drink?" I caught him checking out Marisa's ass as she walked away. "One of the sweetest asses in this whole place," I told him. "And trust me, she ain't interested." I gave him his schedule and was surprised he had stuck around. He had to have heard the yelling and seen Tyler's face. He didn't flinch, so maybe he had some balls. My shots were gone and so was one of the beers. Marisa was on the way with more. "Look," I started while I told him his shifts." I don't know how this is going to play out, but he definitely needs another DJ. Stick around, see what happens."

"What about you?" he said.

What about me? Maybe he heard more than I thought. "Don't worry about me," I said, slamming my fourth shot, now officially drunk, "I'm like the Phoenix. I'll rise from the ashes."

He just looked at me funny. Millie was walking towards the bar. As I saw her coming, I instructed the new guy "Why don't you go double check everything with Vince?"

Millie approached the bar and asked for some red wine for something in the kitchen. When no one was around, she dropped her car keys in my lap. "What was that all about?" she asked.

"What?"

"That I'll-see-you-tonight crack," she said sternly. "I thought we were keeping it quiet."

"Yeah, but ..." I started.

"Whatever," she replied. "You can't drive. Wait a half an hour and meet me at my car. You can't drive." She took her red wine and walked away.

What the fuck was I doing? Hammered in the middle of the day, sneaking around with a woman almost twice my age, thinking of quitting. Could I handle going back to school like this?

I finished drinking and told the new guy to make sure to be on time for his shift.

Vince told me to be up by 11 tomorrow, that we were leaving before noon.

As I walked out the main door, I looked back at Tyler. I had made my point.

I went out to Millie's car and passed out waiting for her to arrive. She hopped in, kissed me and sighed, "We gotta get you something to eat, or you're gonna be of no use to me later."

I just nodded and passed out.

Chapter 3
Millie

Millie lived downtown in a nice little house. We usually ended up there, which made it easier for both of us, I guess. It was so nice, in fact, that it seemed above the level of income for someone running a kitchen in a strip club, but I never asked her about it. Tastefully decorated, always spotless and with a fridge constantly full of food, I certainly didn't mind going there instead of my own place. Some guy rented out the basement, but it had a separate entrance, so I never saw him.

The only thing of mine in Millie's house was a toothbrush. She was adamant I brush my teeth before sex, and then immediately after. Again, I didn't ask.

It was made abundantly clear to me from the beginning that this was her place, not ours. When she was done with me, I went home, sometimes with her practically rushing me out the door. Maybe there was another guy, I don't know. She knew we weren't exclusive and had to know about the other girls I was involved with, so I wasn't really in any position to complain about our arrangement.

She pulled into the driveway, shut off the car and turned to me. "You know you're not staying the night," she asked, "right?"

"When do I ever?" I replied.

"Well," she said, grabbing my arm, "maybe that should change."

"Tonight definitely isn't the night to start," I answered. "Vince is picking me up before noon. We're going to Toronto."

Unlike a regular girlfriend, she didn't ask questions. "Well, I'll get done with you early, so you can leave," she laughed, making her way to the front door.

I know most guys would say they would love the kind of situation I was in, but for some reason I couldn't exactly pinpoint, it was starting to really bother me. Maybe it was the booze. Fuck, I was going to get laid, have lunch, get laid again, and then sent home. Honestly, I really didn't have much to complain about.

As usual, we both entered the house through the garage, and I flopped down on the couch. Millie started moving things around in the kitchen, trying to decide what to make for lunch.

I was still pretty drunk, so I would have been happy with a microwaved burrito from 7-Eleven. She always insisted on cooking and having something good to eat as soon as we got home, no matter what time of the day or night it was. It could be 4 a.m., she would light up a joint and start cooking.

I haven't smoked that much lately, and the smell of weed actually kind of bothers me now, but what was I going to say?

I put my feet up on the couch and turned on the TV. I instinctively turned it to American Movie Classics and The Sons of Katie Elder was on. Good old AMC. Always a John Wayne movie or The Godfather or something else good. I was just dozing off when I looked up. Millie was leaning over me, wearing just an apron. "Before we eat ..." she said, took off her apron and climbed on top of me.

Once we were done, she went back to the kitchen and started chopping up steak, peppers and onions to make us some hoagies. Watching her, again dressed in just an apron, was a little distracting. It was also her way of saying we weren't done yet. If she wasn't interested in another round, she would have gotten dressed and started cleaning something. That was usually her tacit way of saying I could leave. Better than telling me to get the fuck out, I guess.

"So, what was the deal with slapping Tyler around," she asked as she bent over to get a mixing bowl. I can honestly say

I didn't hear the question while watching her, so she had to repeat it.

"Uh, nothing," I answered. "He's just an idiot."

"So, he's back?" she asked before going off on her own tangent. "He's creepy; always trying to get my number." Then she laughed.

"He's back, I guess, but I'm not thrilled about it," I answered. "It's actually making me think of quitting."

At my mention of quitting, Millie put our food on the table, but suddenly got quiet. "So, if you leave, that's it?" she finally asked.

"What?" I asked back. "You mean us? Why would that change?"

"I don't know," she answered. "It seems like you're here more and ..." she trailed off.

"And what?" I asked. "Why would anything have to change?" I wasn't sure where she was going with this, so I began to eat and didn't pursue the conversation. Was she saying it was over? Or was she looking for more? I didn't understand her attitude and didn't really want to deal with it.

After another long pause, she changed the subject. "Anyway, James called from SEN the other day." SEN was an English language course I had taught at Brock University a few times. It was mainly rich European kids whose parents sent them here to learn conversational English. Since it was a university teaching gig, it paid ridiculously well, and it wasn't all that hard. I had done it for a few summers when I began thinking of going back to school.

"If I'm going to get fucked around at the bar," I told her. "I'll just take the reduced shifts, work part time, and teach for the summer." The plan always was to finish my teaching degree, but it had been interrupted quite a few times since I left school with my bachelor's.

Millie had stopped talking, which — for her — was odd. She was usually always going on about something. And not in an annoying way. She usually had something intelligent to say, and I've always enjoyed our talks. You can only fuck so much. Somewhere down the line, you have to like the person at least a little, or you have to pretend, at least. Millie looked up from her plate, "Have you told Jenny?"

"What?" I answered.

"You fuckin' heard me!" she screamed and threw her sandwich in my face.

"What... the ... fuck!?" I yelled back at her.

"She called looking for you at the bar ..." she started, "... and I answered it." There was a glitch with the phone system. If no one answered the phone in the DJ booth, and I rarely did, it would ring through to the kitchen. I really had to get that changed.

I never hid Jenny, or any other girl, from Millie. I never tried to throw anything like that in her face either, but these girls were insane and pressed too hard. Usually, the first thing a dancer does after nailing some guy is to call the guy's girlfriend and tell her. I kept some of my things at Jenny's, but that wasn't permanent either.

Max had a strict "no second night" rule at the house we shared. You could bring home whoever you wanted, she could stay the night, but she absolutely had to leave the next day — no exceptions, no excuses. She could come by for a few days, but they couldn't be consecutive.

Since Max was on a roll himself lately, it was just easier to stay at Jenny's sometimes. We hadn't brought over a girl who had spent the night with both of us, but it was bound to happen.

"First off," I started, "since when do you care about Jenny, or anything else I do?"

Millie didn't answer. She started wiping my face, taking off the bits of pepper that were on my cheek.

Now it was my turn to get annoyed. "Answer me," I started. "What is this all about?"

"If you leave," she answered, "I won't ever see you. You're always off somewhere, I try not to ask ..." She trailed off.

She was picking up my habits. Fuck, we were even starting to talk the same way. I had a bad habit of not finishing my sentences when I was talking on the mic, but then again no one was listening. Things were getting really fucked up and this wasn't helping. "Look, I'm probably not going to quit," I told her. Who else is going to put pickles on my club sandwich instead of tomatoes?"

She looked up at me and smiled. Why was all this coming up now? What the fuck was she expecting of me?

"I'm not asking you for anything," she explained. "It's just hard seeing you get fucked up over a job that doesn't really matter."

She was right. The club was a lot of fun at the start, but now it wasn't really all that great. It had turned into a job, which I guess was inevitable. But still I had to answer the primary question at hand. "Look, as far as Jenny goes ..."

Millie cut me off. "I don't care about her," she said. "She's a stupid cunt."

I broke out laughing. While there was a bit of normalcy — even something of a relationship — with Millie, everything with Jenny was purely physical. Most of the girls in this business are missing something, which is usually why they're doing it for a living. I'm not talking about the ones with emotional issues, I'm also talking looks. Body is a 10? Her face looks like a frying pan. Great legs, smoking ass? Her stomach is blocky. Gorgeous tits? Big ears.

Jenny was damn near perfect body-wise. And she never did a thing about it. Never hit the gym, smoked a pack and a half a day. If she didn't have a glass of wine in her hand, it was a coffee.

Her big problem? She was dumb. Not run-of-the-mill stripper dumb, but deeply and incurably stupid. It was hard even trying to talk about mundane shit, like TV or sports, with her. But I knew I couldn't give her up, not yet. Maybe I was leaving my stuff at the wrong house.

"I feel like an idiot even bringing it up," Millie admitted, "but it bothers me. I can handle the other girls, but not her.

"So, stop answering the phone," I said.

She started to laugh again and punched me lightly in the chest.

"I'm going to talk about it with Vince tomorrow," I told her. "Honestly, I haven't decided what I'm going to do. I'm definitely taking the SEN job. That's for sure."

Maybe not being in the bar would force me to change. I really had to think about all of it.

But I didn't have time now. Millie took off the apron and threw it in my face. "Time for Round 2," she giggled, and pointed towards the bedroom.

For the first time ever since we started this deal, we both fell asleep afterward. It was dark outside, so we slept for a bit. Maybe it was what I needed. It was the first time I enjoyed a good sleep in a long time. Maybe it was some kind of reset button.

Millie stirred, rolled towards me and asked: "Can you put the coffee on?"

I told her I would, put it on and grabbed myself a Coke from the fridge.

She walked into the kitchen and abruptly turned off the coffeemaker. She turned and asked: "Why don't you stay here tonight?"

That was new. She grabbed herself a Coke and sat at the table. "Look," she said, "you're going to do whatever you want, but do it for you. You can do it, don't worry about those other guys. If money is a problem ..."

"Money is not a problem," I answered. "My dad and I talked about this years ago; if I can keep up with my bills, he'll foot the school fees."

"How much would it cost?" she asked.

"Well," I answered, "school, books, then I had to work for free as an intern teacher, so I won't be able to work. Probably $30,000 with everything included."

She looked at me and smiled. "He's got that kind of money laying around?" she asked. "Maybe I should meet your dad."

"Be serious," I answered.

"I am," she said, "I've been with the wrong guy." She got up and sat in my lap. "Round 3?"

"Three?" I answered. "I don't know about that ..."

When I woke up again, it was already morning. What a difference a good night's sleep makes. Didn't need a few beers or a sleeping pill to go down, or even a joint to wake up.

When Millie heard me moving around, she came back to the bedroom. She had her workout clothes on, a little pair of red shorts and a blue tank top. She looked amazing.

"You're alive," she commented. "I thought you slipped into a coma. I even checked your breathing."

"Fuuuuuuuuuucck," I said as I stretched, "that was a good sleep."

She jumped up on the bed and kissed me. "It wasn't all sleep," she purred.

"So that wasn't a dream." I said.

She smiled and jumped off the bed. "Wanna go to the Old Castle for breakfast or eat here?" she asked.

"Yeah," I yawned, "let's go to the Castle. I don't feel like breakfast food. I want a burger." The Old Castle was a popular diner that had been on the Lane since the late '60s. It had started as a drive-in, but it now had a dining room with a liquor license. For years, it was the place to go after the clubs closed. Every night, it was full of bikers, cops, hangarounds, hookers and those who wanted to see what late night was all about. They also ran the same menu for 24 hours. Want a lobster at 8 a.m.? No problem. Once they knew you well enough, the liquor laws were just a theory, rarely put into practice. It had become a little more kid-friendly recently, but I always felt comfortable there. You weren't going to get a flambé or crepes Suzette, but I didn't eat that shit anyway.

After a quick shower, I got dressed and made my way out to the car. Millie was already out and watering the front lawn. I put my hands on her ass and scooped her up. "Let's go!" I yelled.

"Wait!" she screamed, laughing at the same time. "I have to turn off the water!"

"You can do it from up here," I replied, not letting her down, but carrying her over to the tap. She giggled all the way there.

We had attracted an audience. The old couple across the street was watching. They were in their 80s and friendly enough. The old man looked on disapprovingly at our little game, but the wife had a smile on her face. Millie waved to them. The old lady laughed and waved. The old man stormed off.

We got in the car and left the driveway. "Somebody is happy," Millie said.

"Yeah," I started. "Yeah, I am."

She reached over and grabbed my hand. I felt like I was in the seventh grade again. Maybe things weren't so bad. I took her hand and put it on my crotch. She screamed: "Knock it off!"

I laughed and leaned back. Maybe things wouldn't be so bad. Fuck Cody, Tyler and Arnie. Even fuck the new guy, whose name I couldn't remember. For the next few months or so, he was just the FNG — Fuckin New Guy. And that would last until there was a new FNG.

We drove up Ferry Street until it turned into Lundy's Lane. I could drive this part of town blindfolded. First there was the Dairy Queen, then the Admiral Hotel (probably the last place left in town that would still rent rooms by the hour). Then I passed the Busy Bee convenience store, where Ferry turned into Lundy's. After that, the fast-food joints came one after another — McDonald's, Burger King, Wendy's, Arby's. They were all here when I first moved in with Max, and I quickly gained 25 pounds because I was always stopping to eat.

We pulled into the Castle and walked in.

We walked in and the hostess came up and kissed me on the cheek. "Hey," she said, "you're up early." She ignored Millie and walked us to our table. I watched her walk away.

Millie caught that, and said "What? Her too?"

I looked at Millie and said: "Please, she's, like, 15."

Millie picked up the menu and said: "She's 19. I went to school with her mother." She knew I was lying. I hadn't been too discreet lately.

"She is?" I asked. "Well, that changes everything ..."

Millie threw the menu at me.

"Order me a coffee," she said. "I need to use the bathroom." She got up and walked by the hostess. With a big smile on her face, she stopped in front of the hostess and hugged her, whispering in her ear. Stunned, the hostess stood still for a minute, turned white and walked away. I made sure to not ask what was said.

Lorraine came over to take our order. She was in her 60s and only ever worked the day shift now. Some of the old timers told me that, in her day, Lorraine was the hottest redhead in town. When the Castle was packed all the time, it seemed like she was always there. All those hours had got her a nice house in Mount Carmel. Her doctor and lawyer neighbors probably never figured out their nice old lady neighbor was a waitress who was juggling the chief of police and the president of the local biker gang as her boyfriends back in the '70s.

She asked us if we wanted the usual. Yup. Club with extra bacon, but with pickles instead of tomatoes. Fries with a mix of gravy and Castle sauce. Not everyone's idea of breakfast, but I was set. I ordered Millie four egg whites and a slice of melon.

As Millie walked towards the table, I could see she wasn't happy. Chris and Stevie were standing behind her. Both dressed in full regalia: Steel-toe boots, leather pants and jackets, their heads covered with bandanas. At one time, guys looking the way they did wouldn't look out of place, but times had changed. They both had something else on that was new. As they got closer, I noticed Stevie now had full Burnt colors on, and Chris had a prospect patch.

"Look who I found," Millie said, forcing a smile.

I got up and hugged both of them. “Promotions, boys?” I asked. “Congrats.”

Stevie was beaming, Chris not so much. There must have been a reason Chris hadn’t fully patched in yet. A reason I was thinking I would not ask about.

Stevie glared at me, and asked: “You talk to Vince today?”

“Uh, no.”

“His wife said he was going to your place today.”

Why the fuck were these guys calling Vince at home and bothering his wife? Against my own better judgment, I lied and said that it was news to me.

Chris tried to snatch a few fries off my plate, and I slapped his hand. I couldn’t pull that sort of thing on Stevie anymore since he was a full patch, but I could still get away with it with Chris.

“When you see him,” Stevie said, “have him call me.”

I answered that I would, and Chris leaned down and kissed Millie on the cheek. “When you get tired of this guy,” he said, “call me.”

Millie smiled, and the boys walked out.

Millie waited until she saw them outside, then announced: “I know they’re your friends, but Stevie scares me.”

I actually hadn’t considered him my friend for a while. With Stevie fully patched in and Chris’s status still a question mark, Stevie could push him around since he out-ranked him. He probably wouldn’t, since they had been friends since we were all kids; but with most guys, a patch is like a new toy. Who knew what he would act like now?

My bigger worry was how much of an asshole Chris would be when he made it. People get hung up on all that bullshit about what guys have to do to get patched in, and when he didn’t get his, there had to be a reason. These guys weren’t angels, and his not getting his patch when Stevie did could be over something as small as not paying a debt, or some perceived slight of another member. The further I looked into their world, the idea of living as a 1%er — as bikers call themselves — was like a fairy tale. They actually set themselves up for a much tougher life. A regular person can fuck up all the time and not much happens. Doing it with these guys, it could cost you your life.

I leaned over the table and kissed Millie. “Don’t worry about those guys,” I told her. “Pretty soon I won’t have to deal with them.” I waited for a few seconds, and then shouted: “I love you!” That turned a few heads in the restaurant. For the first time ever, I caught Millie blushing.

She looked around and then said: “You’re full of surprises today.” We spent the rest of our time eating in silence. Someone left a copy of the Sun on the table. I read the sports section, she read the entertainment section. Fuck me. I was happy.

Chapter 4
Vince

Millie and I left the Old Castle, after making sure Stevie and Chris were no longer in the parking lot. I wasn't worried about them doing anything to me, it was just becoming more and more uncomfortable talking to Chris.

It was clear that he must have been pissed that Stevie patched in before he did. To me, they seemed to represent the recent divide I had seen between the old and new style of biker. Chris was old school, His game was purely muscle, the kind of guy who would cave your head in over a $50 debt.

He was also pretty tied up in the image of being an outlaw. So much so that I joked that when he got his full patch, he would probably even wear it to bed, because he'd be so proud of the fucking thing.

That's how some bikers get. I've seen guys wear them to funerals, at sporting events and even to pick their kids up from school. I didn't see the point. The patch is a symbol of intimidation, pure and simple, but its impact had been eroded over the years. In the old days, seeing a patch immediately meant "don't fuck with that guy." Nowadays, it just meant the asshole would come back with a bunch of guys and yell and scream like jerks. Don't get me wrong, these organizations have power, but their rapid expansion made them weaker. They lowered their standards to take over more territory, patching over guys who never would have made it into the club in the old days, and it showed. The end result was guys like Chris, and to a certain extent, Stevie. All balls, no brains.

The flipside of the expansion created guys like Stevie. While he had some tendencies that made you think he might be a flat-out nut job, he was a little more restrained than guys like Chris. Stevie could smash your face in, but these days he was a little more apt to leave that threat on the table instead of actually doing it. That's how the club wanted it. Better to be known for violence, they contended, than to actually have to do it.

Gone was the Stevie that wore a tank top and Crazee Wear pants everywhere he went. He cleaned himself up and found it a little easier to fit in just about anywhere.

I was surprised to see him with his patch on in a place as mundane as the Castle, but maybe he was showing it off. More likely, he was throwing it in Chris's face.

Stevie's status in the club rose pretty quickly, but you'd rarely see him on a bike or wearing colors. He had some attributes that Burnt was looking for. For one thing, he was a local boy. Having someone who grew up in the area is key to the success of most organized crime. They know people and places. With any luck, the recruit wasn't a total douche in his younger days, so the connections he has are positive and valuable. It's easier to have someone look the other way or do you a favor if they remember you as their paperboy rather than that little shit. Being a hometown boy also makes it sometimes look like all of this shit is no big deal. It's just some boys having fun.

We cruised down the Lane to get my car. There was little chance Vince was taking the 'Vette to Toronto, especially since he was probably going to make me drive. There was a massive parking lot that separated the two clubs. I usually parked somewhere in the middle of the lot. If you parked too close to the door, Arnie would get pissed, saying those spots were for customers. That made sense. But if you parked all the way in the back, your car was probably going to get vandalized or broken into. My car was a piece of shit, so I didn't care. A big old green Chevy Caprice Classic that was falling apart, it had a great engine and always started. Eventually I was going to have to junk it, so I might as well run it into the ground.

I always drove past the club once, so that I could check the cars in the lot to see if there was anyone in the club I didn't want to run into. I told Millie to always do the same.

As we cruised by, I could see four or five bikes parked to the side, with a handful of guys milling around them. None of them had a patch on, but I could clearly make out Chris.

"Just keep going," I said, "don't even go back in front of the club. Turn at Garner, and we'll take the long way back."

She didn't argue, but Millie definitely looked concerned. It was probably nothing, but I couldn't shake the feeling that Stevie and Chris weren't actually following me, but they were still keeping a loose tab on me.

Millie turned into Garner and pulled into the parking lot in front of the Abbyford golf course. She turned off the engine and just stared at the wheel. "You know I usually don't ask you ..." she started. I tried to answer but she cut me off. "... are you in trouble with these guys?"

"I can't see how," I explained, "I barely hang with them anymore." That was a conscious effort on my part. As soon as Stevie and Chris started prospecting for the Burnt, I backed off any night prowling with them. I had done a lot of stupid shit but didn't have a criminal record and I didn't want to get one. It doesn't sound like a big deal, but it would become one quickly if I wanted to teach. You had to be totally clean. Nothing on your record. Nothing.

As deep as I had crawled into the life, I'm amazed I was still relatively clean. Sure, people would say shit, and I was prepared for that. But getting a police clearance to teach was still possible, and that's all I needed. At one time, I had flaunted the fact that I hung out with Jimmy and his crew, but so did a lot of guys.

Working in a strip club was one thing, but I really needed to distance myself from all the other shit. Maybe taking the teaching gig and bouncing at a regular club wouldn't be so bad.

I definitely wouldn't be able to straddle both. It was becoming clearer by the second that I had to leave.

"It really doesn't have anything to do with me." I told Millie.

"What doesn't have to do with you?"

"Whatever it is they're doing." I responded.

"And what are they doing?"

"How the fuck do I know?" I waved her off. "Just drive the long way around, I don't want them to see me."

She didn't answer, just kept driving. I was really hoping we got to the house before Vince did, or I would have to explain why I was in the car with our 47-year-old cook. I hadn't even told him about Millie and me – but he probably knew anyway.

Vince had a pretty decent home life for a guy in this business. His wife, Pat, was smoking hot and came from old money. They had met in college and seemed to have a good deal going on. She didn't work, and that's the way Vince wanted it. He wasn't too bad with the girls, but I'd heard stories. It was impossible not to have a few that you slept with. We were in the proverbial candy store, and the candy was rock-hard ass 24 hours a day, and you didn't even have to put in any effort to get it.

We made our way down Drummond Hill and turned on the first right after the highway overpass. I could never remember the street name. Everyone in town called it Crack Alley. It was where you could get whatever you wanted, anytime.

We had to drive down this shitty street to get to Max's neighborhood, which was only a couple of years old. New houses were popping up all over town, supplanting these old ones.

The rumor was that Burnt was going to open their clubhouse right in Crack Alley. That made sense. It was right by the overpass to the highway, and no one in the neighborhood would talk.

Stevie grew up right on the corner, with an aunt who seemed to sleep all day, and an uncle who fixed cars out of his garage. He was also selling whatever came his way: drugs, booze, car parts, even the occasional gun. Stevie would feel right at home in the clubhouse.

Of course, the neighborhood will be buzzing with the usual bullshit about how great it is to have a club house in your area because it scares away all the local criminals. Yeah, it's great until a rival gang blows up your garage with a rocket launcher because they were too stoned to hit the right building.

Millie pulled into the driveway and said nothing. "I gotta go," I told her, kissing her on the cheek.

She looked up at me with tears in her eyes. "With all this shit going on," she sniffed, "is that why you're going to Toronto?"

I'd never seen her cry before. "No," I began, and she looked away. "Look," I started again, "Arnie's lawyer's kid is having her bat mitzvah and he offered us up as security guards so he could look like a big shot."

She stopped crying, and slowly started to laugh. "You're going to Toronto for some kid's bat mitzvah?" she asked, stressing the word Toronto, and then broke out laughing.

"See?" I said also laughing. "Could I possibly have made something that stupid up?"

She grabbed me by face and told me: "I'll leave the back door unlocked for you."

"I don't know what time I'll be back."

"Doesn't matter," she said. "You know what to do."

Millie always wanted me to crawl into bed and just start having sex with her. I can't say I didn't like it. Otherwise everything else was pretty normal with us.

"You got it," I agreed. "Now get out of here before I change my mind and go back home with you." I really wanted her gone, because Vince would arrive any minute.

She peeled out of the driveway, stopped the car and yelled, "Hey!" I looked back. "I love you, kid!"

I looked up and smiled. "I love you too, you nutty old broad," I told her. "Now go."

She waved and laughed. Her laugh made me want to run after the car, jump in, and forget all this Toronto shit. But that wasn't going to happen. Not today.

Max was already up; I could smell the coffee and the cigarettes. He looked at me and said: "Max has already called to say he's on his way." After a short pause, he added: "I lied and told him you were in the shower."

Good ol' Max. Best personal security anywhere. He never told anybody anything.

"I was just gonna call your cell ... you at Millie's?" he asked.

He was probably the only person that really knew about us. Once we tried to do the real "date thing" and went out of our way to eat at this little place in Grimsby. Who was at the only other table in the place? Just happened to be Max and his ex-wife. As he explained at the time: "I really fucking hate her, but the sex is too amazing!" I laughed and the four of us sat together.

"He said he'd be here by 12," Max added.

Fuck, it was 11:52. "Gotta clean up," I said and headed for the shower. Vince wouldn't be on time anyway. He never was.

After a quick shower, I was at the kitchen table, stealing one of Max's cigarettes and drinking a can of Coke. "Let me ask you something," I started. He looked up from his paper. "Have Stevie and Chris been assholes lately? I mean, more so than usual?"

Maybe all that shit this morning was coincidence. Why would I have to worry about their shit? I thought to myself as he pondered his answer.

"Well," he answered, "they did slap Herb around last night."

Herb was my replacement at the old club, and about 55 years old. It wouldn't take much to smack him around.

"Why?"

Max rolled his eyes and said, "he disrespected them."

That was the old biker cure-all bullshit answer to everything. Didn't say hi to me when I came in? Disrespect.

Bam! Said hi to me when I was talking to one of my brothers? Disrespect. Bam! Answered my question too slow? Disrespect. Bam! You've been fucking the same chick for five years and now I want her? Disrespect. Bam!

The only good thing about Herb was he had been around forever, so he wouldn't make an issue out of it. From hearing the rest of the story from Max, it sounded like Herb only got a few slaps in the mouth. Humiliating enough, but sometimes you had no choice. Raising your hand or making a scene usually isn't a good Idea. It happened a few times when I was still at the door. It would be some old timer with a patch on running his yap, but you had to take it. As one of the old timers used to tell me, you can disrespect the man, but not his patch, because then he's gotta do something about it. It's all about saving face. Look weak, and your brothers will eat you alive.

I could hear the 'Vette rumble up the driveway. "I slept here last night, if he asks," I whispered.

Max nodded.

Vince didn't knock, he just walked in. "Max" he said noncommittally. Max nodded. "Idiot," he said, looking at me. He then pulled out a 26-ounce bottle of Crown Royal and a six pack. "Whiskey for me, beer for the pussy," he said as he threw me the six pack. He poured almost the entire bottle into a giant 7-Eleven cup and added some ice. With the remainder, he poured out three shots. "Shoot 'em up!" he yelled.

Max just laughed and poured his into his coffee.

I wasn't a shot guy, especially this stuff.

"Get whatever you're bringing," Vince ordered. "We're leaving in five. Where's your car?"

I told him it was at the bar, said I had too much to drink.

He narrowed his eyes, and said: "Funny, I just passed Millie on the way here. What's that old cunt doing up so early?"

I shrugged and said nothing.

"Well," he started again. "We'll have to go get it. We're not taking the 'Vette."

I got my things together and made it towards the door.

"Max," I heard Vince say. "I might just leave your roomie in Toronto."

"Just send me his rent," Max replied sardonically.

Fucking assholes, I thought to myself.

We made our way to the 'Vette. "In the interest of saving time," Vince said, "we'll take the 'Vette. But if you mess it up, scratch anything, even fart in it, I promise you that I will kill you."

"Fair enough," I said, "so I can drive, right?"

Vince let out a huge laugh. "Like you're driving," he bellowed. "Get in the fucking car."

Through Crack Alley to the overpass, and we we're on our way. We drove in silence until about Lake Street in Saint Catharines.

"So," Vince began, "are you serious about quitting, or have you calmed down a bit?"

I didn't answer.

Vince started drinking out of the Big Gulp cup full of whiskey. "So, you're gonna be a dick all the way to Toronto?" he asked.

I didn't know what to say. That I just wanted to run away and move in with a woman twice my age? Fuck, why was I feeling so vulnerable? I never gave a shit about Millie before, and today I told her I loved her? We'd been doing this little game for almost a year, and I never cared before. So why now? And then there was Jenny. I definitely didn't care that much about her, and yet I crashed there a couple of times a week, even looked after her daughter sometimes. She was a good mom, regardless of all the other shit.

Whack! Vince beaned me in the head with a loonie, taking me out of my daydreaming. "What? What?" I yelled at him.

Instead of cuffing me in the head, as usual, he just stared at me. "I asked you a question five minutes ago," he said, "and you've been staring off into fuckin space. Seriously, are you ok?"

"Yeah," I tried to answer him. "Look, I went out to eat this morning" I answered, leaving Millie out of the story, "and I ran into Stevie and Chris. They asked me if I had seen you."

"What did they say?"

"Nothing really," I answered, "they just wanted to know where you were."

He started rolling his hand in a circle, you know, the gesture that meant get to the fucking point. Between his football days and my brief career in wrestling, he and I could have a conversation by gesture that no one else would understand. On the football field or in a wrestling ring it was to your advantage not to have people overhear you. So, we combined the gestures to form our own bar sign language. Gesturing your finger in a circle meant work the room. Doing it counter clockwise meant you were being watched or listened to. To signify that he should knock off his hostility, I put my hand down and waved my fingers, which was the sign for saying slow down and stop being a dick. Vince had waved this many times to me from across the room.

Now the positions shifted. It was my turn to ask the questions. "You're always telling me to stay the fuck away from them, so why are they asking for you?" I asked.

He didn't say anything.

"You know what?" I said. "You're a fucking douche for not letting me know what's going on."

That would usually have gotten me a slap in the head, but he didn't move a muscle. "Fucking football pool," he finally admitted. "I owe Stevie $17,000."

Vince made most of his money running a football book from Niagara Falls, New York, into Niagara Falls, Ontario. He inherited it from his dad; who, in the '70s, ran the biggest sports book in this area, paying off the local cops and the local wops along the way. The casinos opening and the mob falling apart took a big chunk of the old-timer's profits away, but he still did all right. He covered it all by running a football pool during the season and taking the occasional bet on basketball or boxing the rest of the year.

What Vince told me, though, was fucked. There was no way he would borrow more from Stevie, and even a lesser chance that Stevie would lend it to him. “I’ve been getting in over my head for a bit,” he explained, “and some of the local wops were backing me. When the debt got up to $25,000, this old fuck who looked like he was about 90 came to collect. I gave him $5,000 and told him to fuck off.”

I was starting to see where this was going. “So now, these old timers are getting your buddies to collect,” I said. “Right?” That was becoming commonplace these days. Both sides of Niagara were strong with mob influence. Sal Castellano ran all of it for years. But when he died, he left an unclear successor, and both sides of the border suffered. If guys didn’t get shot trying to take over, they got 50 years for selling heroin, the only thing that made any money for a while. The old fucks couldn’t lose face, so they got local bikers to collect their money for them.

“So,” Vince kept on going, “Stevie shows up and asks for the remaining $20,000. I gave him $3,000 and told him to fuck off.”

Now all the animosity made sense. Stevie had to save face and collect the debt.

“If he shows up at my house,” Vince growled, “I will shoot him in the face.”

Chapter 5
Custy and Sweetie

I'm a big fan of simplifying things. If you have to move, finish an assignment, write a proposal, it's all the same shit. Sometimes, if you look at the whole project in front of you, it can be enough to give you a heart attack. But if you break it up, into little parts, anything is doable. You just have to make every little part understandable.

So, this deal between Vince and Stevie? The whole thing was pretty simple. It had nothing to do with mob politics, Vince being a bookie, or the fact that the Burnt had to save face by collecting this debt. It was down to the fact that Vince owed $17,000, and he wasn't going to be able to walk away from it. All the other shit was secondary.

It would all affect how this would be played out, of course, but the big issue was pretty clear. Vince had to cough up. There was no other way.

Explaining it to him, though, that was the hard part. I knew him well enough to know what his next question was. "Do I have to pay him?" Vince asked.

For most people this would seem insane. But then some regular custy – what we called customers – wouldn't owe a couple of bikers $17,000. This wasn't a game with a normal set of rules, at least not to an outsider. And they were the kind of rules you only learned after dealing with these types of people for years.

You always hear a lot of garbage about respect. It's always respect with these guys. Respect my name, respect my colors, respect my brothers. Respect doesn't mean shit. It's all about fear. You can respect my balls all day, but if you're stiffing me on a debt, talking shit about me, or trying to take what I have, how's that respect?

It's fear that runs the machine, and it's fear that keeps everybody in line. If you fear me, you won't fuck with me. If you're strong enough to take something away from someone else, you've got to be strong enough to hold onto it. Respect won't stop me from fucking with you. Fear will. It was a fucked-up game, and there was never a shortage of players. Everybody, I mean almost everybody, knew the rules, but there were always those guys that still thought they could pull a little extra off, steal a little more, intimidate a little more. These were the guys that wound up dead, and I'm pretty sure Vince wasn't looking for it to go that far.

"Maybe," Vince started after a long pause, "you could talk to Jimmy?" I fucking knew it. "... 'cause you know..."

I looked at Vince hard and he stopped. There wasn't much we didn't talk about. Why I had access to Jimmy was one of those things. "And what would that do?" I asked. "Dude, you gotta pay."

He knew I was right. "... well maybe talking to Jimmy could buy me some time," he said. "I could go with you."

That wouldn't work. Things had gone far enough that it was probably a good idea for Vince to be removed from any negotiations, at least for now. But going alone on my part wasn't a good idea, either. I was almost positive that going to see Jimmy was going to be safe, but I wanted everything covered. "I'll get Viking to drive me," I finally said.

"You still talk to that weirdo?" Vince asked in astonishment.

"Hey," I snapped, "if I called that weirdo at four in the morning and asked him to come to my house with a truck and some chains and to not ask questions, he'd be at my place in 10 minutes."

Our conversation had taken up most of the trip. We were now just outside of Toronto, and we hadn't even spoken once about me quitting the bar. I'd let it ride for now. Obviously, Vince had bigger things on his mind.

Once we made it off the highway, we drove down a service road for a while until we came to the entrance of a huge property that looked kind of like a military base. "This is it," Vince said, and we pulled off the road and into the parking lot. We immediately came to a security checkpoint. This was no army base. This was a huge estate that looked like something out of a movie.

A security dude came out of the booth. No dime store rent-a-cops here. Dressed in a nice suit and wearing an earpiece, he leaned into the car. "Can I help you" he asked.

"Yeah," Vince offered, "we're here to do security for the bat mitzvah."

He asked us to wait. After calling someone, he told us to "drive up to the right and park in Lot B — and good luck." Then he laughed. What the fuck did he mean by that?

As we drove around the property, we both decided it was gorgeous. Everything manicured, nothing out of place. "Pretty fancy," I said.

"Too fancy for you, maybe," Vince replied. "I used to have to go to places like this all the time with Pat's family." Vince had said his wife was from money, lots of money.

We pulled into the lot and got out of the car to stretch. We were immediately surrounded by security. I could see why. We hadn't changed yet, and we were both in our gym clothes, sunglasses and ball caps. We definitely looked out of place.

"Can we help you?" one of them asked.

"Yeah, we're here to work the event," Vince replied.

"Just the two of you?" the guy asked, in a pretty shitty tone.

"Well," Vince replied, "I usually handle things like this alone, but Sweetie here gets mad if I leave him alone all day."

I had to try hard not to laugh, but the guy just stood there. After double checking in with the front guard, we were directed toward the main building, where we were informed we could clean up. Vince grabbed our bags, threw mine at me and said: “Let’s go, Sweetie.”

The main building had all kinds of people running around getting things ready. Wait staff, caterers and a lot of others were running around.

We were directed to the basement. The bathroom was massive, so big that it had two attendants. I wasn’t planning on freshening up, but thought, what the fuck, let’s use the facilities. The attendant gave us each towels, soap, a razor, and our choice of colognes. I was impressed. Even though I had showered at the house, smoking and drinking in the car made me feel like I had been out all night.

After I had showered (Vince just read the paper, saying he had already showered), I came out to find our clothes laid out for us.

After we got dressed, it was obvious that we had different ideas of what we should wear. I had on a dark suit, red shirt and no tie. Vince wore a new pair of jeans and a western-themed shirt. He turned and looked at me. “Why the fuck are you wearing that?” he asked.

“We’re supposed to look formal, no?”

We both made our way back upstairs. After walking around a bit and being offered a drink, we saw Arnie’s lawyer. I didn’t even know his name. He waved us over. What a stereotype of a big-city lawyer this guy was. Bad wig, even worse suit, waving around a big cigar. He looked at both of us and let out a huge laugh. What the fuck?!” he bellowed “What’s with you guys? This guy’s dressed up, and this one looks like a cowboy!”

Vince was not amused. But this guy kept going. “You too look like those TV detectives. What was their names?” we just stared at him. “Simon and Simon!” he yelled. “You look like Simon and Simon!”

We all laughed, but Vince made it clear that he wasn’t pleased. “So, what do you need us to do, Marvin?” Vince asked. This guy’s name was Marvin? Now that was funny.

Marvin showed us around the place. "The kids don't get here 'til after the ceremony, so you've got time to eat and look around," he said. "Once they get here, don't turn your back on them, these kids are a handful."

Vince and I shrugged. How much trouble could they be?

Marvin also made it clear that once the kids were gone, the party kicked into high gear.

He promised to get us anything, anything at all. We were told to go right to the kitchen and ask for whatever we wanted. We ordered up two steaks, with fries and vegetables. We waited by the bar until they were done.

"So far, so good," Vince said.

"What about everybody saying good luck and saying how awful these kids are?"

"They're just kids," Vince replied. "We'll just scare the shit out of the first kid that fucks up, and then the rest won't do shit."

I wasn't so sure. I had a little experience working with kids and I knew that if one turned on you, the rest usually followed.

When the food came, the steak took up nearly the entire plate. Then the fries were served in one basket, vegetables in another.

"Fuck," Vince whispered, "think they'll give me a doggy bag?"

I didn't answer, instead deciding to tear into my steak.

Vince flipped his over, cut it in two, and asked: "So are you quitting or not? Don't fuck me around."

I shrugged and grabbed some fries. "I can't turn down that teaching gig at Brock ... too much money and it'll look good on my résumé."

Vince didn't answer at first, just looked outside. "Why don't you do both?" he asked. "Who knows? You might change your mind."

He had a point. The teaching gig was only for eight weeks and it was only from eight in the morning to one in the afternoon on weekdays. If I didn't ask Arnie for more shifts, it would piss him off that I was doing my own thing. And it would piss Tyler off as well. Cody wouldn't care, he would just side with whoever was in charge.

"Well, think about it," Vince said. "Tyler is an idiot and will fuck up again, and Cody is pretty well done. You could be in a sweet spot."

Again, I just shrugged.

"OK, asshole" he said, "we'll talk about it later."

We ate our steaks in silence, enjoying the view, the food, and the silence. The kids and their parents started rolling in at around five, and the shit started soon after. We caught two boys and a girl smoking a joint in that basement. Vince took it and shouted, "get the fuck out of here!" at the kids. They ran.

Vince took a couple of quick tokes and passed me the joint. "Good fucking weed," he said. I took a quick hit, put it out and decided to save it for later. It actually was pretty good fucking weed.

Dinner was uneventful, but we were anticipating trouble once the DJ set up. The kids were going to have the floor until eight, then it was adult time. That's when you could see the staff slowly change, Marvin told us, they were all women and they were hot.

Marvin also said that, as soon as the kids left, any waitress wearing a red bow in her hair was free for the taking. They would also get us whatever we wanted. I wasn't the most virtuous guy, but that whole concept seemed more than a little sleazy.

As soon as the music came on, the shit started. Two kids lit a table on fire, which Vince stomped out.

We couldn't believe how many girls we caught half naked or doing shit I didn't even know existed when I was their age. We finally had enough when one of the girls tried to give us a note. It said we could do whatever we wanted to her, and her friends too.

When I looked at Vince in disbelief, the girl giggled and ran away.

"Fuck this, it's time to go," Vince said.

I was in total agreement. Now I understood all the cracks about good luck from the other security guys. Nobody wanted this gig. We found Marvin, and said that the kids were almost done, and that we should head out.

"But we're just getting started," he grinned lasciviously and pointed to his "waitresses."

"That's OK," Vince said, "Junior here has to get up in the morning." If I was the excuse to get out, that was fine with me.

"I know what a cheap fuck Arnie is, so here," Marvin said, and handed us each $500. That was nice, especially since we thought we were going to get stiffed. We got our stuff and made our way to the car.

"Well boy," Vince drawled like some yokel, "between us, we got a grand. Let's go kick the fuck outta Toronto!"

"Yeah, what the fuck," I answered. "Marty still work downtown?"

"He sure as fuck does," Vince yelled, and we peeled out of the parking lot. After a minute, Vince shook his head in disgust and said: "You know, I'm pretty sure that was Marvin's daughter that gave you that note."

I just shook my head as we headed for the highway. I lit up the joint we took from the kids. Usually that would have got me a shot in the head for smoking in the 'Vette, but Vince just laughed and said: "Pass that fucking thing!"

I could see the Toronto skyline in the distance. It looked different than Niagara Falls. Colder, but at the same time more welcoming. I never had any feelings for Toronto, one way or another. The city meant nothing to me. Too big, too unwelcoming. I never felt comfortable there. I was just a kid from a tourist town.

Chapter 6
Fuck Them, We Run this Place

Vince was driving like a mad man. "Toronto is gonna take a beating!" he yelled out to no one in particular. "We're gonna rip this town in half!"

Fuck, I had forgotten that Vince could be a lot of fun. A quick stint playing for the Argos in the CFL landed him in Toronto years ago. Because the league paid like shit, he wound up working the door on a Yonge Street nightclub, meeting Marty. I had never met the guy, but I knew all the stories.

We pulled into the lot beside Frederick's, the biggest strip club in Toronto. The city had dumped most of the strip clubs, but Frederick's had survived. So, everyone went there.

Vince hated paying for parking, but we considered what we had to be Marvin's money, so he flipped the attendant a fifty, and told him: "Please be careful with her, I don't want to kill anyone tonight."

The guy just nodded and got away from us as soon as he could. We made our way to the front door and asked for Marty. The doorman disappeared inside for a few minutes, then reappeared. "It seems Marty had to step out," he said, "but everything is on him — except the girls — 'til he gets back."

Pretty sweet, I thought. Vince threw him a twenty and thanked him.

Frederick's had three floors. The bottom floor was off limits to everyone but the staff and the girls, but we were immediately led down there to Marty's office.

A well-dressed woman with red hair and pale skin handed Vince the phone. Wow, was she hot. If I could design a girl, she would look like her. About 5-foot-5, with curly red hair and just enough meat on her to make her curvy. She had a couple of freckles on her nose and wore librarian glasses. I was a sucker for the glasses. "I'll see you two upstairs," she said and smiled. Use your head, I told myself, she's fucking working, and she's working you. Maybe so, but ...

Vince put down the phone. "Marty will be here later" he said. "We've got a tab and a private table upstairs with the redhead and her friend. I knew you'd like that."

Obviously, he had planned the whole thing. But I wasn't complaining. I rarely hit Toronto anymore, so I could sit back and relax. The redhead poked her head back in the office. She now had a friend with her. Blonde, almost 6-foot, huge tits and a little ass. "We're waiting" they purred. Each girl grabbed us by the arm and led us upstairs.

The main floor of the bar had the club's main stage, two smaller ones, a DJ booth and a long bar that went right down the wall to the back of the club, then branched out into the middle of the room, almost splitting it in half. Tables everywhere, girls working. I always judged how good a club was by how hot their waitresses were. These ones blew away the dancers. Dancers came and went. But the same custies would come in week after week, just praying that their favorite waitress would get naked. The smart ones never did and milked it for all it was worth. Once they seen it, you're old news.

The girls led us upstairs, which was their VIP section. Nothing fancy, just a little more private. It was pretty obvious that the guy at the table next to us was getting a hand job. The table in the far corner didn't hide the fact the guy at it was getting blown. We were given a table to the side, not too secluded, but with a good view of the stage show.

"So," Red asked, unzipping her top to show a fantastic pair of tits, "a few drinks?"

I nodded yes.

"I've never seen you here before," she said, "or are you friends of Marty's?"

"Vince is."

She let out a sigh. "Whew," she started again, "Marty's friends are fucked up. The things they ask me to do ..."

"I run a club with Vince in Niagara Falls," I changed the subject. "You should come up there sometime." I was always on the lookout for new talent.

When I looked over to the other end of the table, Vince and Blondie were gone. When I looked back, Red already had her dress off.

"Time to dance," she whispered, and began grinding into my lap. In all the years I was in the business, I'd never had a lap dance. You can't go any further unless you paid, and I didn't pay. Red kept swaying in front of me, occasionally grinding her ass into my crotch. After a few songs, she said: "that will be $100." Red had just turned into a cunt in my book.

"For what?" I asked. "Two songs?"

"It was five songs," she protested. "Do you want me to call Marty?"

Just like I thought. I let my guard down for a minute and she fucking played me. "Why don't you call Marty," I shot back, "We'll settle this whole thing, and you won't get shit."

"I thought you were making me ..." she tried before trailing off.

"I wasn't going to make you do anything you didn't want to do."

Just then, Vince and Blondie reappeared. "Fuck this place," he said, "let's hit another club. We'll run up Marty's tab a bit, and then we'll bolt."

Red looked at me and asked if she could come with us. Like a fucking idiot, I said sure.

Once we were all good and pissed, we took a cab to the Black Pearl, a club a little farther down the line in terms of prestige, but hopping nonetheless.

"You call that new DJ and tell him he's working days" Vince told me as we were pulling up to the club.

"And then we can get a place for the night ..." Red said as we got to the door. Yeah, right, I thought to myself, and then I'll wake up tied to the bed with all my shit gone.

As I tried to reach to tell the new guy he was working, Vince was having trouble getting in the club. This wasn't the Falls, and we didn't have any pull here.

As I was trying to get through on my cell phone, I could swear I heard someone calling out my name. This is Toronto, nobody knows me. But then I heard it again.

Suddenly, the guy was standing in my face, "You deaf, asshole?" he yelled. It was my old friend, Chinese Dwight. I got off the phone. The new guy didn't seem thrilled that he now had the day shift, but fuck him, he was the new guy.

"What the fuck are you doing standing on Yonge Street at one a.m.?" Dwight asked.

"Long story."

Dwight started with the Burnt, but moved his way up to an outfit called the Last Knights MC. They were in Toronto and well respected. They had been targeted by another crew; the Royal City Riders wanted to take over and that could mean big money.

Dwight was a computer whiz, kickboxing champion and looked like a samurai. He had black hair halfway down his back, was tall and muscular, and always dressed in black leather. Believe me, people moved out of his way.

"We're trying to get in the Pearl, but we don't know anyone," I said.

"Fuck that, we run this place," Dwight said with a sneer. He started for the front door, pointed at us and said something to the doorman, then playfully slapped him in the face. The five of us were given a table center stage.

Even Vince appeared to be impressed. He quickly disappeared with Blondie, leaving me, Red and Dwight at the table. Even Red seemed impressed now, although it probably had more to do with Dwight lining up enough coke on the table to stun a moose.

Red gladly jumped in, and then held my hand like we were in high school. Dwight and I both snorted a line, and then he whispered into my ear, "a little coke and a walk past the bouncers out front, she'll be looking to marry you before closing time." We both laughed, which made Red laugh, even though the joke was clearly on her.

When the waitress came and I tried to pay, Dwight told me: "What did I tell you? This place is ours." The girl got a ten from Dwight and a slap on the ass.

I settled in for some blow, Coronas and a little catching up with Dwight. Red jumped in my lap and stayed there. I wondered for a second where Vince was, and then I thought – who fucking cares?

By the time Vince and Blondie made it back to the table, he was wearing more of her makeup than she was. And now he was really drinking, with one in each hand.

I told Dwight about school, and he nodded. "You can't do this forever. Get out now."

Fuck, even a hardcore guy like Dwight was telling me to get out.

"You've gone as far as you're gonna go in the business." he said, "without doing this" – he made the shape of a gun with his fingers – "or this" – he pretended to stick a needle in his arm. "And once you do," he continued. "That's it, the fucking real world is gone."

Red leaned in and asked what we were talking about. Dwight just shrugged and ordered another round. This was usually when the girl left me and sidled up to my mysterious biker friend, but Red stayed on my lap. I wondered to myself, was I getting suckered by another pair of tits?

Suddenly, Dwight announced: "This place sucks. Let me show you our clubhouse."

I thought it was a bad idea, but the girls and Vince agreed with Dwight. He leaned over and said to me: "Don't worry about the girls. I'll tell everyone you guys are exclusive. Or we can dump them and get new ones." Boom! Just like that. New girls. It was an interesting concept, but we all went together.

Vince stopped me in the parking lot. "We're not leaving the 'Vette downtown," he said, "and maybe you should drive. Let's skip the clubhouse. You can blame it on me."

"I can drive the 'Vette?" I asked.

"Yeah, but ..."

I interrupted him "... if there's one scratch, anything out of place, you'll kill me, blah, blah, blah."

Vince then turned to our little group, and said: "Dwight, ladies, we should call it a night."

When Dwight began to protest, Vince made up a story about having to meet one of his beer distributors at 9 a.m.

Dwight then hugged me and said to me: "Remember what I told you. Do it now." And then he hugged me again.

To my surprise, Red and Blondie said they were also going to call it a night. Just as we left, Red said "Maybe I could come and work in Niagara sometime?"

"That would be nice" I told her. She kissed me goodbye as I started up the 'Vette. Was she still playing me? Probably. Either way, I was headed back to the Falls.

Vince slept all the way back. That's why he didn't want to drive. He didn't want to look too fucked up if Pat was waiting up for him. I took the highway all the way down to Fort Erie. I could crash at Jenny's and Vince could cut through Buffalo on his way to Niagara Falls, New York. We stopped at a 7-Eleven so I could wash all that shit off his face and have a smoke and a coffee. He then went inside, got two chili dogs, some nachos and two cans of Coke.

"Ah," he bellowed, "the breakfast of champions." Grease always settled Vince's stomach after a night of drinking.

Vince took the 'Vette's driver's seat and we were moving again. "Fun, huh?" he asked.

I nodded, but I was done.

"Look," he said, "I don't want to ruin your mood, but we still got lots to discuss."

I nodded again as he pulled in the driveway at Jenny's.

"She gonna let you in?"

"I got a key."

"OK," he answered. "I know you're off for a few days but call me tomorrow anyway."

I nodded and made my way to the door. I tried to be as quiet as possible, but then I heard a little voice say "Ian?"

It was Jenny's daughter, Charlotte. She was 3, and absolutely adorable.

For all her faults, Jenny was a dedicated mother, and you could see the results in her daughter.

Charlotte ran into my arms and asked: "Where have you been?"

I playfully shook her, and said "Why? Are you writing a book?"

She giggled and kissed my chin. Just then, Jenny came stumbling out of her bedroom. "Uh, oh," I looked at Charlotte and said, now we're in trouble."

Charlotte hid her face in my shirt and kept giggling.

"What time is it?" Jenny asked.

"Time for bed" I answered.

I picked them both up and put them on the bed. Charlotte said, "good night Ian," and cradled herself in her mother's arms. I kissed them both good night and passed out on the other side of the bed, fully clothed, and smelling of chili dogs.

Chapter 7
I'm Hungee

I was woken up by a tug on my shirt sleeve. When I looked down, Charlotte whispered "I'm hungee." She hadn't mastered r's yet.

"You're hungee?" I whispered back. "Go use the bathroom and then we'll eat, ok?"

She ran towards the bathroom. I kissed Jenny on the back of her neck and told her I was going to get something for Charlotte to eat. She mumbled something and gave me a thumbs-up. She wasn't what you'd call a morning person. Charlotte came into the kitchen, in her pink footie pajamas and her Green Bay Packers baseball cap that I gotten for her a few months ago. The first thing she did every morning was put it on. She could not have looked any cuter.

"What would you like?" I asked her, half hoping she would ask for bacon and eggs, so I could wash the taste of Corona, cigarettes and weed out of my mouth. But she asked for Frosted Flakes. Easy enough. Two bowls, some milk, OJ for her and a can of Coke for me.

I told her if she was quiet, we could sit on the couch and watch cartoons. She agreed. We settled in and turned on some cartoons. She was happy. Good kid.

As we were watching cartoons, she started tapping her spoon on my hand, waiting for a reaction. I looked at her and made a scary face. That just encouraged her.

"That's it" I whispered, then I picked her up and started tickling her.

"Noooooooo!" she cried out, trying not to laugh.

Jenny walked out in her bathrobe, smiled and said: "It's like having two kids." She sat on the couch and asked: "What time did you get here last night?"

"Late."

She just frowned and looked away. "You're not working today?" she asked. When I told her what was going on, she said in French — so Charlotte wouldn't understand — that Tyler was a goof. Then she added: "We can stay here after Dale picks up Charlotte."

Dale was her ex-husband. If the term "Canadian douche" was in the dictionary, there should be a picture of this guy. His look and behavior were totally atavistic — rocking a mullet, lumberjack shirt, acid-wash jeans and Kodiaks, he was the kind of guy who cruised around town listening to Trooper on a cassette deck. He lived with his mom and the highlight of his day was getting to be with her.

In an effort to win Jenny back after they split up, he got a job working the door at the club. I had him fired before the end of his first shift. When he asked the other guys why, he was told he should talk to me. Instead, he just left. After that, there wasn't much talk between us.

Jenny got up to make coffee.

We were settling in to our second bowl of cereal when the phone started to ring. I never answered the phone and that drove Jenny nuts. I never answered my own phone, so why, I wondered, would I answer hers? I usually didn't want to talk to anyone. But she picked up, and I heard her tell the person on the other end to "hold on."

"There's some guy named Sean on the phone," she told me.

I said I didn't know any Sean and told her to hang up. As soon as she did, the phone rang again. I heard her say: "Look he doesn't know anyone named Sean." Then she walked back in the room and announced: "He says he's the new guy," and handed me the phone.

"Who gave you this number?" I asked.

"Look," he started, "I can't figure out the lights, and nothing is working."

Fucking new guy. "Is there music on?" I asked.

He said yes.

"OK, I'll be there shortly."

Cody trained this guy my ass, I thought.

"I gotta go fix the lights," I told Jenny. She knew it wasn't some excuse to leave. I was forever bitching about the lights.

"OK," she said. "I'm gonna work days at Heart's ... come by later?"

"OK," I said.

"Promise?"

"I promise."

I took a shower, got dressed and put my stuff together. I kissed them both goodbye, almost like a regular guy going off to work. As I pulled out of the driveway, her ex, Dale, pulled in. We exchanged glances, but that's the closest he would come to confronting me.

I reached under the seat for one of the cans of Keystone Light I usually left under there. I killed half the can in one swig. Now that was breakfast. I tossed the can and lit a smoke. I quickly downed another can and then found myself at the bar.

As I walked in, Arnie was standing in the doorway. "This guy is fucking useless," he told me.

"I thought Cody was training him."

"Just show him the fucking lights," Arnie said, and walked away.

We were building a new DJ booth. The old one had half of the equipment, and we were moving shit into the new one. We had to turn everything off in the new booth, then walk to the old booth and switch the power. Then we had to go to the new booth, turn all the lights on, then switch the power again. The we had to go back to the old booth and manually reset the lights on the motherboard. Then and only then, could we turn on the strobes, the neon that surrounded every stage, then the smoke machine. Unless we followed everything in that precise order, there were no lights.

I told Sean to write it down, because I wouldn't be showing him again. After a couple of times, I told him, it wouldn't seem so complicated.

I went up to the bar and ordered a scotch and a Corona. This day was shaping up to be more of the same ol', same ol'. Marisa put the drinks in front of me and said: "Told you this guy was an idiot."

I laughed and told her to get a shot for herself. Marisa could drink, fight and do just about anything while looking gorgeous doing it. I was starting to think like one of those custies who really wanted to see her ass. She slammed her shot and looked over my shoulder.

The new guy was standing right there. It took a minute to register. I was still daydreaming about Marisa's ass.

"Thanks for helping me out."

"Yeah," I answered, "that's your one and only tutorial." I was starting to like this guy. In two days, he had taken all of our abuse, been forced to drink, and then called at one a.m. to be told he was working the day shift. Maybe he was OK after all.

"Look," I said, "let me make it up to you. Finish your shift and pick me up at home. I'll buy you dinner. My address is in the office. You can pick me up when you're done."

Maybe I would finally get some sleep. I slammed another beer and made my way out.

Opening the side exit of the club, I was hit in the face by a beautiful day. I didn't see sunlight very often, unless I was covering a day shift. Too bad I was going back to bed.

I made it home to an empty house. Nice. Max must have had something going on too. I went downstairs, turned off all the lights and turned on the TV. I just can't sleep without a TV on. I've had people turn it off when I'm sleeping, and it wakes me immediately. Can't explain it. I turned it to the sports channel. It didn't matter what was on, I wouldn't be awake long.

Then I heard Max moving around, so it must have been after five. I didn't feel like talking to anyone, so I stayed downstairs until I heard him leave. The DJ shift change was at six, so maybe Sean would be here by 6:30. Cody was the kind of asshole who came in whenever he fucking wanted to ... 6:45, 7:00, whenever. When anyone would get on him about it, his answer was always: "The night shift starts when the night DJ gets there." So, I made up my own rule. Every 15 minutes cost him twenty bucks and a shot in the shoulder. He started making it in by 6:10.

I went upstairs about 6:20 or so and called Heart's. Ray, the daytime DJ, answered the phone. He was one of my closest friends and an all-around good guy in no small part because he didn't have any of the hang-ups most of the DJs had. He knew he wasn't the star of the show and didn't say too much.

Ray taught music on the side, but business at the club was still hot so he kept three or four shifts. That extra 25 hours a week meant an extra grand in his pocket. It was kinda like my own situation. Ray knew it was in his best interest to leave, but he wasn't ready to give up that cash. His job consisted of answering the phone, playing his guitar, and making sure the broad onstage was naked. It wasn't like we were out digging ditches.

"You seen Mac in there yet?" I asked him.

"Nah," Ray answered, "but he should be rolling in anytime now. You coming in?"

"Yeah, I need to talk to him."

He said he'd tell him, and he'd have a bucket of Export waiting in the booth. More beer, more naked broads, free dinner. I couldn't really complain.

I saw a pair of headlights make their way into the driveway. I opened the door and gave him the "just a sec" signal. I made sure I had my cell, a couple of hundred bucks and no ID. I wasn't driving, so I wouldn't need it. Usually my rule of thumb was that I blew whatever I made Monday during the day, usually between $275 and $350. Since I had no shift today, I had to make sure I had cash on me. Between Marvin slipping me that cash last night and Dwight paying for just about everything, I still had about $320 on me.

The new guy went to get out of his van, and I stopped him. "Where do you think you're going?" I asked.

"Well," he said, "I thought you would drive."

I shook my head no. "New guy always drives," I told him, "and I always get the front seat." I had a phobia about back seats. I've actually taken a cab instead of getting stuffed into a back seat of a friend's car. I don't have too many fears, but I do not sit in the back of cars.

We got back into his van and he asked: "What if I want to drink?"

"I never said you can't drink" I chuckled, "but you still have to drive. We're going to Heart's Desire. Let's roll."

Max's house was almost equal distance to Twilight as it was to Heart's, about two minutes in opposite directions. I told Sean to pull around back near the iron gate.

"Don't we have to go through the front?"

We probably should, actually, because nobody there knew him yet. It was almost seven, so there wasn't much going on. A handful of people were there, maybe six or eight girls, one of them Jenny. She had a huge grin on her face as she came towards us. If she thought I was here to see her, let her think that. The new guy's eyes almost popped out of his head. I forget sometimes how great she looked. I introduced them, and we sat down to eat.

Strip clubs usually have four great things on the menu: a good steak, an all-day breakfast, a club sandwich and a buffet. The old Italian guy who ran the buffet was dynamite. If your man tells you he goes to Hooters for wings, he's an idiot. Might as well actually see the chick naked and get the buffet at the same time.

A bowl of soup, a big chunk of lasagna, a piece of veal, and some pasta. Somewhere down the line I inherited an Italian stomach. After the last three days of chili dogs, drinking and smoking, it would sooth my stomach.

We sat on the riser, second table to the left. We could see the DJ booth, the bar, and both exits in case I had to bolt. It had been a long time since I had to sneak out of a club. I stopped at the bar and got a beer for the new guy and a Coke for me. Love my beer, but not when I'm drinking.

Ray came walking over with the bucket of Export. The drinking would start soon enough. I introduced the new guy and Ray. "So, you're the new protégé?" Ray smiled. It was an old joke with the boys. Most of my protégés snapped, got quirky, wound up in jail, or developed some kind of substance-abuse problem. Nobody said it was easy.

After Ray went back to the booth, I saw the new guy look up and turn white. When I looked back, I understood why. It was Mac, my less than completely legitimate friend, advisor, rabbi, and muscle when the need arose. He looked like Mr. Clean, all bald and buff. He also dressed like a 1960's rude boy, with braces, Doc Martens and spats. He capped that all off with a handlebar mustache that was well past the point of being ridiculous. I hated the kiss and hug thing, but if I didn't do it with Mac, he would pick me up and put me on his shoulder.

Mac was the guy you went to if you had something hot to unload, or you were looking to buy something cheap. You and your buddies got all trashed and stole a U-Haul truck? Mac could find a buyer. Your kid broke his third iPad this year and you need a cheap one? He could get you a replacement. He started as a thief who could steal anything. When he worked at the Tilted Kilt in Windsor, the owners put high-tech cameras all around to see what was up. Mac's solution? He stole the cameras.

He had now graduated to acting as a middleman, brokering deals for anything or anyone, for a price. Heart's was more or less his office, kinda like how Fonzie used Al's men's room on Happy Days. Actually, it was exactly like that. His little office was actually an old bathroom that ran the narrow hallway between the kitchen and the old side entrance, which he had welded shut so no one could sneak up on him. He left the toilet in there. He always joked that he felt like an executive, because he had an office with a shitter. But Mac was also known for something else that I needed. No one talked to Jimmy without going through him.

As he sat down at the table, it occurred to me I'd been calling Sean the new guy for a couple of days because I didn't always remember his name. I couldn't introduce him.

Unlike a lot of hoods who grunted or put on the tough guy act, Mac had impeccable etiquette. He also wanted to know who everyone in the room was. He put his hand out and said: "You'll have to excuse my friend's poor manners. I'm Mac. And you are?" Larry? Lawrence? Lionel? He musta told me."

The new guy shook Mac's hand and said: "Sean, my name is Sean."

This guy now had to start wondering what he had gotten himself into.

"Can you excuse this young fella for a second?" Mac said, pointing at me, "I need his help with something."

We made our way down the hall to Mac's office. He unlocked the door, let us in and locked it behind us. Nothing fancy, a couch and a small table with four chairs. And a huge poster of Kenny Rogers, his all-time favorite performer – everyone has their quirks. On the table were four huge lines of coke. Maybe Mac had his own agenda. The bigger the line, the bigger the problem.

"So," he started, "talk to me."

I laid out the situation with Vince and Chris and Stevie. He almost certainly knew about it anyway, but still allowed me to talk. "So, should I talk to Jimmy?" I asked. "Is that even possible?"

Mac was like Jimmy's secretary, although I would never say it that way to his face. In Niagara if you wanted to talk to Jimmy, you went through Mac. It was Jimmy's way of pulling back. He never wore a patch, didn't need to, but he had Jimmy's blessing to operate in this area. Eventually, that turned into speaking for Jimmy.

Mac pulled down a huge line and slid the tray towards me. I could tell he was contemplating. "Well," he answered, "is there any benefit to you if you talk to Jimmy?" he asked.

I grabbed the tray, did my line. Fuck. So much for eating. "I don't know," I answered, "Vince asked for a favor."

Mac leaned back in his chair and looked at me. We both knew this was a fucked-up situation. "OK," he responded, "I'll ask." He then turned on his Fat Tony from the Simpsons imitation. "And now," he said. "I needs a favor."

It was my turn to play, so I turned into Homer Simpson. "Wait," I said already laughing, "you mean you only did me a favor so you could ask me for a favor? For shame, Mr. Mac." We both started laughing.

"Seriously, though," he replied, "my niece and her boyfriend have gotten involved with some jadrool wrestling promoter in Hamilton. The boyfriend wants to run shows in town, but this guy is giving them a hard time. Tearing down their posters, stealing their guys. The wrestlers are hurting each other, sometimes on purpose. Maybe you could calm these guys down?"

Man, I hadn't wrestled in a while. "You could wear a mask, you know to cover up," he offered. I shook my head no. Masks always made me dizzy. I told Mac to have his niece call me. Since the province of Ontario had let wrestling shows run without insurance, everyone thought they could be a wrestler or promoter. They usually had no skills or understanding of the business. I still had enough amateur skills to put a hold on someone and hold it until the guy settled down.

"And what's with the kid out there?" Mac asked, while snorting up the second line, "you running a Big Brothers program?"

"Well," I answered, "maybe he's OK."

"Since when have you given a fuck about these guys?"

He was right. They were all interchangeable to me. I told him about quitting, or pulling back at least, and the look on his face said he didn't believe me. I wouldn't have a reason to sit in his office, get high and avoid people, if I was no longer in the business.

"We're just starting to make money now, ride it out. Leave the bar but think about everything else."

He was right again. He got up, checked his nose and threw on some cologne. "Now," he said, clapping his hands, "Let's go outside and save your buddy before he offers to buy the waitress a car." We both laughed and left the office.

Chapter 8

Viking

We made our way back to the table. Sean looked like he was in love. I still can't believe how many guys fall for the dancers. Lawyers, doctors, athletes, they all fell for this shit. I've seen guys leave their wives for some 20-year-old, and when the money stops, so does her attention. Then the guy usually tries to go crawling back to his wife. Even worse are the few who just sit in the bar, bitching about their situation. I once had to ban a well-known doctor because he flipped out when he found out the dancer he was screwing was getting married. This fucking guy actually thought that he and the dancer were together — like a real couple. It amazes me how stupid even the most accomplished men can be when they see a hot young woman get naked.

Mac and I sat back down at the table. He only stayed a second. "Sean," he said, extending his hand as he stood, "it was nice to meet you." He then looked at me: "I'll get back to you about that matter. I'll be back here in a few hours with an answer. And think about the other thing."

I nodded as he made his way out the door. Now that the big question was taken care of for now, I had to ask myself if I really wanted to hang out with this Sean guy all night.

I went up to the bar to get another round and to think. When Max the bartender came over, I told him: "Hey, wait 'til

I have time to drink these, then page me to the bar. I wanna get rid of this guy."

Max smiled and said: "So you don't only ditch broads that way?"

I smiled and headed back to our table. I was really hoping Mac could get me an OK to talk to Jimmy. Then I would have to see if I could catch Viking at home. Whenever you ask for a meeting, it usually happens — or doesn't — within the next 24 hours.

I returned to the table with the drinks. Sean looked happy, drinks and broads everywhere. Maybe he wasn't such a bad guy after all. On cue, Max paged me to the bar.

When I grabbed the phone to make it look good, I was surprised to hear Mac say, "noon, you know where." The real surprise was that he said that much. I guess I really did have to go.

I made my way to the table and gave Sean the bad news. "We have to go?" he asked.

"Well," I started, "You don't have to, but I do."

It was obvious he was having fun. I told him I would try to make it back. I left Heart's and walked across the street to a phone booth. It's not that easy to find one anymore, but sometimes you need one, so I knew where all the strategically located ones were. I dialed Viking's number.

It rang twice, and I got his usual "What?" That's how he always answered the phone.

"I'm gonna stop by," I told him.

No reply, no answer, he just hung up. I was on my way to Virgil — a small community in between the falls and Niagara-on-the-Lake. I always liked that end of Niagara. Virgil was small but had the Virgil Arena, where we went every year on May 24 to watch the fireworks. But there was not much else there.

Except Viking's place. It was off Concession 3, out in the middle of nowhere. It was only 15 minutes from Heart's, but it was like I was in the middle of another province. All trees and dirt, not much else.

I made my way up his dirt driveway and parked the car.

Phil "Viking" Burns had lived out here his entire life. The property had been passed down from his grandfather to his father to him.

It wasn't a big lot, but valuable because everything else in the area land-wise was owned by the Harrison family, Niagara's version of the Kennedys, complete with three boys who were all total douche bags.

Phil's family had been holding up the sale of the land for years and that meant that issues had erupted between the two families for years.

A whole crew of us were down the road at the old Polish Hall one night for a stag when Phil's father came looking for him, telling him that, Kim and Justin, the two oldest Harrison boys, had "messed with" Phil's sister, Beatrice. Father and son left together, both vowing in front of a room full of people that they would take care of the Harrison brothers.

I stayed and kept partying. The next day it was all over the news how Kim was shot to death and Justin was wounded out on Concession Road the night before.

The cops came down on all of us. But not a single shred of evidence ever linked the Burns' to the event, even after they threatened the Harrison boys in front of a room full of guys.

Phil was definitely the kind of guy I needed to watch my back. I didn't really think that anything would happen going to this meeting, but you never really know. It's all in how you presented yourself, I thought. If I walked in like some kind of big shot, with not a care in the world, it might send the wrong message.

It would also put a tail on me. The cops weren't watching me, I was a nobody. But if I was going to be sitting outside the Burnt clubhouse with Phil Burns, the cops were bound to notice.

I got out of the car and walked towards the garage. As I made my way into the building, I could see his feet sticking out from underneath a Ford F-150 pickup. I announced I had arrived but got no answer.

After a few minutes, Phil finally grunted: "Hand me a 10-millimeter wrench." I don't know one wrench from another, so I grabbed one and slid it underneath the truck.

It got thrown out from underneath the truck. "Wrong one, Billy," he said.

I don't know why he always called me Billy. "Then get it you're fucking self," I answered.

He slid out from underneath the truck and stood over me. He was almost a foot taller than me, clean shaven, no tattoos, but with red hair halfway down his back. Had we not been friends for years, I would be backing down right about then.

"How 'bout you knock off the bullshit," I growled, poking him in the chest, "and get me a beer, Doug." My response to his calling me Billy was to always call him Doug.

Slowly, I got a smile. Sometimes this game would go too far, and a few punches would be thrown. Never anything too serious, but I always stayed on my toes.

He turned and walked to the fridge, grabbing two beers and Big Daddy. Big Daddy was a bong he had made from an old juice container. It was so big, Phil attached a little electric motor and fan to it. If you were just pretending to take a hit, he'd flip it on, and the smoke would rush into your lungs whether you wanted it to or not. It was pretty fucking funny.

The bowl actually had enough room for an entire eighth of weed. "Uh, I don't know if I got time for Big Daddy," I told him.

He slammed down the beers and Big Daddy and announced: "Too late, he's already packed."

I knew better than to fake it, or he'd flip the switch. Well just a little can't hurt, I thought to myself.

Five minutes later, I was completely high. I used to really love the green until all that hydroponic shit started popping up. It tended to make me edgy and paranoid, which is not something you need from your weed. But Phil grew his own and it did the trick. He also brewed his own moonshine. I found that pretty fucked up. When the rave and Red Bull scene ramped up in Niagara, he sold his moonshine to all the raver kids. Not my sort of thing at all, but it was everywhere for a while. Between the weed, moonshine and the eventual sale of this land, my old friend would be very rich one day, and he didn't give a fuck about anything.

I told him what I needed.

He went to grab two more beers and sat down. "I'll go with you," he said as he tossed me a beer. "But if those guys fuck with me, I'm gonna start shooting."

Most people, even the guys in Burnt, were scared of him. He knew it too. They had tried to recruit him, but he passed on it because he knew it was bullshit, that they would only try to kill him and take his money. He didn't need them, or anyone else. He was pretty much a loner, just him and his wife and kid. If he had his way, he would just stay on his farm.

He always felt that he owed me after the shooting. The cops came to me first, and I told them nothing. Phil always felt that the others followed my lead after that. True or not, I used it to my advantage. We had nothing in common, but it was nice to come here and just get wrecked. After a particularly bad breakup, I partied for three straight days with him and his sister Beatrice. Nobody said anything, they just let me go. I would miss the two of them. Beatrice and I hung out for years as well, but it never went anywhere, not for my lack of trying. It was probably better, I didn't want to be too connected with these rednecks.

"I don't think anything will happen," I told him, "but a little protection can't hurt."

Then we just sat there. No awkward silence, just both enjoying being high.

"Stevie and Chris are a pair of faggots, and I just don't like Vince. Think he would help you? As far as S and C go, you're only doing this to fuck with them."

Pretty astute for a bootlegging, weed-growing hick. It made me ask myself: Why was I getting involved, anyway? Phil was one of my only friends outside of the business, and he saw things more clearly than I did. As I was thinking what Phil said over, we both heard another car coming up the driveway.

As she got out, I could tell it was Beatrice. Man, did she look good. Phil slapped me on the shoulder. "I told her you were coming by," he laughed. "She practically flew here."

As she walked into the garage, I realized I had forgotten how gorgeous she was. About 5-foot-5, she had curly long red hair and green eyes. She was about five years younger than me and had a kid when she was fresh out of high school, although you'd never know looking at her body now.

"Hey, Ian," she said, giving me a quick hug.

I tried to think the last time someone called me by my given name. Not Doc, Harley Richards, DJ, douche bag, Billy or hey you. Even my father called me Doc.

She grabbed a beer and took a haul off Big Daddy. She was bent over, and as she straightened up, her hair flew everywhere, seemingly in slow motion, just like Rita Hayworth, and she broke out laughing. It made me laugh too.

Phil just grinned and said: "Big Daddy gets ya every time!"

We all broke out laughing again. I knew I should go, but after Beatrice walked in, I wanted to stay. We sat at around, talking about nothing. There was no need to impress anyone. Then Phil finally said: "Well that's it. You're not driving. You can stay in the back room. I'll get you up early and we'll take care of your problem."

She never asked what "the problem" was.

I looked at her and asked: "You staying?"

She just laughed, and said, "nice try."

I made my way to the back of the house. The room had a TV, a nightstand and a giant bed. The first thing I would usually do would be to turn on the TV, but fuck it, I thought, and crawled into bed.

I rolled around for about ten minutes. Then I heard the door open just a crack. The house was far from town, so there was no extra light, and I didn't know what was up. Then someone got into bed with me, fully clothed, and put their arms around my stomach. When I tried to roll over, I heard Beatrice say, "knock it off and go to sleep." For the first time in years, I fell asleep almost immediately.

Chapter 9

Let's Go Fucking Do This

As my freshly opened eyes focused, I could see that the clock said 9:30. That would leave me lots of time.

Beatrice must have snuck out earlier, but it's not like Phil wouldn't know. We had done this a few times over the years. No sex, no taking off our clothes, she would just lay behind me. With any other woman, it would be frustrating. I have my own rule with house guests: if you're spending the night and we're having sex, you're welcome to stay in the bed. If you're just over to party, you can find a couch. But I didn't mind bedding down with Bea.

But she and her brother had an annoying habit of telling each other everything. You couldn't tell either something without the other one knowing. Since nothing happened, I guess he couldn't really say anything.

When I made my way outside, Phil, Beatrice and his wife, Beth, and their daughter, Shelley, were all sitting at a picnic table outside.

Phil told me wanted to go to Stacks, the diner down the road. Beth said she wasn't interested, but Beatrice wanted to go. It would be just the three of us. That's good enough for me.

I went in the truck with Phil and Bea followed in her car. As soon as we got in the truck, Phil put a .22 in the glove box, a .38 under his belt, and another pistol I couldn't quite make out under the seat. “If things go bad for you,” he said. “I’m coming in there swinging.”

I knew him well enough to know that he meant it. I didn’t want to say anything at the time, but would have to calm him down after his sister left. I felt like the whole thing wasn’t gonna go bad. But I knew that if it did, I’d be well protected. Or shot in the crossfire.

We got to Stacks and grabbed a booth. Phil made his way to the bathroom. That left just Beatrice and me. “So, what was the deal with last night?” I grinned at her.

She didn’t even look up from the menu. “What?” she said. “Like we’ve never done that before?”

“Yeah, but that was years ago,” I answered, “and what am I gonna have to do to make it happen a little more often?”

She finally looked up from her menu. “Ian,” she replied, “we’ve talked about this before.”

“Not in a long time.”

“And what’s changed since then?” she asked. “You’re still a big kid, working at that bar, with two or three different girls at any time. I got J.R. at home with me now. You ready to help raise a 7-year-old?”

“Maybe.”

“Maybe isn’t good enough,” she answered, getting angry. “I’m not waiting up ’til four in the morning to see if you show or not. You’re not ready for any of that.”

I knew I should’ve started to back off, but I couldn’t. “What would I have to do to show you I’m serious?”

She shook her head and looked away.

The tension was broken by Phil sitting back down. “Let’s order two of every fucking thing!” he yelled. That made Beatrice smile, so maybe she wasn’t too mad at me. We all had eggs and bacon with toast and split a basket of home fries between the three of us. I liked a woman that ate, and she could eat.

By the time we started slowing down, it was going on eleven. “We gotta go,” I told Phil.

Beatrice never asked, but I had no doubt he told her where we were going. “Be careful,” she said as we all walked out together.

“I will, Queen Bea,” I said. “I promise.”

Her eyes lit up when I called her by the nickname I had given her years ago. But she made no promise to see me later, she just smiled and drove off.

The Burnt clubhouse was about 15 minutes down the road. The last mile or so was dirt road; the only way in, and only way out.

As we hit the dirt road, I told Phil: “Drive straight up to the compound. I don’t know if they’re going to let you in or make you wait at the gate. Either way you should stay in the truck.”

“Fuck that,” he replied. “I’m driving into the compound and parking across from the building. If they don’t like it, then those faggots Stevie and Chris can come move me.”

He had a point. Down at the gate, he would be useless if I got fucked over. Phil was itching for something to happen, which was the opposite of what I wanted.

We made our way to the security gate when some hangaround stopped us. He didn’t look familiar, but then there were a lot of new faces around Burnt lately. The Royal City Riders were making their push into the area. The choices for Jimmy’s crew were simple: joint them or fight. Jimmy had formed the Burnt in the early ’70s and was now pushing 60. He hadn’t made a decision about which way to go. The dilemma divided his crew. Guys like Stevie were all for it – it was a chance a move up the biker food chain, more prestige, more money. Guys like Chris were against it. He knew he was expendable and probably would not make the cut into the Royal City Riders. A lot of guys would be told to get lost. To most guys, getting lost means to leave it alone and take off. In their life, it means they take your bike, anything you earned from being associated with the gang, and maybe your old lady, if she was a looker. In more severe cases, it cost you your life.

Unlike what you see on TV, there were no big flags flying the Burnt colors or guys walking around in their patches. The guys dressed work casual, jeans and work boots. And the clubhouse looked like any other building in the area — except for the extra security, of course.

This was the main clubhouse for Burnt. They had another in Port Colborne and a smaller one in Grimsby.

Stevie and Chris met us in the parking lot. There were no handshakes or warm hugs. I began to wonder if I crossed the line asking for this meet. Stevie motioned for me to lean on the car, so he could frisk me. Words would be at a minimum until we were inside. The less said, the less anyone listening in understood.

They knew better than to frisk Phil. Both Stevie and Chris pointed to the truck, which was as close as they wanted to get to him.

He looked at me, nodded and got in the truck. We walked through the parking lot in silence. When we reached the front door of the building, Stevie opened the door and ushered Chris and I inside. The door was then locked. This wasn't looking too good.

As plain as the outside of the building was, the inside was a shrine to the Burnt, with colors and flags everywhere. The wall directly to the left of the entrance was decorated with patches from former members. You never own your patch, you're more or less renting it from the club.

The front room was large and open, with a bar that ran the length of the back wall. On the left, there was a small hallway that led to the bathroom. On the right, a hallway leading to a number of small offices. A long table was set in front of the bar.

Jimmy emerged from one of the offices. Even though he was nearing 60, he was built like a swimmer, tall and lean. His hair was still pretty full, and he had a short-trimmed beard. Just like his clubhouse, everything on Jimmy was tidy.

Jimmy motioned for me to sit down. He sat across from me, while Chris stood behind the bar. Stevie eventually sat down on

Jimmy's left. It was clear he was being groomed to rise in the club.

"What can I do for you, Doc?" Jimmy asked, in a friendly enough tone. He no doubt already knew why I was there but was giving me the courtesy of an opportunity to talk.

I decided to skip any bullshit and get to the point. "Well, Vince is in the hole $17,000," I began. "It didn't start out that way, but I guess now you guys ..."

Jimmy held up his hand. It didn't take long for him to drop the civility. "Your fucking friend," he started, "Is going to get you in a lot of trouble." It was clear there wouldn't be any negotiations.

"Look, he's gonna pay you the money ..." I started before Chris cut me off.

"You're fucking right he is," he said.

I knew Stevie wouldn't help, but I thought Chris would be on my side.

Jimmy turned to Chris and told him to shut the fuck up.

Once Jimmy regained his composure, he looked me in the eye and said: "Your buddy has two days to come up with the money. Good seeing ya, kid."

Jimmy got up from the table and sat at the bar. That was my signal to leave.

As I got up to leave, I knew better than to say anything. Stevie and Chris fell in behind me. If I was wary before, I was downright fucking paranoid now. That whole exchange lasted about 45 seconds. What was the point? It was then that I realized that I was being an idiot to think it would have turned out any other way. I felt like a fucking tool, thinking I could do something.

Stevie leaned over and said: "Your buddy doesn't have the money, and I'm taking the 'Vette."

As I walked towards the truck, I could see it was already running, and Phil was on the phone. Stevie and Chris both looked pretty pissed that he was on the phone. Phil looked pretty pissed too. I didn't want any of these guys to make a move, or someone would start shooting. I walked over to the truck and got in. "What the fuck are you doing?" I said. "You're gonna get us both shot."

Phil just looked at me and said: "Your phone started ringing the minute you walked in there. It was pissing me off, so I threw it in the glove box." He fell silent for a second.

"Has this story got a fucking point?" I asked.

He had been keeping an eye on Stevie and Chris but turned his attention back to me. "I turned the radio on to drown out your phone, when I heard the news ..." he stopped again. "... there's been a shooting in the parking lot at Twilight."

Viking spun the truck into a 180 and headed back towards the front gate. Not even waiting for it to open, he drove straight through it, smashing the gate arm and sending it flying in the air. This fucking nut job wouldn't be happy until they were shooting at us, I thought to myself.

We drove around, not exactly knowing where we should go.

Going to the bar didn't seem like a good idea, especially with Phil and his three guns sitting beside me.

Until I found out what really happened, going to my place didn't sound like a good idea either.

I couldn't totally take off; that would make me look guilty if suddenly I was M.I.A.

I had to find somewhere to sit it out for a while and figure out what happened.

"Let's go back to your place," I told Phil.

He didn't say a word. We just headed towards the farm.

My cell phone started ringing again. I grabbed it and said: "Yeah?"

"Doc, is that you? It's Mitch." Mitch worked next door at the Sunrise, our competition. I always found it strange that two peeler bars were side by side, but it seemed to work. Although the owners hated each other, the girls jumped ship all the time. We would raid each other's staff, and tempers would flare. Then things would go back to normal. Mitch worked with us for a bit, then went to the Sunrise. I didn't think much of him, as a

DJ or a person, but he couldn't shut up, so I was nice to him, so he would feed me info. Sunrise was one of the few places I didn't drink in, so it was nice to have a hook there.

"Mitch, what the fuck is going on up there?"

He didn't answer right away. I was about to end the call when I heard him say: "There's a body on the ground with a sheet over it. Whoever it is ... is gone." He went silent again for a minute, then said what I had been thinking but didn't want to hear.

"I think it's Vince."

I immediately dropped the phone and grabbed Phil's arm and started shouting: "We have to go to the bar! Now!"

Surprisingly, he stayed calm and simply said: "No."

I tried to grab the steering wheel, but he was far too strong. I tried it a second time and he shoved me away so forcefully I bounced off the passenger door.

"What the fuck are you doing?" he asked.

I could barely speak. "It's Vince," I said.

"And going up there isn't going to change that."

I was going to be sick.

He handed me one of the guns, and calmly said, "take this."

Would I even know how to use it? The last time I fired anything was a rifle when I was a cadet, and I was a pretty terrible shot even then.

I was exhausted and didn't know if I was going to throw up or cry.

"Let's go back to my place," he started, "and settle in until we know what the fuck happened. Driving around isn't going to help us." He grabbed both our cell phones and put them on airplane mode. "For now, no one needs to know where we are," he said. "We'll flip them back on when we know what happened."

I just rested my head on the passenger window.

Phil, who was not the known for his affectionate ways, put his hand on my shoulder and said, "we'll figure this out. In the meantime, try not to shoot yourself in the balls with that thing."

I couldn't even respond.
What the fuck was gonna happen now?

Chapter 10

Is That All There is?

On the ride back to Phil's, I had no idea what to do, who to speak with, or anything.

The only thing floating around my head was anger, directed mainly at myself. I thought I was so fucking smart, always laughing at the idiots who took a day job, went to work and gave a fuck about things. I had just been floating along, thinking that I could do as I pleased, and no one would suffer.

Now, I was pretty sure Vince was dead, and there was nothing I could do about it. I was a nobody, a kid who knew a bunch of psychos who had no issue with killing each other. Suddenly, the girls, the late nights, the booze and the drugs all seemed pretty fucking pointless. Walking away always seemed an option. But now I wasn't sure.

I hadn't even noticed that we had made it back to Phil's place. He got out of the truck and said: "Stay here, I gotta talk to the wife and make a quick call." I just nodded my agreement and waited outside the truck.

Within a minute, Beth was loading Shelley into her car. She didn't say anything, didn't even look at me. She jammed the car into reverse, straightened out and squealed out of the driveway. She drove as badly as her husband. It was hard to tell if she was scared or just pissed off. Phil probably just told her she had to go with no explanation.

He began walking towards the garage and signaled me to follow. I could see the two guns in his waistband, and a third in his hand. I guess he felt the need to replace the one he gave me.

Once inside the garage, we both went up to its second level. It had a few couches, a punching bag and some assorted free weights. It also had the storage locker for Phil's long rifles and shotguns. He opened it, pulled out a sawed-off 12-gauge and threw it to me. "Remember how to load one of those?"

I nodded.

He reached down to the bottom of the locker, grabbed a box of shells, and put them on the table.

In the time it took for me to absorb all of what was happening around me, a green pickup backed onto Phil's property and settled itself not too far from the road. He didn't tell me what that was about, and I didn't ask.

We popped on the TV, and it was official. Vince was gone. Channel 11 from Hamilton was the closest thing we had to a local news channel. Most of the stations around here were from across the river in Buffalo, which I'm sure would be picking it up as well.

The announcer reported his death, and his full name, Vincent Joseph Bruno.

Then they trotted out the usual bullshit, tying it to a looming gang war, between the old timers, locals and the Royal City Riders. "Fuck, it don't take long to trot out that old fucking story," Phil said.

Only this time it didn't seem like the same old bullshit. Every act of violence brought out the pundits and the so-called experts. And they each had their own theory of what was going on.

Niagara had been pretty quiet for years, until old man Castellano died in his sleep. He had run the area for years but had been steadily losing his grip. Jimmy and his boys had picked up the leftovers, rebuilt it, and made the wops answer to them. There was some resistance at first, but a few killings put everyone else in line.

Now that it was clear Vince was gone, there was a lot of shit for me to think about, and start sorting out. I reached for my cellphone. Phil grabbed it and said: “Not yet, there’s still a lot to figure out.”

He was right. As much as I played in this world, I didn’t belong in it. But Phil really did know what it was like to have someone hunt you down. He knew the signs of someone fucking you over.

I put the cellphone down, grabbed two beers and pointed at Big Daddy. “You gonna load that bitch up, or what?” While getting high might not be part of a normal grieving process after your friend gets shot to death, I was pretty sure not much was standard behavior in this case.

We smoked solid for about ten minutes, and I couldn’t remember the last time I had ever been as high. I knew I would have to eventually turn on my phone and deal with the world, but it wasn’t time for that just yet. So many questions were running through my head. I couldn’t put them into full thoughts, but I kept wondering if I had been screwed or I had been saved.

Phil grabbed a few more beers and sat down on the longer of the two couches. “You know, pretty soon were gonna hafta deal with this shit,” he said. “The worst of it might not be done yet.”

He was right, but I wasn’t done with what we were doing yet. I cranked up the stereo and turned to Phil. “You ready, Doug?”

“I am, Billy.” Phil rolled up his sleeves and threw me a clothesline.

I ducked it, turned around, grabbed his shoulders, and we started slamming around the room. It might not be what anyone else would do in the situation, but it worked for us. Only stopping to relight Big Daddy or swig down another beer, we kept slamming around until I blacked out.

When I finally woke up, I was dazed and a little bruised, but surprisingly not all that hungover. We had smoked more than we drank; but, then again, we drank plenty.

When I rolled over, I was only half surprised to see Queen Bea laying with me. What was surprising was that she was completely naked. That was new.

I got up, dreading having to listen to all the messages I had avoided yesterday. I got dressed and sat on the edge of the bed. The first message was Pat, Vince's wife. Well, now she was his widow. It wasn't really a message, just her wailing into the phone. Selfishly, I hadn't even thought about how it would affect her.

The next message was from Arnie. I didn't even listen to it. I would deal with the bar and all of the associated bullshit later.

Then came one from Cody, who no doubt only wanted the dirt. I deleted that one too.

After that, it was the usual suspects, people from the bar, family and friends, checking to see I was alive.

Then there was a second one from Pat. She was a little more composed, informing me that once the details were settled, I could come for a viewing, but I was not welcome at the funeral.

The last message was my dad. All he said was: "We need to talk." Short and to the point. That one scared me the most.

While I was checking my messages, Queen Bea began to stir. She sat up, put on my T-shirt, and just smiled at me.

"So, after all these years, we finally did it and I don't remember it?"

She lit a smoke, and laid down with her head in my lap, looking up at me. "Well, that was the plan, but when I snuck in here, you were crying. I've known you since we were kids and I've never heard you cry."

I had no answer to that. Was I really crying, or was this just another excuse to delay our 15-year wait on sleeping together? I looked down at her and didn't know what to say. "I don't know what the fuck to do."

In a flash, Queen Bea was standing in front of me. "I can't believe you. Your best friend is dead, and all you can think about is yourself? Fuck you, Ian."

She started to walk out of the room, and I grabbed her by the arm. She spun around and took a swing, grazing my chin. All the Burns could fight, even the women.

"Hey, come on," I said softly.

"Come on nothing, this is why we never took it further! You don't give a shit about anything. I can't live like that." She grabbed her clothes and stormed out of the room.

When I made my way outside, Phil was sitting at the picnic table with Queen Bea, who wouldn't even look at me.

Phil looked around and broke the silence with "well, now what?"

Good fucking question, I thought. "Well, I guess I should head into the Falls. If the cops are gonna be around asking questions, I should show my face before everyone starts talking."

I had to figure a lot of shit out and had no idea where to start. "It would be nice if I got into the Falls without being pulled over."

Phil thought about that and said: "We'll take the truck."

Yeah, a day after a murder in town and I was gonna drive around with him in his truck full of guns.

Queen Bea, who still wouldn't even look up at me, said, "Take my car. No one is looking for it."

"And you'll drive my piece of shit?"

She waved me off. "My dad was a mechanic, remember? I've driven lots of wrecks." Without looking at me she threw me the keys. Well, one issue settled. Now the big one.

"I think you should stay here." I said to Phil.

"Fuck that," he snapped. "You got no idea what's going on out there." He knew what I was getting at. Driving around with a notorious nut job wasn't exactly gonna help me. "You want the cops snooping around here? You're gone and the old lady and kid not here?"

My big concern was that he would get pulled over with a truck full of guns. Or worse, resist the cops and get arrested, leaving me on my own. I had no idea what was coming, but I sure as fuck needed him around.

He eventually bought the idea. The plan was for Queen Bea to leave, for me wait a bit and then go. They wouldn't pull us both over, or at least that was what we thought.

Queen Bea stood up and started walking towards my car. She didn't look at either one of us. She started up the car and spun out of the long driveway. As she blew past us, she smiled and gave me the finger. Maybe she wasn't as mad as I thought. I'd give her a few minutes, then take off. Hopefully she'd attract the cops. She was totally clean but would flirt with them long enough to let me breeze by.

Phil walked me to her car. "As soon as you get to your place, call me from Max's phone. Don't say nothing, just tap it twice on the table if you're OK. If I gotta come right away, tap it once. Got it, Billy?"

I nodded. It was time to get the fuck outta there. Phil just stood there, like he was trying to say something. He just turned and walked away. "What? No kiss?" I yelled. He just kept walking, muttering about what a pussy I was.

Queen Bea made it about half a mile before she got pulled over. As I blew by, she was twirling her hair, totally playing the cop. Even with all the family history, she was still considered a catch. I could count her boyfriends on one hand, and we had known each other for years. I just smiled and cursed myself at the same time. Fuck, I might wind up with Phil as my brother-in-law.

As I cruised up the hill, it looked like our plan worked. Until I saw the second cruiser gunning towards me, lights flashing like a disco. Fuck me. Time to pull over.

Over the years, I've had to deal with the cops, usually bar-related shit, nothing too serious. Niagara Falls could still be a small town in many ways, so I knew the younger cops from school or the gym.

Most of the people I knew have two approaches with the cops. The first was to be a hard-on, telling them to go fuck themselves. I never understood that. Chances are you're doing shit if they're already bugging you, so ramping them up by being a dick didn't seem like the smartest idea. Then again, maybe it was just a show for any boys who might be watching. Many a cop has told me these guys are all balls in front of their brothers, but most turn into sniveling babies when they're on their own.

The second approach always seems to be the friendly guy, which is actually just as dangerous. If you talk too much, you could hang yourself. Some guys think they're smarter than the cops, but they've heard it all. A minor change in wording, a barely noticeable look and you're fucked.

Most biker clubs won't allow cops as members, but they have no problem dealing with law enforcement to get the whole story. Cops, bikers, wannabes, they all live in the same world. The bikers use some of the same tactics.

I had my own version. Being a dick served no purpose and talking too much might fuck me. So, I would answer the inconsequential shit, and just smile at the stuff I didn't want to answer. By looking in the rear-view mirror, I could see that both cops got out of the cruiser, neither of them familiar. I shut off the engine and put my hands on the wheel.

One of them leaned into the car, while the other walked all around the vehicle. "Thought changing cars would fool us?" the first one asked.

"Nope, just got a bunch of shit to do and my car is on its last legs."

The cop circling the car yelled to have the trunk open. I popped it. No reason not to. He knocked around a couple of things then slammed it shut.

"Where you going?"

"Home, a little too much drinking last night. Couldn't drive."

The cop leaned straight into the car. "How's Jimmy?"

I looked at him, smiled and looked away. He smiled back and punched me in the face.

Fuck that hurt, but I didn't want to let him know. I kept smiling, trying not to let the stinging in my eyes look like tears. "Anything else, sir?" which, as I said it, I was positive was going to get me another shot in the head. I could tell he was thinking about it but pulled back.

The other cop then came to the window. I was still bracing for a punch. He leaned in and smiled at me. Speaking in French, he told me: "Be careful up your way, guys are getting shot." He then leaned in the car, threw a Royal City Riders support sticker on my seat and walked away.

Chapter 11

You Fuckin' Blaming Me?

As the cops pulled away, I just sat there, staring at the Royal City Riders support sticker laying on the front seat of the car.

All the major clubs had some form of support gear, usually shirts or stickers. Some clubs restricted the use of their name to members only, and usually had some kind of ambiguous nickname on their support gear. Not the Royal City Riders. They wanted the name out there, and it was tailor-made for Niagara.

The top of the sticker was orange, which began to fade halfway down, but still hit the bottom of the page on the right. The rest of the page was blue, transitioning its way up, filling the rest of the sticker. In the background was an image combining Niagara Falls, the casino, and Lundy's Lane. Across all of it were the Royal City Riders letters, the first R normal, the C larger than the R, and the last R written backwards. Underneath the logo were the words: "Can't stop the flow."

Not exactly subtle. It was their calling card, which meant they were already here. I had heard stories about the Royal City Riders sending fruit baskets to local police forces just before they moved into their town. I have to admit, I was a bit of a geek when it came to collecting this kind of shit. I had a Double Back MC support shirt, I had a box of Burnt MC stickers, fuck, I even had a Vipers MC hoodie. But Royal City Riders gear? This stuff had never been seen down here before. The Royal City Riders had been making headway into Canada for years, but like a lot of other shit in Niagara, it played out a little differently.

From what I'd heard on the news, from cops, and some of the locals, the Royal City Riders planned on making Ontario their power base, then would branch out across the country. Some clubs would be taken out by force, others would be negotiated with.

A tactic the Royal City Riders frequently used was to let the area gangs fight it out amongst themselves for the top spot and make a deal with the winner. Why take a chance on a bunch of losers? Let the local dummies fight it out, keep what's left, then move your own boys in to run the show.

From what I had heard, Toronto, Kingston, Hamilton, London and Niagara were supposed to be the setup spots. These areas had tourists, strip clubs and jails, all the right places to sell drugs and pimp out pussy. The club had allegedly been working their way through the first four areas before it hit Niagara.

Jimmy had built the Burnt from the ground up, taking almost 30 years to establish relationships with the local cops, the mafia, the hangarounds that did all the shit work, even local politicians. He ran a tight ship and didn't give out his beloved Burnt MC colors to just anybody. He was satisfied running Niagara and didn't see the need for expansion. As he told me himself many times: "Fuck national clubs, going to a meeting every fucking ten minutes, dealing with some asshole in Vermont or California telling me what to do. I'll die for these colors." A lot of guys said that shit, but Jimmy meant it, at least he did up until recently.

Jimmy was pushing 60 and had more money than he could ever spend. He owned a beautiful farm, was attached to his old lady and had the respect of everyone around him. The rumor was his crew were offered full Royal City Riders colors immediately, no questions asked. When Jimmy turned them down, he made it known he would take it personally if any members of his crew made the jump as individuals. It became obvious to everybody watching that the complicated situation would have to play out, and that neither side was assured of coming out on top.

Of course, that all meant fuck all to me, while I was sitting in Queen Bea's car, staring at the sticker the cop left me. I threw it in the glove box.

I was going to go see my dad, to make sure he knew I was all right, but then it hit me: If anyone knew what the fuck was going on, it would be Mac. I remember a while back when the Royal City Riders reached out to Mac to talk to Jimmy for them, it caused a lot of friction.

All that bullshit you hear about clubs not dealing with each other, is just that, bullshit. They all have contact numbers for one another and knew exactly who to get a hold of someone when they needed to iron some problem out.

I drove towards Heart's to talk to Mac. What the fuck, I thought to myself, it was noon. I'd grab a beer and the buffet.

I parked around back and went in through the rear entrance. It was a staff-only entrance, but I didn't want anyone to see me. When I came out, I was standing right behind the bar. My eyes were still adjusting to the light, when — whack! — I got hit in the head with a shoe. My vision blurred for a moment. When it came back into focus, Jenny was standing in front of me, hitting my chest and screaming at me.

"Where the fuck have you been? You don't even call me? You're a fucking asshole!"

Man, she was loud. The day doorman, some big fat kid, came running over, when Mac grabbed him by the arm and told him he had the situation under control. He then stood in between Jenny and I, trying to put an end to our little fight. He asked her nicely to get us both a plate from the buffet. He then turned to me and smiled: "Always gotta cause a scene, don't ya?" Besides being hung over, getting punched in the face and assaulted with a shoe, I was actually starting to feel a little bit better, a bit more normal. I just laughed.

As soon as we sat down in his office, he looked up and said: "I'm sorry about Vince — what the fuck is going on?"

I grabbed the support sticker out of my pocket and threw it on his desk.

Mac picked it up, looked it over and threw it on the table in disgust. “Where the fuck did you get that?”

“Cops.”

“Cops?”

“Yeah, cops,” I told him. “One punched me in the face, the other one threw that in the car.”

“Who were they?” Mac knew just about every cop in town; some were his best customers. He could provide steroids, a second piece, body armor – you know, the kind of stuff you didn’t ask your staff sergeant for.

“Neither one of them looked familiar, but the one spoke to me in French.”

Mac seemed to mull that over. “The boys are finally here,” he said with no small degree of gravity.

“What the fuck does that mean?”

“It’s all their PR bullshit. These guys don’t just show up in town and open up shop. This has been in the works since the ’80s.”

I knew most of that already. Had Jimmy not been so well respected, the Royal City Riders would have bulldozed their way into town, killed Jimmy’s toughest guys, chased off the weak ones, and dealt with who was left. Every biker says they’ll die for their colors, but if they get a better offer, they’ll drop their patch on the floor in an instant. Maybe Jimmy was thinking the same.

It was all above my head. You hear all kinds of shit, and you see things when you’re working in the bar, but you never really knew what was actually going on. It’s a shitty old joke, but when do you know when a biker is lying? His lips are moving.

Mac was probably the only person close to me who had an idea of why Jimmy ran interference for me sometimes. I had a feeling he knew the whole story. “So why did Jimmy take the meeting with me only to make me feel like an asshole yesterday? The whole fucking thing took about 45 seconds.”

Mac stopped eating, lit a smoke and put his feet on the desk. “You tell me, Doc. He puts up with a lot of your shit, for a guy with no patch.”

That was kind of true. I tried not to drop Jimmy’s name, but it saved my ass a few times.

But Mac was angling, trying to figure out why Jimmy pulled strings for me. He looked me dead in the eye, then stared at the ceiling and blew smoke rings: “You’re never gonna tell me, are you?”

After all this shit, I wasn’t in the mood. “That’s between me and Jimmy.”

Mac continued to blow smoke rings. “Jimmy and I, Doc, Jimmy and I,” he said in French. Hearing the French set me off. It was something he’d do in front of the idiots, and sometimes he would do it in Italian, although I only caught half of that. Today it felt like an intentional taunt.

But I couldn’t shut up. I switched over to French as well. “Do I need this now, tabernac? Stop talking in your little riddles. That French cop a buddy of yours, esti?”

In a chaotic burst, he had me backed into the wall. I’d seen him fight three guys at a time, so I wasn’t making any moves. He once tossed a Royal City Riders ass-kisser through the front window of the Castle for disrespecting Jimmy. I’d seen him stare down cops and some of Jimmy’s own guys. Always had a gun in his jacket, a knife in his boot, and a length of chain in his pocket. I was frozen.

He looked away, then had that old Mac, my best buddy, look on his face. But the words weren’t any softer, and they were now back in English. To add to the menace, he used my real name, something I had never heard him say apart from the first time we met. “Ian, you think I’m in on this shit? Do you have any idea what everybody’s laying on me, and all I have to do to see it doesn’t turn into a fucking disaster here? You can skip and jump outta here, this is my fucking life.”

He slowly backed away from me, never turning around, just shuffling his way back to his desk. It was obvious he was furious and trying to calm down.

He popped another smoke in his mouth, lit it, and looked at me. “Ian, mon homme, what a couple of fucked up days, eh? Why don’t you go clean up, you look terrible. I’ll make some calls.”

He held up his hand, pinky up and thumb down. It was usually our way of walking through the bar and using it as a “everything is good” hand sign. I couldn’t shake the feeling that today it meant “you’re pushing your luck boy, beat it.”

I stood up and left his office. Not wanting another shoe in the head, I decided to go out the front to avoid everybody. I walked around back to the car, and really thought I should go see Millie. But what was really nagging me was that I had to deal with my dad.

I walked down the alley that separated Heart’s and a laundromat, making my way to Queen Bea’s car. I hopped in and started it up. Just about to drive away, I could hear thump, thump. What the fuck now? Jenny was standing in the parking lot — in a G-string and heels, nothing else — throwing shoes at the car. “Fuck you, Ian! Get your shit out of my house, we’re done!”

It should have bothered me more, but it happened about once a week. I actually laughed, blew her a kiss and drove away.

I pulled onto Main Street and made my way down Barker Street to Drummond Road. It was almost 2 p.m., so Dad would be either on the way or already at the Dorchester Arms. Retired, still married, and in decent health, he was the local who made it. Everyone in the area had known him since the ’70s, some even from when the family moved to the region in the ’50s. Everyone in that bar had a story about Dad lending him 20 bucks, telling him to go back to his wife, to stop drinking so much. Fuck, two of my mom’s best friends for years had been a Scottish couple that my dad met drinking and insisted they stay with us instead of a hotel. A house with a wife, four kids, two cats and himself, and he brings home two people who wind up staying with us for two weeks and becoming family. My parents even went back to Scotland for the couple's wedding.

Dad always called it down the middle and had seen enough to know how things work on both sides. He'd lived in Staten Island, New York, as well as Scotland and Canada. He smelled bullshit a mile away and let you know. He got mad quickly, and then dropped it just as suddenly. If it sounds like I idolized the man, I did. He always seemed to do the right thing while still having time for a beer. As I drove up, I could see his baby blue Mercedes convertible parked in his usual spot, third down from the left.

Dealing with Chris and Stevie, Jimmy and Mac's bullshit, getting punched in the face by a cop? None of that was as intimidating as disappointing my dad and telling him I might be involved in a murder. I turned off the car and threw my wallet in the glove box. Dad always paid.

Chapter 12
Tell Me You're Not Involved

The Dorchester Tavern had been around since 1988. And I had many an underage drink there.

It was originally up on Lundy's Lane, in a smaller building, and was called Drury Lane. An old-style English pub, I didn't know much about it, because it was just before my time. I do remember waiting in our station wagon with my brothers and sister while mom went in to pick up fish and chips. Greasy, wrapped in newspaper, we weren't just a fish-on-Friday crew. I didn't mind, I could have had it every night.

The original pub had been opened by five drinking buddies – usually not the greatest reason to form a business partnership. But with tourism and the huge number of people in the area of Irish, Scottish and English ancestry, it stayed busy for years.

What eventually destroyed it was five middle-aged partiers who started with a dream, but now had some cash.

One went nuts, divorced his wife and married some 22-year-old fresh from Glasgow. Another died from a heroin overdose. A third one just packed up and left with what he thought was his share of the cash.

That left just Willard and Ben. Ben got tired of the bullshit, took most of his customers and established the new place on Drummond Road. He had been a friend of my father's since the late '50s and was a pretty nice guy. He also had two gorgeous daughters who both worked behind the bar. One was okay, the other was kind of a princess. That wouldn't have stopped me, but neither were interested in me.

My dad always hung out to the left of the bar under the huge Manchester United banner, not that he ever gave a fuck about soccer or most sports. Very rarely did I ever come home to find him watching a game.

He saw me walking towards him and ordered a beer that was on the bar before I sat down. He always stood at the bar. I couldn't, I was too exhausted.

He looked around to see no one was standing too close before he spoke. "Tell me you're not involved in this."

"Dad ..."

He wasn't on a slow burn, he was full on pissed. "Did you even try to call your mom or me? Did you? Why the fuck didn't you take my offer to get out? You're involved in a murder." He slammed his beer down. It quieted the entire bar. He slammed it again and signaled for two more. He stormed over towards the washroom.

Princess came over and pretended she was wiping the bar. "He came in last night looking for you. He hasn't been in here at night in years," she told me. "Then your mom showed up looking for him. She hasn't been in here for years. I sure hope you know what you're doing and how it's affecting those two." Princess might have been a cunt, but I couldn't deny those words hurt.

Dad walked out of the bathroom and motioned me over to a table. That wasn't a good sign. Even my mom always stood at the bar. He sat down and pulled his chair close. "I'm really sorry about your friend."

As he said that, he made the sign of the cross, which made me do it as well. I could just see Vince in my mind, laughing at us, but doing it as well.

"Do you know what happened? I know he's your friend, but he was no bar manager."

When I looked up at him, he smiled. "Cut the bullshit, kid, save it for your mom," he admonished. "I was a teamster for 37 years. You think I didn't know who your friend's dad was?"

"You knew Vince's father?"

"I didn't know him, but I knew who he was." Dad was never a big shot in his union, but in a shop of 200 guys, he rose to No. 3 on the list, and that gave him some pull.

I vaguely remember going to pancake breakfasts with him and seeing some of these guys. They were too over the top to be cast in a gangster movie. All draped in gold, shirts unbuttoned halfway down their stomachs, they would bear hug him and turn their attention to me. "Steve, this kid looks just like youse! Lissen to your dad, kid, he's no dummy." The conversation always ended with them putting an American $5 bill in my shirt pocket. I thought I was rich.

My dad downed his beer and signaled for two more. Fuck. he drank fast. My own drinking had to slow down.

"His dad and his boys ran Niagara Falls, New York, for years."

Even Vince hadn't told me this stuff.

"They kept it small; numbers, betting, unions. I'm sure there were drugs, but I had four kids, so I never was interested."

I always knew my dad was a teamster but never really consider anything exciting about what he did for a living.

"Do you need my help?"

I didn't know what he was asking.

"It's a small town and I've heard shit about the bars and your friends. No one gets murdered without a good reason, usually anyway. It's almost always over money, a broad, or just bad luck. Tell me what's going on, Ian. Maybe I can help."

"Want me to start at the beginning?"

Dad signaled for two more beers and punched me in the shoulder. "That might help, smart ass."

It took almost an hour, but I told him everything and was, by the end, thoroughly drunk. I told him about switching bars, Jimmy, Stevie and Chris, about all the girls, the drugs, the drinking, the gambling, and the few not-so-legitimate things I was involved in.

Dad just took it all in, and then spoke. “Well, I was always pretty sure you didn’t make all your money being a bouncer. See how easy it is to get involved with these guys? Trust me, in the long run, they don’t get any further ahead. It cost your friend his life. You should quit now, and I’ll float you some money until you figure out what you’re going to do.”

Dad was right, of course; but could I just walk away? “Dad, at the very least, I owe it to Vince to find what the fuck happened.”

Dad grabbed a hundred out of his wallet and put it on the table. “You’re a grown man and you were always stubborn, so I’ll just say this: Be careful trying to figure out what happened to your friend but go get cleaned up and go see your mom sometime today. I’m not gonna tell her what we talked about.”

That was the only time I never believed my father. He was going to tell her everything. She wasn’t going to give him a choice. Mom called the shots in the house.

He stood up, put his hand on my shoulder and walked out.

As I stood there, I began to piece all the shit together. Most of what was going on had nothing to do with me. But by calling Jimmy for that favor I got myself involved in a fucking mess that killed Vince. I didn’t think I was responsible, but it definitely felt like I was being used to divert attention away from how it went down.

In the middle of my contemplation, Viking plunked himself down at the table. “What the fuck, Jimmy? What happened to calling?”

“How did you know I was here?”

“You’re not that complicated a guy, Doc. You’re too wrecked to go to the gym, you weren’t at home or at Heart’s so I figured you came to see your dad.”

“I’m pretty fucking predictable, eh?”

“Yeah,” he laughed, “You are. And seeing how this is practically your dad’s office, I made an educated guess. Saw your dad outside. Asked about the kid, then he told me to get a haircut. Same old dad." He looked around and turned back to me. "Fuck, I can't remember the last time I was here." He then ordered two beers and two Sambucas.

"Okay," I protested. "But after these, I'm done."

"Shut up," he replied, "Big Daddy is in the truck and ready to go. And if that don't work, Mr. White is in the glove box. So, suck it up, douche bag." I couldn't argue with that logic.

We left the bar and dropped Bea's car at Max's. He was sleeping, so I just left my keys and hopped into the truck. I had to go to the bar and face the bullshit. Poor new fucking guy. I'd called him in the middle of the night from Toronto, and now he's working at a bar where one of the managers was murdered. Fuck, if he stuck it out this far, he just might make it. Arnie, Tyler, Cody, they're all gonna be up my ass — and rightly so.

At least, I was pretty sure I still worked there. If I had been fired, one of the idiots would have called to rub it in my face.

Viking pulled in and parked right out front. Today, I didn't care and realized we wouldn't be there long anyway. We both walked in. I made my way to Arnie's office, while Viking hung out in front of the DJ booth. I walked through the kitchen. Millie didn't say a word, but I could tell that she was fuming. I gave her the not-now look and went to talk to Arnie.

He could barely be bothered to look at me. "You got some balls showing up, Doc."

"And why's that?"

"What do you fucking mean, 'why's that?' Cops are everywhere, Jimmy and his assholes have been in and out of here, I'll be lucky if I don't get shut down."

You're worried about getting shut down? I thought to myself, then stop selling coke, you fat fuck. Stop fucking every 18-year-old that comes in to dance. But I didn't have the energy to say it out loud. I spun on my heel and walked out.

"And you're off until you prove you had nothing to do with Vince!"

I stopped for a second and wanted to go back and knock Arnie the fucking Hutt out. But I kept thinking that if I burned every bridge I had, I just might have to go back.

On my way out of the kitchen, Millie stopped me. "You know you can stay with me for now."

I reached over and kissed her on the forehead. "Thank you." So much for keeping that quiet. But it didn't seem that important now.

I went to the booth to talk to the new guy. The look on his face when I walked into the booth was off the map. He looked frightened and disgusted at the same time.

"Looks like you'll be covering my shifts for a while."

Before he could respond, I heard Tyler's voice from the change room. "Don't worry about that, tough guy, I'll be here. Maybe he doesn't want to stand too close to you ... might get shot."

The last thing I needed now was this fuck, but he had an audience. He followed me right out onto the floor. "What's the matter? You finally got nothing to say?" I went to the bar and got a beer for Viking. He was already sizing Tyler up. We had a signal we use if we need to fuck someone up, which was rubbing your thumb on the side of your head. Viking did it, questioningly. I shook my head no.

Tyler wouldn't stop. "What you got a bodyguard now? Think you're next?"

In the time that it took me to turn towards him, I could see Viking on top of him, gun in hand. Fuck, he was gonna shoot him. Tyler didn't know Viking, so he probably didn't see it coming.

Tyler was thrown to the ground, then got the gun smashed into the side of his face.

"Who's the tough guy now, asshole?" Viking growled. "Say something else!"

With that, he smashed Tyler in the face again. Tyler looked terrified, and I can't honestly say I didn't like it.

Viking got up, and we both stood at the bar. No one moved or said a word. Within seconds, everything was back to normal, except for Tyler, who was looking for his teeth on the floor.

"You thought I was gonna shoot him, didn't you?"

I slammed down my beer. "Yup,' I said. "Let's go get some suits."

I knew I was gonna have to deal with what just happened later, but I couldn't resist taunting Tyler: "Looking good, fuck face."

Viking and I walked out the bar and into the sunlight. We hopped into the truck and lit up Big Daddy. Whatever happened to me next, at least I would be wrecked for it. It would make it easier to deal with the next catastrophe.

Chapter 13

38 Wide, 30 Long

Viking skidded on to Lundy's Lane and pushed the pedal to the floor. You'd think assaulting a guy, carrying a few guns and being fucked up would slow him down, but you'd be wrong.

"Look there's no way the cops aren't watching us. Fuck, there was probably one in the bar when I fucked up that idiot DJ. Why do you put up with that goof anyway?"

I just shrugged. "The more you bitch about somebody, the more Arnie will bring him back, just to fuck with you. Besides, he's harmless."

Viking was steering with his knees, so he could hold Big Daddy and still see the road. He blew a huge cloud of blue-gray smoke towards the roof of the car. "Those are the guys you gotta watch, the fucking weasels who skulk behind your back, getting other people to fuck with you. I don't think he'll be bugging you anytime soon."

I wasn't so sure.

As we were talking and toking, my cell went off. I was getting a call from the 716 area code, which meant either Buffalo or Niagara Falls, New York. I was pretty sure I knew who it was. "Hello?"

"Ian? It's Pat. I wanted to call you with some details."

"Okay, hold on." I punched Viking and made a writing motion to get him to give me something to write with.

His answer was to punch me back. Thanks, asshole.

"There will be two viewings at Montessi's on Pine Street." This was the funeral home of choice for friends and family of the "club" — what the boys over the border called themselves. "You're welcome at the viewing, but I don't want anyone at all from the bar at the service. The viewings will be on Thursday."

Before I could answer, she hung up.

It was already Tuesday. One extra day to clean up and then say goodbye to my friend.

Viking looked over and lifted his chin, as if to ask what's up?

"Details for Vince's funeral."

Viking raised his eyebrow. "She's letting you go?"

"No, only to the viewing."

"Well, you definitely need a suit. Let's go to Artucci's."

Fuck, I hadn't gone there since I rented the tuxedo for the prom I never went to. Artucci's was down on Victoria, almost in Silvertown. When most of the businesses began to leave the downtown area in the '80s, the old man dug in and stayed. He'd weathered the new malls, the fashion trends, whatever hit him. Almost every kid in town rented their tuxedo from Artucci's. Weddings, formal functions, his shop was still the place to go. It was a little odd that he had a picture of Mussolini on the wall, but his politics weren't my concern. He still made the best suits in Niagara.

When we got inside, the old man was sleeping in his chair. He looked up when he heard the bell above the door, nodded and pointed us towards the counter. A young Italian girl came over to take the basic measurements. She seemed to like Viking, which would've given the old man a stroke had he been paying attention. Here's Viking, ugly as fuck, and this chick is checking him out. I just laughed to myself and took a seat as she began taking out suits, shirts and ties to show us.

Viking sat down beside me. "Cute, eh?"

"Don't you have enough going on?"

"Listen to you, judging — all those broads of yours, my sister ... Don't you worry about me, Billy."

I wouldn't spend too much time worrying, I thought to myself.

Viking had been done up in a dark three-piece, with no tie. He came very close to not looking like a nut job. "So?" he asked, shooting his cuffs, "how you gonna play this tomorrow? You know you're gonna get one fuck of a reception at the funeral home. Will Vince's old lady make a scene?"

Pat would have no issue making a scene. She had no problem showing up at the bar and losing it on Vince habitually, although that had slowed down in recent years as he tried to keep her out of the club.

"It'll be interesting to see who shows up," I diverted.

"Not really," Viking replied. "A lot of times the fucking guy that shot you will show up at the funeral to make things look nice. A lot of guys will show simply 'cause they don't want anybody to think they did it. If you're going there to play detective, you won't find out shit. You know better than to ask questions."

It was my turn to get suited up. I turned down the three-piece. I wasn't tall enough, didn't think it was the right look. I settled on a dark blue suit, no vest and no tie. "What do ya think?" I asked.

"What am I, your chick? And buy a fucking pair of shoes. Don't wear those fucking Doc Martens you wear with everything."

I turned to look in the mirror. "Think Chris and Stevie will show?" I asked.

"They're just the kind of guys that would. But if they don't, you know they're gonna know everyone who showed."

We changed back into our regular clothes and just sat for a moment. Viking eventually got up, put everything on the counter and told the girl to ring it up. He came back over and sat down beside me. "Why don't you go to the funeral, say goodbye and then forget all this shit? Your old man is fucked up over all this shit, and I've never seen him shaken before, even with all the crap you've pulled over the years. You know he'll float you 'til you get started again."

I looked up at him. "To do what? Can I go back to school now? I don't know if I can pull it off."

"Fuck off with that shit. You're the geekiest guy I know, and you rose up in that job to deal with people who should have eaten you by now. Can dealing with kids be that hard after all of this? You know what's coming – jail, rehab or death, Billy. Fuck, even I'm almost done ... just waiting for the land deal to go through."

Viking had paid a bigger price than I did. He would never admit it, but the shooting fucked with his head. He was a regular guy who protected his family and that made him a murderer. And he was positive it wasn't all over. He put all the clothes on the table and started sorting his cash. "who knows, maybe there's a book in all this shit for you to write. I'll pick up the tab, you might not have a job anymore."

I didn't need to be reminded. He grabbed all the clothes, paid the girl and tipped her with a fifty. We loaded everything into the back of the truck. That's when he shoved the receipt in my face. The girl, whose name was apparently Deanna, had written out her number. "Suck on that, Billy!" Viking shouted as we peeled out of the parking lot.

"Staying at my place?" he asked after an awkward silence.

"Yeah, but let me go to Max's and grab some things. He's gonna want to know what the arrangements are for Vince."

"How is your wop roommate?"

"First and only roommate I ever had that wasn't a chick. Doesn't hassle me for the rent, and the fridge is always filled with Italian food – one of the benefits of having six sisters I guess."

"Yeah, Max is okay," Viking mumbled.

That surprised me, because he hated just about everyone. I was almost never at the house, so our arrangement usually worked in Max's favor. I felt bad for all the shit that he got pulled into because of me, but he would never complain.

Besides, he had his own connections. He would be fine. I started worrying about myself again.

When we got there, Viking elected to stay in the truck, so I went in to talk to Max and grab a couple of things. When I walked in, I almost shit myself. Jimmy and Stevie were sitting at the table with Max. Max was impossible to read, but he didn't look uncomfortable, at least not yet.

"Well, well," Jimmy said. "Look who's still alive. I was beginning to worry."

Yeah, I'm fucking sure he was worried.

"Stevie, why don't you take a look at Max's front lawn," Jimmy said, with a false casual tone. "He's done a great job."

"Viking is out there," Stevie reported.

I didn't intend his presence to be a threat. I didn't want any shooting to start, or for anyone to think I was planning something. With cops on either side, any conflict could get ugly quick. Max has a garage with an obscured entrance we all used, so no one knew Jimmy was in the house, or that I was there either. Every single thing about the situation told me to worry, but I wasn't ready to panic just yet.

"Sit down," Jimmy said.

I remained standing.

Jimmy pushed the chair with his foot, and it slammed against the wall. He never raised his voice. "I said, sit down."

I grabbed the chair and sat as far away from him as possible. If I was getting it, I was gonna make him work for it. I learned years ago that if you can't touch me, I might get away. Nice idea in theory, I guess.

"I know you think that your friend going down was my doing, but it ain't. Then again, you'd be an idiot to believe me. There's bigger things going on and your friend got stuck in the mix."

Why was I being told this? Was the old man trying to assuage his guilt?

"We're still taking the 'Vette, and Stevie is going to be at the funeral."

"You want me to show up at the funeral with Stevie?"

Jimmy was obviously trying to clear himself of any suspicion. And he wanted to let me know he was serious, and I wasn't getting out so easy.

If he wanted a representative to go with me, he could have sent Chris. He was sending Stevie, so I wouldn't fuck around or think of not telling him everything that happened while I was there.

Jimmy got up and put his hand on my shoulder. "Your buddy was playing a game, kid, and he lost. Don't make this any harder on yourself than it has to be. Stevie will pick you up Thursday at Viking's. Don't try and dodge him."

So much for hiding. Jimmy knew everything: where I was, what I was planning.

Jimmy began walking towards the door. "After this is all done," he called over his shoulder, "we're gonna need to talk. But for now, you should keep your distance and only talk to me through Stevie."

It felt like he was making every effort to cut me away from Chris. He got to the door and turned to face me. "Take care kid, and none of your famous disappearing acts. Say hi to your dad for me."

When I followed him outside, things seemed cordial enough. Viking, Max and Stevie were all standing together, not saying much. I was to only deal with Stevie from that point forward.

A black Lincoln Town Car pulled up. Stevie looked like he wanted to say something, but Jimmy stared him down. Jimmy wouldn't even look at me. They got into the car and it took off.

Max lit a smoke, and said: "Hey, it wasn't that bad. I can make some calls if you want."

Viking looked up, and asked: "Who you gonna call, Sonny Corleone?"

We all laughed and realized that he diffused the heavy fucking scene.

I could almost hear the cameras clicking from both houses where the cops lived. All this surveillance wasn't a bad thing. If I was lucky, they wouldn't let me get shot.

Jimmy and Stevie had gone out of their way to come in quietly, but to make sure everyone saw them leave. I got the feeling Jimmy wanted everyone to see him and I together. I was being played, that was certain.

Phil and I hopped in the truck, and he pulled two cans of Keystone Light from underneath the seat. I told him what was said inside the house and asked what was said outside.

He started loading Big Daddy but stopped and set out two lines of coke the size of Bic pens. He snorted his in one breath and passed mine over, saying: "There's no fucking way you're getting in a car with Stevie." He jammed the truck into gear and peeled out of the driveway. No sense taking it slow. Almost every cop in Niagara must've been watching us by now anyway.

Chapter 14

Queen Bea, a Hose, a Tractor, Some Acid and a Case or Two of Beer

"So now what?" I said to no one in particular as I tossed my beer can out the window and dug under the seat for another.

Phil reached under his own seat and pulled up two cans of Keystone Light. "Well, there's no way you're going over there with Stevie. It fucking screams set-up."

I cracked open my beer, and downed half of it in one gulp. The line between who was helping me or fucking me over was getting stepped on and less clear by the moment. "Why did Jimmy tell me I had to go with Stevie?" I asked Phil. "Why couldn't I just go with Chris? Or by myself?"

Phil slammed on the brakes, jammed the transmission into reverse and drove backwards through the intersection at O'Neil Street. Still in reverse, he cut through two lanes to A.N. Myer Secondary School and floored it through the parking lot. He then shifted back into drive and tore right through the football field.

"What the fuck was that?" I asked as we turned back onto O'Neil and drove almost politely back in the direction we came from.

He threw his beer can out the window and had me hold up Big Daddy so that he could put both hands on the wheel. For reasons I couldn't comprehend, that seemed very important to him at that moment.

"Just making sure no one is following us, Billy. After Jimmy's remarks at Max's, he's probably gonna have someone watch over you so you don't pull one of your disappearing acts."

There was precedent there. I didn't take vacations or snap easily, but I did work six days a week in a stressful environment of bikers, cops, whores, drugs and booze. My way of dealing with it was to remove the bikers, cops and whores, disappear for a few days and just focus on the drugs and booze. My last disappearing act lasted three days and involved Queen Bea, a hose, a tractor, some acid and a case or two of beer. That wasn't going to be an option before seeing Vince, but it would be pretty fucking tempting after I said goodbye.

We made our way to Fireman's Park and parked the truck. Viking grabbed a six pack out of the cab and pointed to the Pavilion. If you grew up in the Falls, you had a story about bringing a girl here, partying with your friends, or simply hanging out there. Some nights it was just cool to sit there and talk. I spent many a night here with Phillip laying on our backs, staring up at the stars. Big Daddy had his own history with the Pavilion. Many an amateur got stoned fucking stupid when Phil would switch on Big Daddy's fan.

"Going to the funeral with Stevie is gonna fuck you," Viking said, stating the obvious.

"So how do I get away without him finding out? And what happens to me after?" It seemed pretty clear that getting rid of me wouldn't be an issue for Stevie. I was a nobody, just one of the guys hanging around. I couldn't count on our years of friendship to mean fuck all. These guys killed each other all the time. You had more to worry about with your "brothers" than you did cops or citizens. Everybody remembered what happened in Buffalo in the early '90s. When the Royal City Riders brass decided that the boys in Orchard Park weren't doing enough to expand the organization into Southern Ontario, the bosses decided to kill a few of their own guys to discourage anyone from sitting back and not participating in their "expansion drive." Expansion, how fucking cute. There's your brotherhood.

Viking shotgunned a beer, threw the can in the air, then kicked it halfway across the Pavilion. "Well Billy, you've got to hide without really hiding."

I was getting too drunk and high to decipher his hillbilly wisdom. I lifted my chin and stuck my finger in my ear, which was our wordless way of saying, "Please elaborate, asshole."

Viking grabbed a beer, stuck his knife in the side, getting it ready for a shotgun, which I knew was coming my way. He shoved it in my face and made sure I drank the whole thing. He smiled approvingly and announced: "We hit the Shack."

The Shack was in one of the corners of Viking's property. It had a generator and windows on every wall that you could see out of but not into. It had nothing around it, but a clear view in every direction so you wouldn't get caught flat-footed.

We partied many a night in that fucking Shack. Viking hid out there when the cops came after him after the shootings. He made it clear he would give himself up, but only wanted Scotty Reynolds, a cop we used to hit the gym with, to be the one to come get him.

We would pull onto the property, wait until dark and make our way out there, hopefully with everyone thinking that we stayed in the house. There was no plan after that, but we would have time to decide how I made it to Niagara Falls, New York, in the morning.

We made it back to Viking's to see the same truck with the same guy parked out front. Again, no introduction and I didn't ask. No wife or kids around, so we hung in the kitchen. "You fucking hungry?" he asked.

Actually, I was. In the last couple of days, I think the last time I ate was at the diner with Viking and the kid. He was actually a pretty good cook. "Yeah. Steak?"

He looked in the fridge and laughed. "Nope, frozen pizza." I would have much rather had an extra-large from Volcano Pizza with extra cheese and hot sausage, but I'm sure we didn't need anyone delivering anything to us. He threw two frozen pizzas in the oven and a bag of Doritos on the table.

What the fuck, in the meantime we might as well light up Big Daddy. "Grab me a beer Doug," I barked. Before I had all the words out there were four cans on the table.

As he was taking the pizzas out of the oven, I grabbed two cans of Coke out of the fridge. I can have a can of beer for breakfast. Fuck, I could brush my teeth with it, but I didn't like it when I was eating. Seemed like a pretty good time to start sobering up, anyway.

Viking took his can, downed half of it, and filled the rest with rye. I kept mine clean.

He cut up the two pizzas and grabbed the bottle of rye. "So, Doc, you got a fucking plan yet?"

"Actually, no. Is there any way we can hide at the Shack, then sneak out of here around 5 a.m. to get ready?"

Viking chewed on a slice while thinking. "Yeah, but we can't go to your place. Or any of your chicks'. Or Bea's. We gotta come up with something."

I grabbed a slice and another can of Coke. "Maybe I don't go at all?" Too many fucking voices in my head thought it made perfect sense just to skip the whole deal.

Viking shook his head. "Makes you look bad to Jimmy and to Vince's family."

I understood his point. But he was also showing a bit of himself. Viking might be a crazy outlaw fuck, but he was a very careful, cautious and meticulous crazy outlaw fuck. Just because you don't punch a clock every day doesn't mean you don't care about people or want to do the right thing.

We kept eating in silence, Viking trying to figure out how to get me to the funeral home, and me trying to figure out how to avoid the whole fucking thing.

We sat around the kitchen talking shit and trading stories until the sun went down. There were so many stories. My favorite was about getting a second interview as a teaching assistant a few years back. I really wanted that job, but they were putting me through the wringer. After two interviews, I got a little snippy about the situation, and decided to drink the night away with Viking and his family to forget about the situation. At about 8 a.m. and just as I was getting ready to open a second bottle of Sambuca, my phone rang. It was the school. How about I come in this morning and fill out the paperwork to start the next day? Fuck! Not a wink of sleep. Who's gonna fucking drive? No problem. Viking's solution? We take the tractor.

"I'm gonna pull up on a fucking tractor?" I asked him. "No, no. I'll drop you off a block or so from the school, so no one sees." Great idea, except one the cars stuck behind our ride saw me chugging a beer then using some mouthwash on the back of the tractor.

Just as we were both trying to remember another story, I noticed that it was around 9 p.m., which seemed as safe a time as any to make our way to the Shack. I grabbed a two-liter bottle of Coke. Viking took 12 beers and Big Daddy. Only 12? I thought to myself — at least we were attempting to slow down.

"Ready, Billy?"

"Ready, Doug."

We locked up the house and made our way outside. As soon as we stepped out of the house, the pickup truck sped off. At the same time, a red Honda came up the driveway. Viking instinctively dove behind a tree and pulled out one of his guns. I wasn't so quick. The car slowed down, skidded sideways and hit me. It sent me flying.

For a moment, everything was peaceful. I thought maybe I was dead. Just as my head began to clear, intense pain shot through my legs.

I managed to open my eyes and saw that two guys were pointing guns at Viking. They kept their distance, not giving him a chance to touch them.

That's when I heard the click. A pistol was definitely being cocked and pointed at my head. Looking up, I saw Stevie standing over top of me. No patch today, just a track suit. He looked at me and growled: "Get in the car."

Chapter 15

So the Border has a Hold-My-Piece Policy?

As Stevie pulled me up from the ground, I made a quick scan of my body to make sure I was still in one piece, with nothing broken, sticking out or where it wasn't supposed to be. It seemed like I was intact, but I sure fucking hurt.

The car hadn't been coming all that fast, so I took the brunt of the impact with the front of my body. All I remember is turning my head to the left with my chin down to protect my face, teeth and eyes. Maybe all those karate lessons paid off.

When I flew backwards, I landed flat on the ground, feet apart, arms out. That was pure instinct. I had been thrown around enough in the ring and at work, so I knew how to fall with minimal damage.

Stevie had me by the hair, which always looks painful on TV, but isn't that big a deal when it actually happens. He threw me in the front seat. It was only then that I realized Chris was sitting in the back. He immediately put a gun to my head. "Don't get cute, Ian," he instructed.

Stevie got in the driver's side and immediately tore down the driveway.

"What the fuck, Stevie?" I shouted. "Didn't think I would show?"

"Shut the fuck up. I wasn't allowing you to back out on me."

I grabbed my head, which was now throbbing. "Tu decides de me frapper avec ton char?" I asked. "T'es vraiment une plotte." Without realizing it I had slipped into French.

Stevie understood, but Chris had no clue what I had said. Chris cuffed me in the back of the head. "English, idiot."

Just to piss Chris off, I decided to keep berating Stevie in French. "Man, you're full of fucking surprises, mon esti. This is RCR etiquette? Slow down your friends by running 'em over?"

Stevie lit a smoke and laughed. "Tabernac, I wanted to shoot you, but Jimmy said no. The old man still puts up with your shit. Pretty soon, I won't have to."

"Now, what the fuck does that mean?" I asked.

Chris started whining from the back seat. "I fucking hate when you guys do this."

It was always our little inside joke. Stevie was fluent in French but usually only answered back in English. I always used to joke that I kept up my French because before all the Russian girls showed up, the girls at the strip clubs were 80 percent French, mainly from some little towns in Quebec, far away from Montreal. Gorgeous, far away from home and no one to talk to. Not exactly what I would tell any school looking for a French teacher, but it served me well.

"Everything is changing, and pretty soon you, Jimmy and a whole bunch of shit won't matter." Stevie said in French, and Chris's ears perked up hearing Jimmy's name.

I didn't want to play anymore, so I switched back to English, hoping Stevie would say something stupid that Chris would catch. "So, you're the king of the hill, now?" Then realized it might be advantageous to switch back to French. "C'mon, mon chum. Maybe Chris is that stupid, but you know better."

Chris was getting pissed, especially after hearing his name. "I will shoot both you fuckers if you don't keep it in English!" Despite the fucked-up situation, Stevie and I both laughed, with Chris eventually joining in.

"What happens to Phil?"

Stevie threw his smoke out the window, then grabbed another. "Nothing, unless he does something stupid ... and he is pretty stupid. How the fuck do you hang out with that guy?"

"Well, he's one of the few friends I have who isn't trying to kill me."

Stevie shook his head. "You think this is all about you, don't you?"

"Well, hitting me with your car seemed pretty fucking personal, I would say."

It seemed like we were heading for the south end of Niagara, not too far from the Square.

"We got a few things to talk about, you and me" Stevie muttered.

"What about me?" Chris must've been feeling left out.

"You're gonna stay with the car 'til I tell you," Stevie snapped at him.

We passed the Square, headed down Montrose Road and turned at the White Pigeon Garage. It looked like we were taking the back way into Welland.

I knew Welland a bit, but not really. A couple of bars, the French high school we chased girls at, not too much else. We cleared the bridge after East Main Street. Now I wasn't sure of the area – not a great feeling. Getting away now wasn't going to happen. It was time to sit back and play along. Chris went silent and Stevie just kept smoking and looking at the road, grinding his teeth. We pulled up to an older house, with no garage and no lights on inside.

Stevie killed the engine and looked back at Chris. "You stay here 'til I come get you." He turned his attention to me and threw me a key. "Go up to the front door and unlock it. Don't fuck around."

I walked into the house, flipped a light on, and sat down on the couch. The whole place looked very clean, like nothing had been touched in a while. The wallpaper, furniture, everything screamed 1968. I plopped down on the couch and stared at

Stevie. “So now what?” Stevie asked as he sat on the recliner across from me.

“What do you mean, now what?” Fuck, he was starting to piss me off, but I couldn’t be too insulting. “Did you think any further than hitting me with the car? We’ve got to be in Niagara Falls, New York, in less than 12 hours. You think I’m gonna go in my ripped jeans and T-shirt? I’ve got nothing here. Maybe you’ve got a room full of suits back there?”

Stevie called Chris into the house and instructed him: “Wait ’til the other guys get here, then go back to Viking’s and get his shit for tomorrow.”

I looked over at Stevie. “Other guys? We having a party? I’d like to get a little fucking sleep.”

Stevie didn’t answer but soon enough a truck pulled up. Three squareheads got out. Not one of them familiar to me. Two of them parked themselves on the front steps, the third stood by the side door.

Stevie threw his jacket on the floor and turned on the TV. “Take the back room, I’ll wake you when we’re leaving.”

“Fuck that, Stevie; you said we would talk. How ’bout telling me what the fuck is going on?”

Stevie lit a smoke and threw me the pack.

“Vince? That’s what we’re talking about?” Man, I was trying not to lose my temper. Instead, I said nothing. Of course, I wanted to know about Vince. The Royal City Riders, Burnt politics, why he patched in and whether Chris was still striking, I didn’t give a fuck about any of that.

“Why did Vince have to die? He owed you $20,000 —that doesn’t mean shit to you. And you know he would have paid it. Even if I didn’t know the whole story, how long would it be before the cops figure it out?”

Stevie hadn’t said a word since I started my tirade.

“Now, I’m involved in a fucking murder.”

Stevie lit another smoke, and finally erupted. “What do you care? You’re leaving. Getting out. Gonna teach retards or some shit. You didn’t want to ride. You wanted a straight job. How the fuck is running a strip club, playing the middle man to whores and coke a straight job?"

He wasn't gonna tell me anything unless I went for broke. "So, it's all just a big game, killing my best friend. What if I decided that you gotta go?"

Stevie laughed out loud, got up and went to the fridge. "You don't have the balls. You finally got in over your head. Just be thankful you didn't go down already for some of the shit you've pulled in the last few years. If I hadda gotten the OK, there would be a double funeral tomorrow."

It finally dawned on me that I still had the gun Phil gave me in my boot. Stevie or Chris would never have frisked me, I was never known for carrying a piece.

While he still had his face buried in the fridge, I pulled the gun out and got up.

When Stevie turned around, I had it pointed in his face. "Please," was all he said and walked towards me.

I had nothing to lose. I'd fucked up everything. At the very least, I wanted to know why Vince of all people. "Why did Vince have to go? Tell me, motherfucker."

Stevie was starting to sweat. I couldn't understand why he didn't try to signal the guys outside. We both knew I wasn't going to shoot. Things were pretty fucked up, but I wasn't about to kill anyone, not even a guy I grew up with, who hit me with his car, and probably killed my best friend. I realized the insanity of what I was doing. If I did shoot, and I had no idea how, I wasn't going to make it out alive. One of these guys would kill me, dump me in the river and then go for breakfast. I put the gun on the table and sat back down.

Stevie picked it up and put it in his pocket. "Everybody gets one," he said solemnly, "That was yours."

Stevie lit another smoke. "This RCR shit didn't start overnight. It's been in the works for years. Everyone got pushed aside, killed or chased off. Jimmy is still on the fence about their offer. If Jimmy doesn't take it, they'll push him out. You have no idea how much power these guys have. Jimmy is nothing to them. If he don't play their game, someone else will take his place. It's all business, dude, pure and simple."

Where was this going? My old friend baring his soul, or just rubbing it in my face before he shoots it off? There was no way he was going to admit to killing Vince, he wasn't that stupid. I was no Perry Mason, there would be no dramatic confession, but his story had to be leading somewhere.

"You're talking in circles. What the fuck are you trying to tell me? I just want to know why Vince died. Because of some stupid feud between you, Jimmy and the RCR?"

Stevie started playing with the gun I left on the table. "These RCR guys cover all the fucking angles. When Jimmy wouldn't give them a straight answer, they started looking at other options."

Options. Nice euphemism for murdering your competitors. "And you're the option?" I finally asked.

"These fucking guys are taking everything over. The broads, the bars, the coke, everything. The money all runs to the top. And we had to show 'em we could take care of business."

I had to read in between the fucking lines. He was telling me something here, but three or four days full of coke, weed, booze and no sleep weren't letting my brain put it together. Business, taking over, I couldn't think.

"Look I need sleep." Stevie moved to the couch and stretched out. "Take the back room. And don't give me any reason to shoot you with your own gun."

I walked down the hall to a tiny room. It had a small bed, and a dresser with an old TV on top. I flipped on the TV. Before my eyes could focus, I was asleep. Although I crashed immediately, my dreams were brutal. Viking getting shot repeatedly, Viking carving up Stevie's guys, me getting shot beside the 'Vette instead of Vince, even Vince shooting me in front of the 'Vette. That one jarred me awake. I've never been one to sleep well, usually tossing and turning all night. But that shit was enough to unsettle anyone. I bolted straight up in the little bed, covered in sweat and sucking in air like I had taken a baseball bat to the chest.

I got up and wasn't sure if I had to puke or pee first, so I began looking for the bathroom. I noticed in the spare room, someone had put out my suit, shirt and tie, and some brushes and shit. Must've been Chris. Stevie would have just tossed it all on the floor.

I thought that I might as well shower and get ready. I hadn't showered in two days, so there was some grime to scrape off. The bruises were forming on my thighs and stomach, but I didn't seem to have any major cuts. I was definitely sore and was thinking about some serious payback for hitting me with a car. I dried off and looked at myself in the mirror. I really needed a shave. I had grown my hair when I was wrestling, but now it was getting long. I hated tying it in a ponytail. Those fucking things are for pretty boys and Steven Seagal. Since almost every biker I knew had hair down to their shoulders with a beard to match, I wouldn't look so out of place at the funeral. For the first time ever, I noticed a few gray hairs.

I had gotten dressed, except for my tie and my shoes, although it took longer than usual. Slipping my feet into my Doc Martens (I don't wear any other shoes, not even to the gym) I couldn't get my foot in the right one. When I flipped it over, Viking's gun fell out, the one Stevie took. I had no explanation for that. I put it in my pocket and sat down across from Stevie.

He was wearing a three-piece suit and didn't look all that bad. For some reason, every biker I knew thought the height of dressing up meant wearing a three-piece and they usually looked ridiculous in them. But he was kind of pulling it off.

Stevie was eating a bowl of corn flakes and reading the Welland Tribune. We looked like a happy fucking family. He even put out a bowl and spoon for me. No orange juice though. Asshole, he knew I loved orange juice.

He pushed the cereal box in front of me without looking up. "You found it in your boot?"

No big words, the less said, the better.

I nodded.

"Even though you think you know what's going on, you don't know everything. We're gonna leave here and you're gonna take that with you. If anything happens from here to the bridge, you're on your own. Just before we cross, someone will collect it."

That plan sounded incredibly risky, it not downright stupid.

"The border has a hold-my-piece policy now? What the fuck, Stevie, do you think the cops aren't watching us?"

Stevie grabbed the cereal box and dumped more into his bowl. "It's not the cops I'm worried about. I told you last night, you don't know everything. Besides, the cops want us to cross. They don't know what the fuck is going on either."

I was becoming less and less confident that he gave a fuck if I got shot or not. In his mind, he's doing what he was told. He's bringing me to the funeral. If I get shot on the way, that's not his problem.

"So, all three of us in a car, guns on all of us, driving to a funeral. What could go wrong?" I started eating my cereal.

Stevie kept reading the paper. "Chris isn't carrying; and he's going in the truck." They were adhering to a pretty standard plan. If we get pulled over, and Chris and his boys would cause such a scene or accident that the cops would have to ignore us and bolt to take care of them. It didn't always work in the big cities anymore but would be sufficient for our local cops.

Aware of the plan, it occurred to me that Chris was still being relegated to the sideline. If he didn't fuck up his little assignment, maybe he wouldn't be viewed as such an idiot. If he got shot in the process, oh well. One fewer guy around.

"Eat your fucking cereal, we're out of here in 15 minutes. You drive, I'll be beside you." Stevie put down the paper and stood over top of me. "If that gun comes out in the car, you better be shooting out the window. Let's fucking go."

Chapter 16

I Can't Believe We're Wearing the Same Fucking Suit!

There wasn't much discussion as we gathered our things to leave. I threw all my shit in a plastic bag and put it on the couch in the front room.

Stevie immediately grabbed it, dumped everything out and searched through it. Can't be too careful, I guess. "Put your shit back in the bag and let's go."

While I was doing that, Chris walked in.

Stevie started in with the plan. "You, Chris, you're going in the truck with Dumb and Dumber." Nice nicknames. "You stay behind us, and make sure Doc here doesn't try and take any shortcuts. If we get pulled over, you know what to do."

Chris just nodded and looked at the floor.

"When we get to the Falls, we'll pull over in front of Simon's on Bridge Street. You take all the gear, then give it to one of the idiots to get rid of. You and the other idiot wait in the restaurant." Chris didn't look too thrilled but listened. "Everybody got it?" Stevie asked. Without waiting for a reply, he barked: "Let's fucking go."

I climbed into the driver's seat of the truck and waited for Stevie to get in.

He locked up the house, lit a smoke and jumped in. He adjusted his vest and then looked out the window. "Straight to Simon's, no bullshit, no distractions. You keep your eyes on the fucking road, I'll keep watch for anything else. Let's go."

I pulled out and watched the truck instantly fall into line behind us. Chris was going to make sure I wasn't going anywhere but to Simon's.

We both sat in silence as I made my way to the Falls. I was starting to think I was beginning to get all the shit pieced together. Stevie and Chris couldn't have been the ones who shot Vince. They were sitting across from me during that bullshit meeting with Jimmy. But Stevie put everything into motion – I was sure of that.

"So, what was achieved by killing Vince? You guys got to build a rep? He fucking owed you $17,000. The 'Vette is hardly a great substitute."

I had Stevie's attention now.

"The 'Vette is gonna last a few years, tops," I continued. "You coulda bled the juice off that $17,000 for fucking years. Not exactly a great business plan."

Stevie was slowly getting agitated.

"Burnt, RCR, whoever you wind up working for probably would have let you take over the football pool, bleed Vince for the money, the winnings and the fucking juice," I went on. "And all you got is a fucking Corvette ..." I shook my head and laughed under my breath. "... a fucking Corvette."

My mentioning the car so often was clearly pissing him off.

"Got it all figured out, eh, Doc?" Stevie lit another smoke and threw the empty pack out the window. "I got his car, and you're gonna run the pool for me."

That made me laugh again. We were just passing the Square, about halfway to the bridge. "Really? I'm gonna run the pool when I'm teaching full time? Maybe I'll write up all the receipts at recess."

Now it was his turn to laugh at me. "Fuck, Doc, like you're getting out now. You've been talking that teacher shit for years. You're not going anywhere now. We made sure of that."

We were now on McLeod Road, about six blocks from where I grew up. For a second, I considered crashing the car and running. If I made my way to any of the side streets, I'd be gone. But the comment about making sure I would never get out fucking played in my head. Stevie had planned this to fuck me over. He was thinking one step ahead of me, and I had no idea what to do.

"So, I guess I should have just joined in with you and Chris?"

"You never would have made it, although Jimmy would have sponsored you. You got too big a mouth, that's what your fucking problem is. You never would have made your way up," he looked like he'd wanted to unload all of this for a while. "Plus, you're a pussy. You shoulda shot me last night."

Man, was he playing with my mind. "How would have killing you helped me out, you fucking psycho? Shooting the guy I thought killed my friend wouldn't have helped me."

"It would have proved you've got balls. Did you check the gun last night? It wasn't fucking loaded. You probably wouldn't even know how to put the fucking bullets in."

No wonder he was so cool when I pointed it at him last night. Phil would have never given me an empty gun. I reached over to my pocket, but Stevie knew what I was going to do, and already had his gun out.

"Ah, no. Leave it where it is for now. And, yeah, this time it's loaded," he said, then went back to his tirade. "You always thought too much, that's your fucking problem." He then grabbed a new pack from his jacket and lit two, handing me one. "Sometimes, you just gotta react, no matter what goes down. You never had that in you. But you still might be useful, if you get through all of this."

It felt like I was being groomed and set up at the same time.

"Jimmy always said I should keep you around. You'd make a shitty biker, but you'd be useful when the answer wasn't violence."

Had I lasted this long simply because Jimmy thought I'd become some sort of consigliere to Stevie? If Jimmy stepped out, I would be expected to follow Stevie. It didn't feel like Jimmy had been helping me at all.

"We hit this funeral, and I'm gone." We were turning onto the bridge. "We're gonna be at a wake surrounded by cops, bikers, all kinds of shit. I'm paying my respects and walking, Stevie. You gonna start shooting, and cause World War III?"

We pulled in front of Simon's and Stevie opened my jacket and took the gun. Chris pulled up directly behind us.

"We'll see about that, Doc," Stevie said just before he got out of the truck.

Chris walked over and handed us a box to put everything in. Stevie held up the gun I had and laughed. It had never been loaded, not last night, not on the way here.

"Empty your pockets and show me you've got all your ID," Stevie asked. "I'm not getting turned around at the border because you forgot it or try to pull out some roach to get yourself busted."

When Stevie was satisfied that the car was clean, he made me get out of the driver's seat. "I'm driving, and if you do anything stupid, they're gonna turn us around and we'll have to come back together ... just remember that."

I watched Chris place the box in the truck, then walk into Simon's with Dumb, or maybe Dumber, I wasn't sure. Within seconds, we were on the bridge, with only maybe ten cars ahead of us. With two border inspection booths open, it wouldn't be long.

"What's our story?" I asked.

"What do you mean, what's our story? We're going to a fucking funeral."

I started rummaging inside my wallet. "Good thinking, we're going to a fucking funeral that every local cop, Canadian cop, a whole bunch of bikers and, yeah, the local boys are gonna be at." I handed him a business card and a plastic slip key from my wallet. It was my pass and a card for Dusty's Gym on Pine Avenue on the American side. Vince and I worked out there all the time or used to anyway. Maybe I would luck out and know the guy in the booth. They change them up all the time, but it might work. "Tell them we're going to Dusty's."

Stevie grabbed the two pieces and stared at me. "if this is some kind of trick ..."

I cut him off. "It'll work. Just do it." If we got turned back through no fault of mine, Stevie would still blame me. It was worth a shot.

Two cars to go. I was trying to look ahead to see if I recognized either of the guards when, all of a sudden, a third booth opened and waved us over. A woman, about 35, who didn't look familiar at all.

I punched Stevie in the arm and told him: "Turn on your charm."

We rolled up and Stevie handed over our ID. She asked for our citizenship and where we were going. "Dusty's. Gonna hit a quick workout." She looked at the ID and didn't even glance up. We got waved through by her swinging her arm.

"Good thinking, Doc," Stevie said as he threw my ID and the door key at me, "maybe I won't kill you."

The funeral home was a local landmark in Niagara Falls, New York. If you were Italian or Irish, your family had your wake here. If you weren't, it was politely suggested that you fuck off and have your wake elsewhere. In the glory days of the "boys," a funeral meant a line of limos, cops helping with the traffic, and mobs of people paying their respects. It wasn't totally crime-related back then, but everyone knew these guys weren't the Shriners. Some families had known each other for generations. Maybe someone did you a favor, big or small, but you always had to pay them back.

We pulled into a parking lot two blocks away. Stevie was scouting shit out, trying to see who was watching who. In the old days, you had the cops snapping pictures of the bad guys. Then a lot of bikers turned the tables on the cops, taking pictures of them to identify which cop watched what. Then sometimes the cops took pictures of the bikers taking pictures of the cops taking pictures of the bikers. It was like a fucked-up underworld Salvador Dali painting.

Stevie lit another smoke and straightened out his vest. “We’re going in together. His old lady is gonna want to see you, so you go right to her. You’re the one who’s gonna tell her I’m taking the ’Vette.”

“We gotta do that today?” I asked.

“She doesn’t know who I am. You’re gonna take the heat.”

It was all part of Stevie’s little game to make me look involved.

“What if they recognize you?”

“They won’t unless you draw attention to me. I’m just another douche bag mourning my old buddy Vince.”

I gotta say, he had thought the whole thing out. My only hope of escape was if someone recognized him. The criminal world is pretty small in this area. If someone got all over him, I could possibly sneak out.

But the fucking guy could read my mind.

“No bullshit, no trying to get away. Just stick to the plan and maybe I’ll buy you breakfast at Simon’s when we’re done.”

As he was laying down the law, some big guy with almost the identical suit as Stevie’s leaned in the car. Before Stevie could react, Viking punched him twice in the face, knocking him out.

“Now we’re even, asshole,” Viking laughed as he watched Stevie slump down in his seat. To say I was shocked didn’t begin to cover it. When I tried to sputter out why? or how? Viking just looked over and grinned. “C’mon, let’s go before he wakes up. I can’t believe we’re wearing the same fucking suit!”

Chapter 17

Now What?

"How the fuck did you get over here?"

Viking pulled on his lapels and looked down the street. "C'mon, let's move, I'll tell you on the way."

From Viking's story, Stevie didn't hire the greatest set of thugs. A lot of guys think they can do this shit, be a tough guy, but it's not a movie. Usually the guys you're going after aren't exactly pussies.

"When you fucking guys sped off, these two idiots started talking shit, blah, blah, blah, we're gonna kill you. They barely knew how to handle a gun."

And I thought I was the only one.

"They spent more time looking at each other, trying to outdo one another with tough-guy lines. While they were lipping. I just kept crawling up an inch. If Stevie woulda sent some real tough guys, they woulda shot me the first time I moved."

I looked at him and laughed. "Fuck, even I woulda shot you."

Viking got a kick out of that. "My only friend, shooting me. Thanks, Billy."

We went a little further and walked down a side street, so I could tell him all the shit Stevie was trying to put into place, and how, win or lose, I'd be fucked. Stevie was creating backstops for himself everywhere: Jimmy, me, the RCR. It didn't matter what happened, Stevie would wind up with some kind of place in the new Niagara order. I told Viking about my theory of how stupid Stevie had been by throwing away the cash instead of just bleeding Vince out.

"Stevie don't give a fuck about the cash. Those guys make a bunch, lose a bunch, then go make it again. They always think they'll find another score."

The more he talked, everything Stevie said was blasting between my ears. I learned a bit over the years, but I couldn't compete with these guys. I didn't have the willingness to risk it all, my life or my career. Some did, and it paid off. I just didn't have it in me. Jails are full of guys who took their shot.

We started walking back toward the funeral home.

I had been just processing all this shit while walking the last bit. We were right in front of the funeral home, when I saw Stevie on the sidewalk looking ready to explode. All of his meticulous planning, and he gets knocked out. Viking had played it right.

Stevie wouldn't take on Viking without a weapon, so we walked right by him. "Nice suit, Stevie," Viking taunted. I tried not to smile.

"You think this is over, you fucking idiots? You still gotta make it back to Canada. Did you think about that?" Stevie was practically hyperventilating as he was issuing threats.

But for the first time in days, no one was assaulting me. It just drove home how useless these guys were without a weapon in their hand or a gang behind them.

Viking and I walked in together, with Stevie on our heels. "Do what you gotta do," Viking said to me. "I'll be out here."

There was no way Viking was signing the registry, but I sure did. The mass cards they made had a picture of Vince standing beside his beloved Corvette. I stuffed a few of them in my pocket. Fuck this place could've been owned by the same old fuck we got our suits from on the Canadian side.

Just in case you forgot who ran this town, there was a giant painting of old man Castellano right in the front foyer. He owned the funeral home until sometime in the '80s and everyone knew him and heard the jokes about him being his own best supplier.

I tried to prepare myself for what I thought was coming once I entered the main room. Pat's family had money and Vince's father wasn't an out-and-out gangster, and the room definitely had a fucked-up dynamic. Throw in the undercovers, hangarounds and old-timers from the area, and I was consciously trying to make myself as small as possible in the hope that no one would notice me.

That tactic ground to a halt when Pat screamed out my name as soon as she saw me.

I always got along with Pat. A smart, sexy woman, she always kept Vince on his toes. Between her family and what Vince was making, she stopped working a year or two ago. I always told Vince that if he dropped dead of a heart attack, I would step right over him to get to Pat. That didn't seem so funny now. She was 31 and widowed. I had no idea what I would say to her.

As I stepped forward to grab her hand, I was met by a wall of flesh. Vince was big. These guys were fucking gigantic. I had no idea if they were family, bodyguards or just Vince's football buddies. It was clear they were protective of Pat. When she whispered to them that I was OK, they all backed up, but not much. It was clear they were protecting her. No introductions were made. She grabbed my arm and led me in front of the coffin. I had no words to console her.

"That guy in the back," she had no problem pointing Stevie out, "says he's taking the 'Vette. First my husband, now his car?"

I had nothing to say that wouldn't make me sound like a piece of shit. "Pat, that's the way these guys operate."

She knew what Vince did to make most of his money, how much she knew or if she had started to hear stories or put shit together, I didn't know.

"Let me see what I can do." We both knew I was lying.

"I don't want to see that car ever again, but I don't see why I have to just give it up. They've taken enough from me."

I had no idea what to do at that point. I couldn't exactly mingle. Who the fuck would want to talk to me? It was obvious Pat could barely stand to look at me.

"I still think it's better you don't come to the funeral. I should get back in the receiving line. Take care of yourself, Ian." A quick hug and she was gone.

Our talk was shorter than my meeting with Jimmy. I turned to kneel in front of the coffin and stopped, then continued. Fuck everyone. Vince was more than just my friend. He was my boss, my workout partner and a big brother all in one. I knelt in front of the coffin. No tears, no fake dramatics, I just said goodbye to my friend. Regardless of all the fucking insanity of the last few days, it was the right thing to do. If I was the guy in that box, I'd like to think Vince would have barged in, all dramatic, and cried on my coffin. That's how he was. But it wasn't me.

I lifted my chin toward Viking as the signal for us to leave. I had the feeling I was going to be arrested or shot; like something was going to go down in that foyer.

Viking stood and put his hand on my shoulder. "Let's go, Billy."

We were immediately met at the door by Stevie. He was back to his cocky old self. "What? You think you're just walking out of here? Nice little display, but we're not done."

Viking was ready to stand in front of me, when I put my hand up. "You can do whatever the fuck you want when we get back to Canada, Stevie. But I'm not going back with you."

We had a nice little stare-down going. He realized he couldn't do anything. I was fucking myself by doing this, but it didn't matter. Stevie had put me in the middle of everything. He knew what I would do, how I would react. This was the only way I could get some measure of control back, to maybe figure my way out. Stevie had no reason to keep me now. Getting in the car with him was going to finish my little story. Maybe I could change that ending before it happened.

Stevie moved aside just enough so that the two of us could get by. Viking engaged in a pretty intense staring game with Stevie, but nothing was said, no contact was made.

We both walked out into a beautiful day. We both ripped off our ties and just stood around for a moment.

"You think he's really gonna let me go?"

Phil looked up at the sky and stretched out his arms. "What can he do? But you're gonna pay for this later."

I had no answer, although I was pretty positive Phil was also going to pay for the shiner that was already forming on Stevie's face.

We walked over to his truck in silence. We both piled in, and I had no idea what my next move was. I turned to look at Viking. Whatever was gonna happen to me was also going to happen to him for showing up here. We might as well go out in style.

"Norm's?" I asked.

He jammed the truck in gear. "Norm's it is."

Down Main Street up through the avenues, almost to Buffalo was littered with bars, pool halls, betting shops and liquor stores. There weren't many I hadn't been in. To this day, Norm's still sold ten-cent drafts. It was close to the bridge, so a lot of guys just walked over the border. Getting home wasn't a concern. The place had about ten tables and one long bar that ran the length of the place. Nothing much, but every couple of years it came back into style, packed with college kids. When it died down, it had enough regulars to keep it alive until it was a hotspot again.

We sat down and got a tray — thirty small glasses of draft. Without even speaking, we both downed three in a row. I took off my jacket and put some money in the jukebox. Fucking country music. Didn't matter, I just didn't want anyone listening to us talk.

Viking, on the other hand, loved it, whooping and hollering along with the words. Fucking hillbilly. We both downed a few more each before we got to talking.

"So, what happens now?" I wondered aloud. "Should I try and talk to Jimmy?"

Viking downed another glass and put another in front of me. "At this point, what's that gonna fucking do? Sounds like Jimmy has his own problems, one of which seems to be Stevie. I think you're fucked, Billy."

Unless I planned on running away, I had to go back to Canada. Even that wouldn't work. The Royal City Riders had chapters from Buffalo to New York City, with a few others in Boston, Alaska and the Carolinas. If it was really such a concern, some idiot might try to off me just to make some points. It was starting to occur to me that Stevie kept putting me in all those situations, so I would look like a problem. I try to get my friend out of trouble by talking to Jimmy, then disappear when my best friend gets shot. Then I have to be kidnapped and dragged to his funeral. Then I escape. That all made me look like quite the liability.

Viking was pretty drunk, and I wasn't far behind.

"I should settle this by shooting Stevie in his nice fucking suit." He was only half kidding. It would sure solve most of my problems.

Viking yelled to the bartender for two shots of Sambuca and two shots of scotch. He thumbed his nose at me and walked towards the bathroom. That nutty fuck had brought some coke over the bridge. I couldn't say I wouldn't partake.

The bartender put all the shots down. A nice little blast would help those go down.

Viking came back to the table and said: "top of the paper towel rack." I hated it when guys just dumped their coke on the back of the toilet. Who dumps their drugs on top of a shit-and-piss device?

I slammed one more draft and made my way to the can. I pulled the coke out of the paper towel dispenser. To my surprise, there was quite a bit left in there. I'd do some now and come back. We weren't leaving right away.

Stevie hadn't had us followed, so it was probably safe to sit for a while. He would be heading back to the border to wonder where the fuck we went. Fuck, maybe we'd even take the Rainbow Bridge back to really make it look like we were gone.

I checked my nose, then my phone. Messages from Shelly, Millie and my dad. Fuck, there was still all of that to deal with.

As I made my way out of the bathroom, I saw that Viking had taken my seat. He always sat with his back to the farthest wall, viewing the whole room. If you couldn't get out the front at Norm's, you could take off out the back and run off their loading dock. I knew the American side of Niagara as well as I knew my hometown. If I got to the loading dock I could disappear. But I also noticed that Viking wasn't alone. It looked like he was sitting with two local cops. He had changed seats to warn me. He had his arms crossed and gave me a quick look that said: "Keep walking and get the fuck outta here."

I tried not to break stride so I would look like I was just some drunken idiot coming out of the bathroom. I just cleared the table when I heard: "Tu vas où? Assis toi."

What the fuck? What Niagara Falls, New York, cop speaks French? I kept walking until I saw a glass fly by my head.

"Je te dis pas un autre fois." I was just told I wouldn't get another warning.

Walking back to the table, I could see two state troopers sitting with Viking. What looked like state troopers anyway. One was beside Viking, the other behind him. They knew what they were doing. Viking wasn't going anywhere, and for the first time ever, he looked intimidated, if not a little scared.

I sat down, slammed another beer and tried to look tough. When I tried to stare down the cop, I realized it was the French-speaking regional from back home who had thrown the support sticker in my window.

Chapter 18

It Would Have Been Easy

The cop helped himself to one of the drafts and grabbed a shot of Scotch. "You don't mind, do you?" he asked Viking.

Viking had no threat or snappy answer. He was clearly intimidated. He downed the shot and spoke to the other cop. "I'm going to speak to our friends in French. Don't take it personally, you just don't need to hear what I'm saying. Actually, I'm done with you, but why don't you stay and keep an eye on the other guy. This shouldn't take long." He slid an American hundred to the guy and gave him the other shot and a beer. Even this other guy, cop or not, was intimidated. "Relax, you've done good. I'll make sure he knows."

Who the fuck was this guy? No threats, all business, which made it scarier. And who the fuck was 'he'? This guy's boss? Another biker?

The guy smiled and put beers in front of all of us; he even offered Viking a cigarette. "Relax, we're just gonna talk. Try to be a little more reasonable than your friend ... leaving behind such a beautiful wife." Viking and the cop weren't his problem, I guess. "Let me show you something ..." he started in French, "... a little slide show." He slid a cellphone across the table. "Pick it up, esti. It won't work if you just stare at it."

I grabbed the phone and had no idea what to expect. It started with a Royal City Riders support sticker, just in case I didn't get the fucking point. Some assorted guys in colors, bikes, the usual. I put the phone back on the table. "Thanks."

"No, no," he said, "it gets better."

I reluctantly picked it back up. Pics of Millie and I at the Castle, the outside of Max's house, Vince and I in Toronto, Vince dropping me off at Shelly's, Viking and I in the Burnt clubhouse parking lot waiting to get in. His little show had been a repeat of my last week. Watching it made me start to feel sick, remembering when and where they were all taken.

"See, here's the thing," he continued in French, "we knew every step of the way what you were doing. I wanted to kill both of you in Toronto. Cops would have never figured it out. You've got some pretty loyal friends. I just don't know why Jimmy gives you so much leeway."

I wasn't fucking biting. I also had the feeling that no matter what I answered, I was going to be hit or shot. I stayed silent.

He lit another cigarette and laughed. "Maybe you really are smart. But it didn't help you. No matter what you try to pull now, you're fucked. Merde, if I were you, I would think of joining. You might have no other option when it's all done."

The cop and Viking hadn't said anything. "I just want to walk out of here," I answered.

He shook his head. "Too late for that. You know what happens when you leave?"

I didn't answer but I had a pretty good idea.

"When we ask a guy to leave, we take his bike, his shit, maybe even fuck his old lady. If the guy was really a problem, he doesn't get to leave. But you, you're not a member."

He handed out another round of beers. "Killing you is easier in our game, no one would care, but you're actually protected by being a nobody. It will look like we're animals picking on some loser."

He looked at me directly and switched back to English. "After everything you've done, you won't look so innocent anymore.

I couldn't breathe. I thought I was going to pass out but settled for puking all over the floor. Viking and the cop pushed their chairs back. Frenchie didn't flinch. The bartender threw us a dirty rag and pointed to the mop bucket in the corner. I puked, it wasn't his problem. Actually, it was my problem. Smelling puke or cleaning it up made me sick immediately.

Frenchie pushed our table back and told the cop to clean it up. It was obvious to both of us that Viking wasn't going to do anything stupid.

Frenchie brought his attention back to me. "With your little games, these pictures and a little luck, you're gonna look guilty, or at least involved. Anyone who might have helped you will walk away. You might get out if you do what I say."

No matter what I did, it seems like I was fucked. "So, what do I do?" I had to at least get back home. Maybe I could get Viking cut loose. After helping me and his interactions with Stevie, he was gonna have his own set of problems.

"Well, going back home with Stevie with be a start." Frenchie offered.

"No fucking way." It was the first time Viking had spoken up.

Frenchie seemed surprised and a little impressed. "Maybe your friend here does have some balls. He knows when to speak." Frenchie seemed to mull the situation over, lighting another cigarette and lighting one for Viking before handing it to him. Fuckers hadn't even offered me one the whole time we had been sitting there.

"You go back to the Falls with your friend here. I'll deal with Stevie. I can't follow you over, but I won't be far behind. It won't be hard to find you. Just drive back over to Simon's."

He looked directly at Viking and spoke in English. "You drive him to Simon's and you leave. Simple."

Viking nodded.

The conversation flipped back to French. "He's gonna have his own bullshit because of helping you. Killing both of you wouldn't be a problem." This guy had it all covered. He knew we were gonna try to bolt.

Frenchie got up and nodded to both of us. "Finish your drinks, boys. You've got thirty minutes to get back to Simon's."

"What if the bridge is busy?" Viking was getting a little confidence back.

Frenchie stared directly at him. "I'll take that into consideration." He walked to the front door, flipping the bartender a coin like he was John fucking Wayne riding into the sunset.

The cop walked out behind him, because it seemed pretty clear he was no longer needed.

Viking grabbed a beer and exhaled like he'd been holding his breath during that whole exchange. "Who the fuck was that guy?"

I still had no answer, so I grabbed another beer as well.

Walking back to get the truck was a fucking nightmare. Drunk and a little high, we both thought every single person was watching us, waiting to fuck us up. We were paranoid about everything. Who else was watching? Would we be allowed to make it back to the Falls? Frenchie obviously had connections here too. Fuck, shoot us in the parking lot and let the Americans deal with it. Why not? Just two morons in over their heads. They spent the day drinking, shot their mouths off, got shot. Just another day in the fucking city.

We made it back to the truck. I took off my jacket and threw it in the cab. Viking stripped off his jacket, vest and shirt, wearing a wife-beater and his pants.

"I say we go to Simon's," he said. That was not exactly what I thought would come out of his mouth. He reached under the seat and grabbed the mouthwash. When you drink as much as we did, it was always under the seat with the beer. The rest of the coke would at least make us appear sober. We'd done the same drill a million times.

"Why Simon's? Why don't we just cut out the middleman and shoot ourselves?"

He swigged the mouthwash again and passed it over. "'Cause no one is thinking we're gonna go. Everyone has to be pissed at Stevie, so he might not even be there. If we beat that French fuck there, maybe you can figure something out."

I didn't know if we were thinking the same thing, but Chris came to mind. He'd been shoved to the side. Plus, he wasn't all that fucking smart. If we made it to him first, maybe we could tell him how Stevie fucked up and see if Chris would bite. It was worth a shot. It was pretty fucking slim though. "What if we get there and everyone is there? Stevie, Chris, Frenchie, Jimmy, and who the fuck knows who else"

Viking looked over and laughed. "Then we're both fucked, Billy," and kept laughing uncontrollably.

We made it to the lower bridge with only a few cars ahead of us. This might fucking work, I thought to myself. I told that to Viking. He agreed, in no small part because we had nothing to lose. If we made it to Simon's, then we'd go for broke.

"Let me take the lead," I told him. "He might still think this is just between me and Stevie. I'm fucking positive he doesn't know all of it."

That was usually the part where Viking tells me to go fuck myself, he'll take care of it, but he just nodded. He knew he might be fucked now, and I knew Chris way better than he did.

We pulled up to the border crossing and dealt with another bored bridge worker. He couldn't even be bothered to look at us. "Buy or receive anything?" he asked reflexively. We both said nope in unison. The fucking guy waved us straight through. Viking shook his head. "I would bitch about national security, not pulling over a fuck like me, but let's be thankful he was a lazy bitch."

I shook my head and smiled to say I agreed. I couldn't believe our fucking luck.

You can actually see Simon's from the bridge. Viking drove by once to check it out. If he would've kept driving, I might not have stopped him, and he was aware of that. He turned in the Via Rail parking lot and straightened himself up. He drove back down Bridge Street and parked directly in front of Simon's. Chris was in the window, sitting with Dumb or Dumber, couldn't tell which.

No sign of Stevie or Frenchie, just these two. We had to do this quickly. It seemed off; too fucking easy. But we had to go for it. Everyone else might be on the way. I fucking hoped that maybe Stevie had been taken out of the picture for letting me get away, but it wasn't likely. He was still valuable and hadn't fucked up enough to be chased off or killed. For the first time since all this started, I felt like I was in charge. I punched Viking in the shoulder. "Let's go."

As soon as we walked in, Chris jumped up. "What the fuck?" We both put our hands up and offered no resistance.

"Sit down," I whispered. "Don't make a scene. It's cool."

Chris hesitated and then briefly frisked Viking. "Where's Stevie?"

"That's the fucking thing," I said, starting out my big lie, "We go to the funeral and Billy here shows up" I start, pointing at Viking, "Stevie makes a fucking scene, and Billy punches him in the face!" It was kind of true, I guess.

Chris broke up my speech. "You're gonna pay for that!"

Viking played right along. "I know, fuck I'm an idiot."

I continued my bullshit. "So, this fucking guy walks up to Stevie, slaps him and hustles him right out of the funeral home."

Chris's eyes were wide-open and unblinking at that point. "So, we went for a few drinks to calm ourselves down. What the fuck is with him anyway, Chris?" C'mon, I was thinking to myself, bite, god damn it.

"I don't know" he answered. "I don't get told shit anymore. I ain't his bitch."

Viking and I both nodded our heads, in sympathy and agreement.

"Anyway, look. I don't want you to burn for Stevie's bullshit. But Phil here has to split. You can take me home, to Jimmy, whatever, but I gotta crash. I'll work on getting you guys the

'Vette. I don't want no hassle, dude. You seem to be the only one I can talk to lately."

Chris was evaluating what I was saying, and I could tell he was still on the fence.

Phil spoke up. "What's up with your partner anyway? You should be calling some shots. It would make more sense."

That fucking sold it. "Yeah, yeah," Chris looked at Dumb (or Dumber), then Viking. "You guys get outta here, I'll take Doc home. I just might have to talk to Jimmy about this shit. Someone has to step up."

He bought it. Phil bolted the fuck out. "Later, boys," he yelled.

Chris and I walked outside. "Thanks for being reasonable, Chris." It had fucking worked. Out the door, in the car, worry about the rest later. What would happen next, I didn't know, but I knew I had to get away from Chris. Maybe I'd try to meet up with Jimmy. As fucked as it was, I still thought that was my best bet. Maybe it was time to cut Viking loose. I didn't have any idea. It all hinged on what Chris said or did in the car.

We both got in. Chris put on his seatbelt and looked over at me. "Put yours on too. You've been through a lot." Fuck, the man truly was an idiot.

Chapter 19

You Got Big Daddy in There?

As we left Simon's, I wasn't sure what my plan would be. Viking had bolted, not giving me any indication that he had a plan. Maybe he was just sick of all this shit and realized that his help could only carry me so far.

He was spooked by Frenchie — I'd never seen anything like that in him ever. Taking a beating, even taking three shots to land one, that never bothered him in the least. But he was clearly rattled.

And he would definitely need to deal with Stevie somewhere down the line. Their little game was getting personal, and that's when people always get sloppy and stupid.

Phil had his own life and family to worry about. In the beginning, helping me was a game for him. Now, he would have to deal with Stevie regardless of what happened to me. He was helping me because he was my friend. He had no other motive, which in its own way was reassuring. I thought he'd stand beside me no matter what happened. But maybe I had pushed it too far. I had only made it this far because of his help. Alone, I would have been eaten alive.

We drove up Victoria Avenue, past the library, and past the Shopping News office building that had been part of the landscape since the '70s. When we reached the old Armory, it reminded me of our time as cadets. We had all made cadet sergeant rank, and Stevie used it every chance he could to throw his weight around over the younger guys. Chris developed an aptitude for mechanics, helping the militia guys fix their trucks and clean their old rifles.

"Remember when my mom used to drop us off, thinking we were going to cadets, but we'd fuck off to Silvertown to chase the Biamone sisters around?" I asked, hoping to lighten the mood.

Chris only grunted. He wasn't the type for reminiscing. "Pull into the 7-Eleven," he said.

Most of us cadets spent as much time at the 7-Eleven as they did at the Armory.

"Grab me a Coke and some Tylenol," I blurted at Chris. The non-stop activity, getting punched, hit by the occasional car and a lack of sleep had ruined me.

Chris put out his hand and stared. The fucking guy didn't have any cash. Prospecting for the Burnt hadn't improved his financial situation. Full-patch members are always telling prospects what to do; and they had better do it at their own expense and without complaint. It's usually something like "hey, pick up my old lady at the hairdresser; and, oh yeah, bring me some smokes too." If a prospect is told he's going to be escorting the guys to dinner, he might not eat, but he's definitely picking up the bill. It's a struggle and how any of them pull it off is beyond me.

Chris took the keys out of the ignition and made a big show of pocketing them. That didn't make much sense to me. Maybe I couldn't drive away, but I could just get up and leave.

Instead of musing about his motives, I stretched back and closed my eyes. Adrenaline from the last few days was working its way out of my body and now all I could feel was pain. I still had no plan. My only idea was to maybe get Chris to talk about all the shit that had happened. It wouldn't change much, but maybe it would clear my own head.

I was just about to doze off when Chris swung the car door open and plopped his ass down. Before handing me the Tylenol, he downed about ten of them and chased them down with an entire can of Coke.

I took three.

"Where to?" Chris asked.

I had no idea and told him that. "You're driving, dude."

Chris pulled out of the parking lot and drove towards Clifton Hill. We passed the spot where the new casino was going to be built, where Maple Leaf Village once stood. Then we went up through Centre Street, past the Memorial Arena. At the four-way stop, he turned to me and said: "We gotta talk, I need your help."

Shocked, I wondered why the fuck Chris would need my help.

But there were no further words from him. He just kept driving, heading towards Highway 420. Once we hit the 420, Chris floored it. In no time, we were going 100 miles per hour.

"Trying to scare me, Chris? You gotta do better than that."

We were heading towards the fork that allowed us to go back toward Niagara Falls or head to Toronto. Chris wasn't veering one way or another. He was driving straight towards the median.

"OK, OK, whatever you're trying to prove, I got it. Pick a fucking lane. Now."

Chris wasn't even looking at the road.

"For fucks sakes, Chris!"

At the last second, he veered towards the exit for the Falls, so close to the median that his mirror smashed off into it. We practically left the ground, as we careened toward the ditch. Chris plowed straight on through, landing in the dry patch of land that separated the highway and Dorchester Road.

He stopped in the dirt, looked both ways like he was at a crosswalk and drove over the curb back onto Dorchester like it had been his plan all along.

Once my fear and rage had subsided, I began to punch the dashboard. “What the fuck, motherfucker! Fuck!”

Even in my rage, I knew better than to punch Chris. Fucking with Stevie was one thing. Hitting Chris would get me knocked out cold. He was always the toughest of the three of us.

With no trace of a smile, Chris looked over at me like he was talking to a child. “I told you I wanted to talk. I had to be sure that fucking Viking or anybody else wasn’t following. Fuck, you’re becoming a pussy.”

We looped back around Dorchester, got back on the 420 cut-off, but headed down Stanley instead. We drove down to Palmer Park, just before the bend where Stanley turns into Thorold Stone Road.

The park had four baseball diamonds and always had someone there. Chris pulled into the parking lot and again made a big show of putting his keys in his pocket.

“What now? You wanna make out?”

Chris held up his finger and spun it counter-clockwise, which always meant to us someone might be listening. It also meant he didn’t want to talk in the car. As we walked across the field to the benches, there were some girls who looked to be about nine or ten playing ball.

Suddenly, one of them yelled out my name. It was Maddie Kraft. Her dad, Gene, was in our little crew before he opted out for a day job, wife and two beautiful little girls. Gene was just as tough as Chris, but he had traded in our bullshit for a happy little life, and I had tutored his kid when she needed it.

We sat down on the benches near the end of the park. Chris lit us both smokes and handed me one. Without any build-up, he dropped a bomb on me: “I want out.”

We both knew what he meant. At first, I thought he meant just to leave the Burnt. Most guys get chased out by the point he was at. Chris hadn't really fallen behind, but he still resented Stevie being promoted first. "I done everything they asked me to do, those fucking assholes. Remember Trippy Zip?"

Trippy Zip, or TZ, was an old-time Burnt member who basically sat around the clubhouse and watched Dr. Phil all day. He was allegedly the club's version of a jailhouse lawyer until someone dosed his drink at a party one night and he lost his mind.

Chris lit another smoke and threw me the pack. "You know what I did for my first three months prospecting? I had to pick him up every morning. That fuck is retarded now. I had to help him get in and out of the shower, he's so fucking weak. Then I had to chauffeur him to the fucking dollar store, where he looks at every single fucking thing on the shelf. Then we gotta eat at the Castle. Same table, and if people are sitting there, he'll just sit down with his patch on and make grunting noises 'til they leave. All with his patch on!" He emphasized that last bit to make it clear how much it offended him.

I rolled my eyes. Being at the bottom, like Chris was, a lot of guys dump their responsibilities on you. You'll hear about how they've got more important things to do, but usually once they get their patch, they just can't be bothered with them anymore. They can always get a prospect to do what they want.

"So, what's the problem I asked? You don't love the Castle?"

He ignored me. Then, then ..." Chris didn't usually stutter, but he began repeating words when he got frustrated. "... then, we'd go to the clubhouse to watch Dr. Phil all fucking day. The same episode all day. Then the next day he wants to see the same episode. I know he's got a lot of time in the club, but he's a fucking vegetable."

He paused, then continued with his rant about how the club had treated him. "And that's just my day. At night, we're fucking cruising bars, looking for RCR supporters to beat the fuck out of. The other night at Hearts ..."

"Whoa, wait," I cut him off. "Why are you guys punching out RCR supporters? Aren't you guys working out a patch-over?"

Chris immediately stopped talking.

I rolled my hand towards myself, giving him the old yeah, yeah gesture. He's not supposed to talk about this shit with outsiders, but that rule seemed pretty fucking pointless now.

He hesitated for a moment, then started again. "Jimmy says they're fair game until the patch-over. Those idiots shouldn't be wearing colors here." As hard as it might be for a regular guy to understand, bikers have been killed for wearing their patches into the wrong bar. Wrong club, wrong bar, wrong sideways glance and someone gets shot. As far as the supporters went, they were mostly idiots with no real chance of getting any kind of patch. Some of them might, though, so beating them indiscriminately didn't make sense.

Whatever Jimmy's plan was, it was confusing. Or, like the rest of us, maybe he had no plan at all.

"And these RCR guys?" Chris continued, "They're ... they're ... they're fucking scary. It's like they got little armies and groups like we had in fucking high school."

I told him I didn't understand.

"One guy does one thing, that's it," he began explaining. "I asked a guy for coke a few weeks ago and we partied. When I couldn't find the same guy, I asked another guy. I got told I could only deal with the first guy. They got guys that only do their fighting, other guys seem like nothing more than errand boys. Fuck that noise."

I tried to explain to Chris that maybe he was only seeing what they wanted him to see.

"I don't fucking like it," he said. "Do this, do that, don't talk to this guy, go here, go there."

"Chris, you knew that's how it was gonna be in the beginning."

"Nah, man, it's different. These guys don't give a fuck about anyone here. Remember how we could go anywhere, anytime,

Doc? I ain't having outsiders tell me where the fuck I can go in Niagara. I'll take them all out, one at a time."

"Chris, this is serious. These guys are a major club around the world. If Jimmy agrees to the patch-over, it's their rules, their game."

Chris got up and stretched his legs. "Yeah, well fuck Jimmy too. He's no help. One minute he's kissing their asses, and the next minute he's telling us to fuck up their supporters. I don't know who to trust."

We both stood up and I put my hand on Chris's shoulder. "How much contact have you had with the RCR full-patches?"

"Not much. Stevie usually keeps me away from them. I get all my orders from Stevie now."

"Would you recognize any of the guys?"

"Maybe, maybe, I don't know, why?"

It was my turn to unload. I told him about the run in with Frenchie as a cop, then our fucked-up drinking session after Vince's wake. I told him about Frenchie seeming to know all my moves and knowing the situation Vince was in. "My best friend got killed for $17,000. What the fuck? These guys drop that in a weekend on blow and broads."

Chris got agitated at the mention of the money and really started to trip over his words. "Vince, he ... he ... he ..."

Yelling at a guy who was stuttering didn't exactly show my compassionate side, but I couldn't help it. "For fuck's sakes, Chris, he what?"

"He ... he ... he didn't owe Stevie the whole 17. He got it down to like four grand."

I didn't know what to say. It's easy to say shit once a guy is dead. Sure, sure, I paid him, just before he got shot 36 times. He must've have forgotten to drop the cash off to you. But saying a dead guy paid, and then he got killed anyway? That didn't make sense.

"When did he pay? He never told me shit."

"He paid us that morning."

"The morning he got shot? Why didn't you ever tell me this before?" That was a pretty fucking stupid question on my part. Chris wasn't going to implicate himself in a murder. Before he could attempt an answer, I asked: "Why tell me this all now, motherfucker? Feeling guilty?"

Both of us unloading reminded me of why I used to like Chris so much. He wasn't a bad guy, usually pretty upfront about his shit.

Stevie and Chris had both been my friends so long I forgot how I met him. He didn't go to the French school like Stevie and me. He went to the worst school in Niagara, Heximer Public, where I had heard that the kids routinely attacked their teachers.

Chris was a tough kid among real fucking delinquents. When a bunch of them tried to steal my bike, all it took was a look from Chris and they all backed off.

Chris had his good points. In my first year of university, my grandmother died. Chris showed for the funeral and openly wept beside her coffin, saying she was the only lady that was ever nice to him.

Grandma had no time for Stevie, but had a soft spot for Chris, calling him her lost little Wayne, whatever the fuck that meant. Finding him disheveled with a dirty shirt and hungry as a kid, she fed him, got him a new T-shirt and marched him home, telling his grandmother that if she ever found him that way again it would be a problem.

Sitting here pouring our bullshit to each other, I began to think I wasn't the only one being fucked with. Chris was being played, dealing with all of the day-to-day mundane bullshit of being in a club, while Stevie was playing the big shot. Stevie wasn't technically doing anything wrong, just taking advantage of the rules. Nothing but upsides for Stevie. If Chris made it through, well hey, it was all due to Stevie guiding him. If he didn't, fuck that guy, he couldn't cut it.

"So, when did Vince give Stevie the cash?"

Chris hesitated.

"C'mon, man, you owe me that much."

Chris stood up and shoved me in the chest. "I don't owe you shit. I always been the third wheel between you and Stevie and now I want out, irregardless of your fucking feelings."

I didn't think this was the time to point out how much I hated the use of the almost-word "irregardless," but it struck me anyway.

"Vince gave us the money the day you and Viking came to see Jimmy."

"So, you both talked to Vince that morning?"

"No, Stevie went straight to the clubhouse so he wouldn't be late."

Yeah, late. Stevie is at the clubhouse, Chris does the shit work. Vince is gone, Chris looks guilty. Fuck, Stevie can even argue Chris didn't even get the money. Stevie is a full-patch, Chris isn't. Shit, who are they going to believe?

Stevie had fucked over his two best friends, had Vince killed and still got paid. He made sure he was nowhere near the actual shooting. He was with Jimmy, who was no doubt under some kind of permanent loose surveillance. Business taken care of, he proved himself to the Burnt and the RCR. It was pretty fucking brilliant, I had to admit.

I couldn't bring myself to ask, but the obvious question hung in the air.

"I didn't kill Vince, fuck ... fuck ... fuck you, Doc."

I immediately believed him. I don't know why, maybe I was being an emotional idiot, but there wouldn't have been any drama with Chris, no long, drawn out back-and-forth. He just would've shot Vince.

"So, what do we do now?" Chris asked.

Just walking away wasn't going to work. If Chris just got up and left, Jimmy would kick him out of the club. Most clubs called it being in "bad standing," but Jimmy preferred his own title, that you were "put outside." If Jimmy put you outside the club, it meant your protection was gone. Worse, anyone with a patch or connections to the club was expected to fuck you up on sight. With the Burnt-RCR thing going on, that made for a lot of guys who would go after you just to score a point or two.

"Let's go see Jimmy and sort this shit out."

Our running and ducking Stevie was going to burn us eventually. For now, it seemed the safest place would be with the only guy who might be able to call off whatever was going on.

I was pretty sure we weren't a big concern to anyone but ourselves, but circumstances and Stevie's maneuvers had stuck us in the middle of the whole thing.

Chris didn't seem too sure about what to do next. But he didn't have too many other options. We sat around a bit talking and bullshitting, me remembering at one time that Chris and I had been pretty tight. We never had very much in common, but we had been through a lot. Chris didn't open much or let anyone know what he was thinking very often, but it was clear he wanted out. I thought, at first, that it was because he wouldn't make the cut for the RCR, but it was clear now he was just fed up.

As we were talking, what looked like a family was walking towards us. It was pretty easy to spot Viking in any crowd, since he was legitimately two feet taller than his old lady. They even had the kid with them. She ran up and jumped in my lap. She didn't know Chris, but she didn't seem afraid, she just buried her head in my chest.

"What a lovely day in the park," Beth said, her voice dripping with sarcasm.

I gave Viking the old raised-chin look that told him just to stay cool for a while.

"The kid starts T-ball today. Beth, go get her ready, I'll be there in a minute." Viking then opened the workout bag and pulled out a six-pack, tossing two beers each to Chris and me.

It was his turn to give me the raised chin.

Chris and I went through everything we had discussed.

"Well fuck, what are we waiting for?" he said.

I thought maybe we should make up some sort of plan.

Chris looked at the sports bag and asked: "You got Big Daddy in there?"

"You know I do."

Big Daddy was packed and ready for duty.

Once sufficiently buzzed, we got up to go.

"Let me tell Beth we gotta go," announced Viking.

Poor Beth. She didn't bitch, she knew the deal.

We gathered all our shit and walked towards Chris's car. Viking put his hand out for the keys. He always did the driving, drunk, stoned, whatever. Chris didn't hesitate, he simply handed them over.

As Chris got in the car, I grabbed Viking by the arm. "How did you know I was here?"

Viking smiled, looked over at his kid hitting the ball for the first time, then started cheering. He then looked back at me. "Ian, my kid had T-ball. This isn't all about you. Get in the fucking car."

Chapter 20
Plan?

After talking with Chris and Viking, it was pretty easy to blame everything that happened on Stevie. But really, like all the other shit in my life, it was my own lack of planning that had led me to this spot. More to the point, it was a lack of giving a fuck. Stevie, Chris and Viking all made conscious efforts to follow this lifestyle. But without really paying attention, I kind of just fell into it and wasn't smart enough to know when to pull myself out.

Lots of guys had friends who made their other buddies look like saints, but that didn't mean their old friends from Grade 6 dragged them into murder conspiracies.

I voiced my concerns to Viking, who had somehow become the voice of reason in this fucked-up situation.

"Plan?!" he laughed out loud. "Has there been a fucking plan so far?" He reloaded Big Daddy and handed it to Chris, who was thoroughly fucked up.

We would have to slow down or come up with some kind of fucking idea right away. Guys who live the life literally fry their brains. They get up, drop a few lines to get going. Usually a handful of Tylenol and a little speed will keep the buzz moving. If they pass the point of control, they usually smoke a little hash or weed to even it out. They never think about the havoc on their hearts: up, down, up down, up, down. Then they do their rounds: shaking down pimps, drug dealers, anyone they can fuck with that is afraid of that little patch on their back, as long as it has “MC” on it. The club’s name isn’t as important as the “motorcycle club” part — that’s what scares the fuck out of most people.

Of course, since they’re dealing with pimps and dealers, the drugs and the partying continue from stop to stop. Just making the rounds sometimes with Stevie, I would wind up passed out in the car. I was known for being able to hold my own, but these fuckers partied for days straight. Mix in a blow job here and there, because they needed to keep the party cranking. They also had to stay alert but being straight was considered a pussy thing to do. So, on top of all the other shit, they usually guzzle down about ten coffees a day.

By the time it was all said and done, they’ve usually been up for 15 to 18 hours, ingested more drugs and booze during the day than most guys in a bowling league will see in a lifetime. They’ve also had sex with some of the most beautiful women on the planet, who very shortly turn into skanky used-up pigs because they buy drugs from guys like them.

At the end of their rounds, all these guys want to do is crash. But they can’t. So, what’s their solution? More weed? Doesn’t work for many. More booze? No, for most, it’s sleeping pills. What a way to come down. A handful of barbiturates to keep their asses alive after a day of stimulating drugs. But the good side is that they usually fall asleep immediately. The bad side to the pills is that they make them feel like they just came out of a coma every time they wake up. They’re groggy as fuck for the first hour of their day, but they have no choice but to suck it up, throw a shot of Jack Daniel’s in their coffee and blow off a line the length and thickness of a man’s finger.

And then they do it all over again. It’s because the life is where the money is. They’ve got to hustle — and if they fall asleep beside that knockout brunette they picked up last night at Hooligans — someone else is gonna be out there making their money. Besides, she's going to look like a dried-up old trout after fucking guys like them soon enough.

This was what Chris, Stevie and a million other guys were running towards. Viking too, I guess, just in his own way.

Working your way up the ladder is hard, and it's a lot harder when everyone involved is a liar and potentially a murderer. This isn't 1972, you don't die in the garden with a fucking orange peel stuck in your teeth. You're gone, and some other kid is already working your corner, fucking your whore. If you're lucky, the boys might send a wreath to your funeral.

How did I know all of this? I was living it, although on a much smaller scale. I'd take shit to wake up, and different shit to go to sleep with a million distractions in between. I knew it was wrong and that it wasn't going to lead to anything substantial; but, fuck it, for a while, it's every geeky kid's dream.

I looked over a Chris, pleasantly baked, like the weight of the world got left on those bleachers in the ballpark. One minute, I'm looking to sacrifice the guy for my own good, and the next minute I'm looking up to him. I had really become a piece of shit.

Viking was screaming something out the window. When I began to pay attention, and focus on his words, I realized he was doing a really horrible Colonel Klink impression. "Ze best plan is nooooooo plan!" he shouted. It was nice to see he was going all Zen on me.

"So, we march in there without a plan ... maybe we should at least think about what we're going to say?"

Viking mulled that over and sparked up Big Daddy. "Look, we should both be dead, probably fuckin' Chris here too. We've been lucky and caught a couple of breaks." He didn't elaborate, but I understood. We caught a break when Frenchie thought we would do anything other than run straight across the border. We caught a break when Chris bought our bullshit. Maybe Chris having a change of heart was a break too.

Certainly, driving around like a couple of hicks in a pickup truck had caught us a couple of breaks too.

We weren't involved in a murder, we were just some local morons blowing off steam. "You always say, 'let's play this out,'" Viking drawled, passing me Big Daddy, "Well, then, let's play this out. It can't get no worse. Fuck, we might not even die." I couldn't argue with that logic as I sparked up Big Daddy.

We decided to stay at the Red Rhose Inn on Queen Street. Far off the beaten path, it might very well have been a half-decent place to stay back in the '50s when Queen Street was still the main drag. Why Red Rhose was spelled that way I never understood.

It had seen far better days and had become little more than a shooting gallery for the local junkies. The lady at the desk was pleasant enough, looking like she had been here since the place's good old days. She wasn't being too discreet checking out Chris passed out in the truck. She cheerily asked about our plans for the next few days.

We both looked at each other and shouted: "Ze best plan is no plan!" Viking decided to amp it up by goose-stepping out of the office. I just shrugged and followed him out.

We had taken a room on the ground floor. Viking dumped Chris on a bed and pulled the truck in backwards to make for an easy escape.

Fuck, I needed a shower. The bathroom was relatively clean, so I drew a bath instead.

"Fucking pussy," Viking hissed as he threw me a beer and went out to sit on one of the ratty chairs outside of our room.

It was time for me to return some calls and see who still wanted to kill me.

First up was my dad. His message was about an open house at D'Youville College in Niagara Falls, New York, for immediate entry into the Master of Education program. His message said to get all my shit together and he'd drive me over. God bless him, he was still trying to help me.

Next was Jenny. I heard her voice and immediately erased it. Nothing she said could be of importance right now.

On to Millie. The usual. Where are you? Fuck you! Call me! I love you! Where are you now? Thank God, she knew I was cheap and only had a certain amount of message space or that long-ass diatribe would have been all separate messages.

The only message I took seriously was Jimmy's. I was actually amazed that he even left a message. "This is getting old, kid," he said ominously. "You should go swimming." I had to take him seriously. "Go swimming" meant I should get my ass to where he was, or I might be found in the water.

I dried off and put on my suit pants and undershirt to sit outside with Viking. I lightly shoved Chris as I walked by. No response except a long grunt. Chris never was much for weed. Big Daddy got him every time. I didn't bother tying back my hair. No one to impress in this shit hole. Probably not a bad idea to look a little different anyway.

Viking kicked a chair towards me, throwing me a beer at the same time. I lit a smoke and crushed the can in one gulp.

"Fuck, you're a lightweight pussy when it comes to the hard stuff, but you could always slam your beers." He threw me another. I caught him up on all the other shit Chris had said. He just looked away from me.

"So, Chris can figure this all out, but you can't? What the fuck is it with you? You're not gonna be able to keep this pace up."

"What about you?" I asked.

"Don't worry about me. Me and Big Daddy will be fine."

Typical. No mention of his wife or kid, or the few million bucks he had coming his way. Nothing was going to change for Viking. He was right though. Not much would change for him or Bea; they would just have more money and more excuses to do what they wanted.

"I don't know what the fuck to do. Maybe just marry your sister and run away."

We both sat in silence for a bit. Chris finally dragged himself off the bed, and immediately pointed at Big Daddy. Hair o' the fucking dog, I guess. After a few rounds for himself and a few for us, he slowly came to life. "What were we talking about?"

Without missing a beat, Viking said: "Doc here becoming my brother-in-law," which was his way of saying it was all right with him if I married his sister.

"Bea have a say in this?" Chris asked.

"Maybe," I grinned.

We then discussed my call from Jimmy, not even bothering to mention the others. "do we go see him together, separately, what?"

Chris spoke first. "It don't make no sense to separate now. Let's fucking do this. Whatever happens, happens."

We were all pretty much in agreement that it had to end, good or bad, Chris was the one with the most to lose. He would probably have to pack up and leave if he told Jimmy he was done.

The RCR might give him a position just to fuck with Jimmy. They would try to get info out of Chris. Once he was used up, they would probably kill him. At least Jimmy would let him live. As much as I bitched about my own situation, Chris had to carefully weigh out his options as well. I might still get out with a shit-kicking and a warning not to talk to any of my friends. Chris might lose everything, including his life. He seemed resigned to the fact that his only ticket into the RCR would be to fuck over Jimmy and Stevie. After all of the deceit, duplicity and destruction Chris had witnessed, he still stuck to his own code. The RCR needed dudes like Chris in every chapter.

"Look, nobody gives a fuck about you or Doc. Just stay here. I'll deal with this." Chris wasn't looking for friends. It had never been that important to him anyway.

Viking took a haul off Big Daddy and then handed it to Chris: "Can't let you do that, Billy." Chris genuinely looked confused. He had never played our Billy/Jimmy game, always thinking it was stupid. But Chris was just as high now as he had been when he passed out.

I couldn't resist joining in. "Billy is right about that Jimmy. How can we expect Jimmy to go see Jimmy if Billy doesn't have his back? I think Billy would agree."

Viking just nodded.

Chris laughed and kept smoking. "You two are fucked ... Doug."

Hearing Chris say Doug sent the two of us over the edge. We all rolled around on the ground, barely noticing the pizza guy standing there. Viking must have ordered earlier. He quickly stood up and handed the driver cash. "Sorry, Jimmy, looking after Billy and Billy here. Good guys, but both a little retarded."

That sent Chris and I back to the ground, howling and rolling around.

Viking stood there, stone-faced and earnest, looking over the two retarded Billys.

As we ate, the sun was going down. What was happening to Queen Street wasn't unique to Niagara Falls. A nice little downtown with men's shops, a butcher, a pharmacy, maybe a jeweler starts to erode when the big-box stores show up. What began the erosion for us was Niagara Square, the mall that destroyed our downtown. There had been a few attempts at revitalizing the area, but nothing serious. Sitting here after it all happened, downtown seemed like a good place to hide.

"Everybody crashes in shifts," Viking said. "I'm pretty sure Stevie, that weird fucking French guy and a whole bunch of other people are still looking for us."

It made sense. It wasn't like we were gonna get in a big gun battle like some fucking B-movie, but it would be nice to know when people were coming.

As we began to decide who would take the first shift, we heard the start of the rumble. It was in the distance, but all three of us knew what it was. Viking jumped up to start the truck. With Chris and I jumping in the cab, we planned to get the fuck out. Two bikes immediately blocked our path. Two more, blocked Queen Street going toward River Road. Two more blocked any question of us going down Queen Street to downtown.

Viking jammed the truck into park and gave me the old what-the-fuck look. It didn't take long for the bikers, all wearing RCR patches, to surround the truck. As the parking lot began to fill with bikes, the noise was deafening.

Looking around, I didn't see Jimmy or Stevie or the few Burnt guys I knew by name. After the full-patch RCR members, none of whom I knew, there came a few guys I recognized as full-patch Burnt members, but they weren't wearing their colors or RCR colors. These guys just had a bottom rocker, which was the bottom part of the patch set. It was in orange and blue and read "Niagara." The only other thing on their backs was a small patch that said HTMF, which stood for halfway there, motherfucker. It meant you weren't a hangaround, that you had some status with the RCR. These boys didn't want their members-in-waiting being shit on. They could still get voted out, but that was unlikely. You wore that patch until you were a full member. It was then replaced with a small piece that said ALA, which meant all in, always. Once in, your life revolved around the RCR, and you better not fucking forget it.

Behind them, I quickly became certain, were a bunch of local idiots called the Checked. What that meant, who the fuck cared. Jimmy didn't tolerate competition or puppet gangs, but I always thought he let the Checked hang around because their idiotic antics took the heat off his own boys. Dumb doesn't begin to describe these guys. They'd pull shit like small B&E's with their colors on, crashing their bikes into police cruisers – they were just fucking useless. If that was them, they were wearing nothing that identified them, not even support gear. Just leather and denim. They rode at the back, which showed they had no status. They would be errand boys, nothing more.

I would be surprised if any of them ever made the cut into the RCR.

We were allowed out of the truck but were walked back towards our room. Even I have to admit it was impressive. This was a balls-out display of power, from the full patches, with their slow pace, to the pecking order in which they rode. Usually the president or the man in charge rides in front. But the RCR feel a need to put on a show, so after everyone rode in, they took over the entire lot.

Nothing was said until we could hear a smaller rumble approach. Eight bikes, two on each side, full colors, full helmets. If anything I read was correct, it went something like this: While most gangs had their president ride up front, the RCR preferred two bodyguards up front, then the president in the second line and on the left, with a road captain on his right, two more bodyguards, then the vice-president on the right, with a sergeant-at-arms (third in charge) beside him.

That gave them lots of bodyguards and their top three guys together but separated a little if the shit goes down. That way it looks like they stand united, but they can get away with a bodyguard if the shooting starts.

The eight of them rode in, and no one turned their bikes off until these eight did. I don't think any of us were surprised when the guy we took as their president took off his helmet and it was our old buddy, Frenchie.

Chapter 21
RCR Niagara

Well it was fucking official. The RCR ran Niagara. One chapter, maybe two. They might take over the Burnt clubhouse, or they could open their own.

Jimmy and his boys kept it fairly low-key, but everyone knew they were around. The RCR didn't hide, they practically slapped you to get your attention.

Their clubhouses looked like gaudy churches, tall and imposing, with blue-and-orange neon everywhere. Unlike a lot of clubs, who wanted to bury the past, the RCR let you know an area was taken from someone else – usually by force.

The clubs that had lost the battle usually found their old sign upside down, with RCR written across it, the Rs in orange, the rest in blue. It was usually hung near a bathroom or garage just to add a tweak to the insult of vandalizing their old foes' honored symbol. It was a fitting reminder of the enemy's capitulation.

It looked like the RCR entered negotiations with Burnt about a patch-over, but they dragged on. That's usually not a great tactic. These kinds of situations were expected to be responded to swiftly. Taking any time was considered an insult. The RCR sincerely believed that any other club should be happy that their little gang of losers had been chosen to wear the sacred orange and blue.

They always said that not everyone got in. But, to me, that seemed to be a bunch of P.R., if not outright bullshit. In an effort to gain territory in Ontario, the RCR were making deals with gangs that had previously been considered second- or even third-rate. Not everyone got the nod, but it didn't seem nearly as tough as it used to be, or they claimed it still was.

Maybe it was romantic delusion on my part, but the RCR had always been considered a cut above (which, not coincidentally, was one of their slogans). They were the big time, their membership equivalent to being a made man in the Mafia. What most people didn't understand was that being made, or getting your patch, being straightened out, whatever you wanted to call it, was supposed to be a recognition of your efforts to achieve a certain lifestyle.

It wasn't the beginning of a criminal career, it was an acknowledgement that you already had one. You now had the backing of a criminal organization that had financial and political clout. It didn't make you infallible, but it gave the other guy pause because he knew you were in the big time.

Even after working in the bars for years, I still got uneasy when a bunch of patches showed up and started hanging around. It made me downright paranoid when they were out-of-towners.

The RCR had their own mystique, and I was just as guilty as the next guy for buying into their bullshit. They were bodyguards to the stars, they partied all over the world, they seemed to be everywhere. Forget their coast-to-coast slogan, they were international. Even in the areas when they weren't always visible, they still had some control of, or at least a voice in, what went on in the area.

For a lot of guys in the game, every contact they had made in the Niagara area just went out the window. For now, they would still have a place, but that was tenuous at best. They would be used to help the club set up contacts, figure out who to avoid, who'll help, who they'll tell to beat it. Most clubs let patched-over members rise through the ranks, simply because they need the manpower. The weak and stupid are quickly tossed aside. Patch-overs have to pledge their loyalty to the new regime if they expected to survive.

Of course, all that really meant nothing. Most of what I knew about the life was the shit I had read. I had some access to it because of my relationship with Jimmy, as well as growing up with Chris and Stevie. But I always tried to remember that I only saw what they allowed me to see. I had no status except for long-time friendships. It never really helped me as much as I thought — but it saved my ass a few times. I don't think I would be seeing any favors from Frenchie, though.

Frenchie got off his bike and began stretching a little. Two prospects immediately fell in behind him. He looked around, with no expression on his face. Fuck, this guy was scary. I wondered how high up the RCR chain he went. Most new territories get a club "advisor" to show them how things should be done.

He leaned over and said something to both prospects. They positioned themselves at the doorway of our hotel room. They didn't bother coming inside, there was only one way out anyway. Frenchie waved over to us and we all got up.

The prospects looked at me and said in unison: "Just him." They were well-trained, to say the least.

I walked out to meet him. He looked me up and down, not offering his hand or saying a word. I was pretty sure anything I said would get me hit, so I stayed silent. After seeing him dressed as a cop, in a suit, and now in his colors, I had to say the last version was the most intimidating. He stood toe-to-toe with me now. I tried my best not to look afraid, but I could feel the sweat running down my back.

"Just who the fuck are you, anyway? You and your little friends have taken up a lot of my time."

He put three fingers in the air and three more prospects appeared.

"Let's take a walk," Frenchie said, as though I had a choice.

As we left the hotel parking lot, I saw that one of the prospects stood guard at the entrance of the parking lot. One walked in front of us, one behind. Far enough away to make it look like they wouldn't hear, close enough to fuck me up or protect their boss. By now there must have been a ton of surveillance on us, but it didn't stop the pounding in my head. I knew what was coming. I leaned over and puked all over the sidewalk.

One prospect grabbed me by the arm while I was heaving. Frenchie waved him away. "What? He's gonna run away while he's throwing up?"

The prospect went back into position. He threw me a rag and laughed. "What is it with you and the puking?"

We sat down in front of City Hall. Frenchie told one of the boys to get me a can of ginger ale to settle my stomach. Coke, I corrected him, Coke would make me feel better. He just shrugged and said to make it two cans of Coke.

He flipped through his phone while I caught my breath. The prospect reappeared and handed us both Cokes. These guys were pretty efficient. I was going to joke about it, but I thought better.

"Doc, Doc, Doc, what am I going to do with you? Mac speaks very highly of you."

I knew Mac knew something. No one talked to Jimmy without going through Mac. Maybe he thought he was protecting me by not giving me details, maybe he never met Frenchie in person.

"Yeah? What did he say?"

Frenchie crushed up his can and threw it in the trash. "Shut the fuck up and listen to me. You don't mean shit to me or what I'm trying to accomplish here, but you keep popping up and fucking up my plans. The only reason you're not dead is you seem to be fairly normal and getting rid of you would bring a lot of unwanted attention. Jimmy and his idiots should have taken care of you, but they didn't. You wanna tell me why?"

I was going to say that it was because I'm a great guy or something stupid, but I quickly realized that it wasn't going to help my situation. "Look, I'm just a DJ and club manager. I wanted to make a little money before I went back to teachers' college."

Frenchie put his hand up. "Save the I-just-work-there bullshit for your family, kid. You've been selling weed, steroids, and helping that friend of yours with his football pool for years. You wanna pretend you're not involved, but you are. Mac says he's been doing deals with you for years, that you know everyone in this fucking town. Why does Jimmy still protect you?"

I just shrugged.

"I'm gonna find out one way or another. Don't make me ask again."

Jimmy did feel that he owed me, but it had never been discussed with anyone else. Not Chris, not Viking, not Queen Bea, not Mac, not even my dad. If getting me out of this mess meant telling him my story, what difference did it make? I had already proven to myself that I had no morals anyway. I was no better than these guys. It took about ten minutes to tell him the whole story.

Frenchie sat there, not offering any opinion, just listening. "loyalty is important. No wonder he put up with you. But you're still a fuck for telling me all that."

There was no winning with these guys. Play by their rules, break their rules, you're still a fuck. Loyalty died a long time ago. All for one and fuck you if you get in the way.

"Jimmy was right about you. You're OK, although you'd never survive in this game. You're too independent, that doesn't work. Although you seem smarter than that Timmy guy."

I assumed he was talking about Stevie, but I wasn't about to correct him.

"You've outplayed him at every turn, though you have had a lot of help from that nut-job friend of yours."

No doubt we had been lucky, but a lot of our success was the direct result of Viking's balls. He was calling the shots, something I didn't think would ever happen. I usually used him just for muscle.

Frenchie stood up and instructed me to do the same. "I'll deal with him later."

We started walking back to the hotel. "I'll tell you what. I think you were gonna run to Jimmy, so I'll let you and your friends go talk to him."

This guy was good. He was three steps ahead.

"Your other two buddies have their own problems now for helping you, but maybe you can plead your case to walk out of here."

I didn't believe a word he said.

On the way back to the hotel, I screwed up my courage to ask why a French guy was calling the shots for a predominantly American gang. He laughed and shook his head. "I'm from Sept-Îles, it's in Quebec. I've been around, fell in with these guys. We're taking over Ontario before we take on Quebec. I guess you guys are kind of a test run. The problem is, it seems every little town has a guy like you. Killing people isn't going to help our cause."

"Our Cause." This guy spoke about establishing his biker gang in Ontario like it was a Holy Crusade.

I figured I would ask about the cop routine.

"What's this? A fucking movie? I'm gonna tell you everything?"

It was worth a shot. How about Niagara Falls, New York?

"That was easy. We've got better contacts on that side than we do here. Border guards on both sides are fucking useless. You'd be surprised what a hundred can get you with those wanna-be cops." He looked over and got all serious. "I hurt you with that shot to the face, didn't I? I thought you were gonna cry. I didn't even hit you that hard."

It hurt like fuck, but I wasn't telling him that.

"You did the right thing, though. Maybe you can keep your mouth shut if you have to."

We were at the gate to the hotel. It looked like even more of his troops had shown up. Doing anything out of the ordinary would be a bad idea. We were surrounded by guys who would do anything to impress Frenchie. I put my hands at my sides, and looked straight ahead, not giving anyone a reason to think I was trying to stare them down

Back at the hotel, Viking and Chris didn't look any worse off. Chris was smoking a cigarette, and Viking was pounding a beer. Viking immediately stood up and gave me the chin up look again. I kind of shrugged and tried to give him an "I'll-tell-you-later look," if there would be a chance.

Frenchie entered the room and briefly acknowledged Chris. He then began to stare down Viking, who wasn't moving, but wasn't backing down, either. The two prospects took over the door and three more entered the room. One for each of us.

"Frisk them. No bullshit. If they fuck around or cause any problems, you three will go back to pimping broads in South Dakota. Got it?"

All three nodded, but no one spoke.

Frenchie turned back to us. "Grab your shit. We leave in ten minutes." To my surprise, all the prospects and Frenchie left the room together.

"What the fuck, dude?" asked Viking.

I told him to lower his voice. I didn't want anyone to storm in and start shooting. I told them both about what Frenchie and I talked about.

Jimmy had excellent intel and it made me begin to wonder if that was some kind of test, to see what we would do. We all chugged a beer, and I said: "I guess we're going to see Jimmy."

Chapter 22

The Dirty Stuff

We were drunk, stoned and held captive. We came with some weed, beer and Big Daddy, and getting away from these guys wasn't going to happen anyway. Every exit was covered. We put these guys through enough shit, I'm pretty sure that shooting us wouldn't have presented a huge moral dilemma if we tried to leave.

It seemed pointless to go see Jimmy anyway. It was Frenchie's story now.

He came back in, telling us the only stop would be at Chris's to hand in all his Burnt gear. People don't always realize it, but anything given to you by the club belongs to the club. Your patch, your support T-shirt, anything with the club's logo on it. Jimmy wasn't as obsessive about it as some other clubs, but you definitely handed in your patch on the way out — no matter what your position. Asking Chris for his gear didn't sound good: once it was all taken from him, he was a nobody, with no protection. The losers in these lesser clubs were not only allowed to fuck with him, they were expected to.

Chris offered no reaction when he was told. That seemed to please Frenchie.

The three of us would ride together. Maybe we'd get hit by a bus and solve a lot of problems at once.

As we got ready to leave the room, I told Chris and Viking: "I'm sorry I got you guys involved."

Viking slammed a last beer. "Fuck that shit. I coulda left anytime I wanted to." He still hadn't adequately explained if meeting us at the ball park was an accident. "We're not done yet."

I looked over at Chris. As usual, he said little. "Whatever. Let's fucking go."

We cleared out of the room. "It's not all bad," said Viking. "Maybe they'll give us bikes to ride back."

Seeing the nondescript black van pull up put an end to Viking's bike-return theory. Frenchie and his two preferred prospects/bodyguards walked over to talk to the driver. Frenchie walked back over to us. He pointed at Chris. "We stop to get his gear then straight to the clubhouse. No one else gets out of the van. Just to ensure there will be no fuck-ups, I'm coming with you."

Viking flinched just enough for Frenchie to notice.

"You really don't know what's going on, do you?" he asked. Viking knew better than to respond.

We loaded up and made our way down Queen Street. When we hit Victoria Avenue, the van and a dozen bikes turned left. The others all turned right. They appeared to be taking us seriously. Then again, maybe Frenchie just wanted to show off. Talk was minimal in the van, although Frenchie texted on his phone the entire time.

Chris had a nice little house on Arthur Street, just behind Oakes Park. Not a big place, but he lived alone and was never there. Maybe it was because he was always living in a series of shitholes with his grandmother, his house was always spotless. No dishes in the sink, no ring around the bathtub. Unlike a lot of guys, who made some stripper that owed them clean their place, Chris did it all himself.

Frenchie waved the prospect/bodyguards out of the van. "Go with him. No phone calls or any other shit." Chris got out of the van and walked towards the front door. Frenchie lit smokes for all three of us and handed us each one. "Well, our time together is almost over. Can't wait to get out of this town. It's been fun though." I could tell Viking wanted to say something stupid, but he kept himself in check.

"When this is all done, I don't want to see you two ever again." Frenchie stopped short of telling us we had to leave town. "No more clubs, no favors, no dealing a little bit on the side. You won't get a second warning, and you definitely won't get all the chances you got from Jimmy."

He turned to face Viking. "How do I just know that you're not just gonna be a problem again somewhere down the line?"

Viking had stayed quiet, but he was about to spill over. We'd been friends forever, so I knew the signs. "No one is telling me I can't make my rocket fuel. That ain't gonna happen." Not a bad start. At least he hadn't told him to go fuck himself.

"We'll talk about that later," Frenchie answered. "You've got a lot of money coming your way. Maybe your Rocket Fuel could become a brand."

Viking wasn't biting. "It's mine" he replied.

"I know what you're doing," I finally said to Frenchie. "The whole ass-kissing, divide-and-conquer thing. You're not the only one who read Machiavelli."

Frenchie laughed out loud. "The whole ends-justifies-the-means bullshit? That's for wannabe rappers and old wops. You might have read that shit, but I've lived it. You gotta be a little more ruthless than some homo philosopher to survive in this game, mon esti."

Chris had made his way back to the van. He had a box filled with the paraphernalia that recorded his attempt to climb up the Burnt ladder – support stickers, a commemorative 20th anniversary Burnt T-shirt. It struck me as sad, even though I knew he was better off out of the club.

Frenchie grabbed his prospect vest and took out a knife. He cut off all the accessories, the Niagara rocker, the MC patch and those with Chris's name and prospect status. He threw the vest back to Chris. "It's a nice vest. Hold on to it. You might need it later."

As Chris fiddled with the vest, a picture in the box caught my eye. It was one of Arnie, Stevie, Vince, Jimmy and me all standing outside the nightclub in Port Colborne. It dawned on me that it showed the very day that was the beginning of my problems. It reminded me of my big shot to run my own place. Everyone in the photo looked so happy, even though Stevie and Vince were at opposite ends of the picture.

Frenchie caught me looking at the picture. "You know why that place was never gonna happen?" I lifted my head. "You were all too greedy. Arnie, that fat fucking moron, we bought him off for peanuts. But your partner, he wanted more. He was good at borrowing money, not so good at paying it back."

That reminded me of how these guys attempted to control everything. Without the club even being open yet, they already wanted total control over it. The owner was only a name on a piece of paper. They owned it. They controlled who sold the drugs, which girls danced. It was made clear it was their place, so the other boys stayed away. This was all supposed to be up and running by the time they moved in. Or you wouldn't do it and try to keep it running on your own. But that didn't look so good. And even if you could manage it for a while, it didn't matter. It wouldn't last. You'd do your bit and they would come to town and collect.

"So, what are my chances of running that place now?" After everything that had happened, I felt it was worth a shot.

Frenchie just looked surprised. "Maybe you do have some balls, kid. But I already told you. You're out. We don't need you. You don't have what it takes to do the dirty stuff."

Sounds like my talk with my Chinese friend, Dwight, that night in Toronto, I thought. Then it occurred to me that walk was only last week, even though it seemed like a decade ago. No killing or heroin-selling for this here guy, I thought to myself, I've got to draw the line somewhere.

For some reason, Chris was now smiling. It was a rare enough occurrence on its own, but it seemed totally out of place now. It made Viking smile as well.

Frenchie then looked at both and grinned. There was something going on, but nobody was telling me what it was. We drove for a while in silence. We would be at the clubhouse any minute. Frenchie looked over at me and said: “Kid, the game is still on, but you’re not playing. Don’t take it personal, mon chum.”

Chapter 23

Stevie? Jimmy?

What the fuck was everyone smiling about? I was pretty sure that Viking was just joining in because he was still intimidated by Frenchie. But Chris and Frenchie definitely seemed to be enjoying a little inside joke. It wasn't like I could ask what was going on in front of everyone. Something in the air had shifted, and I was maybe the only person who didn't know what it was.

We pulled into the clubhouse, which could have been in limbo for all I knew. A huge RCR sign was on the back of a flatbed out front – it looked gaudy enough to be a marquee for a strip club. The Burnt sign had been taken down and was already covered in RCR graffiti. It hadn't been hung upside down yet, but that was coming.

I guess in a weird way, we were privy to something not a lot of people ever saw – the transition from the old to the new. The only thing I could compare it to would be that scene in the Wizard of Oz when you get used to the movie being in black-and-white, but then after a while, you realize that it's switched over to color.

Did it make things any better? That depends what side you're looking at. There was no going back now, and the moment was fleeting, but the book-reading geek in me still thought it was cool to experience.

When we got out of the van, everything was the same, but tweaked. Guys were in position, but now there were two more at the door; a local and a new guy. Everyone was watching everything, just waiting for someone to fuck up. All our years of friendship meant shit; everything had been reset. No one seemed happy about it. There were no handshakes, no back slaps – it was all business. Welcome to the machine, boys.

We made our way to the front door of the clubhouse. With all the old Burnt insignia gone, it looked like a catering hall. Once inside, every single scrap of club memorabilia was gone, except for a single vest, hung upside down behind the bar. When I looked closer, it was easy to tell it was Jimmy's.

As I was pondering what all this meant, Jimmy and Stevie emerged from the office with four other guys I didn't know, all wearing RCR colors. Each of their vests had the word "president" sewn on. I was trying to look at their bottom rockers without being too obvious about it. One said "New York," two of them I couldn't see yet, and the fourth one clearly said "Niagara."

It appeared as though they weren't ready to claim a province on their patches yet. For now, they were happy with the name of their local territory. If their master plan worked, it wouldn't be long before they all wore bottom rockers with "Ontario" on them. Little steps, I guess, work even in this world.

We were guided to the long table in front of the bar. I sat at that very spot not long before, asking Jimmy for a favor. Chris, Viking and I were all sat to the left side of the table. Frenchie took the top seat, and the guy with the Niagara president's vest sat to his left. It looked weird to see anyone other than Jimmy sit in what had always been his seat.

Instead, he sat across from us with the three other RCR members. Stevie wasn't even asked to sit at the table. The familiar-looking prospects serving as bodyguards fell in behind Frenchie, with two more at the door.

"Let's get this over with, so I can get the fuck outta here," Frenchie said. "First things first."

Stevie was immediately walked over to the table by two prospects. One of them sucker-punched him while the other one pulled off his vest. "You're done," Frenchie told him. "You were asked to take care of business. Instead you fucked everything up, went on a goose chase after these three, and made a fool outta yourself and your club. You're not RCR material, you're not even a biker."

Three other prospects fell in with the first two. "Get him the fuck outta here. He's done."

Things weren't looking too good for ol' Stevie.

Frenchie pointed to the Niagara president, and said: "He's in charge."

Niagara patch didn't say a word.

"If you weren't here you wouldn't know that," Frenchie said, looking right at Viking and me. "But that won't matter soon."

What could we say? We just nodded.

He now turned to Jimmy. "Jimmy, you wanted out, you're out. You know how this works, if we need you, you're expected to help. But don't get any ideas of starting your own deal or working against us." Jimmy simply nodded.

"You," Frenchie pointed to Chris, "stand up." Chris took his time, but he stood up. "You can't wear the Burnt anymore, so why don't you put this on that vest I let you keep. It was a Niagara rocker with blue letters and orange trim.

I didn't know what Chris was thinking, but he didn't say no. The Niagara president and the other three hugged Chris.

Jimmy just sat there, stone-faced.

It was our turn. Viking's mouth had returned. "So, when do I get my patch?"

That actually made the full-patches laugh.

"What to do with you two ..." Frenchie muttered. Frenchie began a speech about loyalty and honor, talking about his cause. I could hear him speak but heard no particular words.

The next thing I knew, I was on the floor. We were being raided. It was all slow-motion and operatic like in the movies. I was on the ground with a rifle pointed at my head. We all were, except Frenchie and Chris. Frenchie struggled to stay up as the response team tried to pull him to the ground. In the mix, Chris attacked the cops. They were both pepper-sprayed, clubbed and pulled to the ground. I couldn't understand what I was seeing, and still couldn't hear anything. Even now, I find it hard to believe I didn't shit my pants.

They dragged us all outside and separated everyone. It didn't matter, I wouldn't have heard anything anyway.

There were cops everywhere. Chris, Frenchie, Viking, all the RCR boys were on the ground. It would take a bus to get all these guys to the lock-up.

I quickly realized that we were probably all going to the jail in Thorold, since the Niagara lock-up couldn't hold us all.

It took a while to sort us out, but it was clear that they intentionally separated Viking from me. Some of the guys were still being hard-ons, taunting the cops and talking shit. Most of the cops got a good laugh out of it. They couldn't resist saying that the RCR wasn't even officially in town, but here they were, all busted.

I shut my mouth and got on the bus. It was a busy day to be a cop, I guess. I wasn't going to talk to anyone, cop or otherwise.

I guess the raid was the best I could have hoped for, although I never would have predicted such a thing could happen. Who knows how it might have played out?

I was so tired and elated I just hung my head. I fought tears, knowing it wouldn't look too good if I got locked up with these guys, which I probably was going to be — at least for a bit.

Just before I dozed off, a cop sat beside me. He looked vaguely familiar, but I couldn't remember where I knew him from.

He broke into the standard cop talk. "Busy couple of days, eh? Funeral, partying, fucking around with your retard buddy's sister."

Well, I was right about being under surveillance. I always had a nagging feeling this little game played out a little long so that the cops could figure out exactly what was up. I had always heard about how they'll go just far enough to prevent a murder. I didn't believe it, but my mind had just been changed.

If I had actually been shot, they would simply play it up in the media that I had "gang connections" and imply I had it coming.

But not all their info was totally correct. In all this mess, I still hadn't slept with Queen Bea.

The cop kept yapping according to their standard playbook; first playing my friend, then saying shit to get me going a little. He must have said "Where's Stevie?" about a dozen times. But I didn't know. How could he have gotten out with so many cops around?

But the cop kept it up. "Maybe you'll run into Stevie soon enough. You know they were going to kill you, right?"

There wasn't much I could say to that.

Chapter 24
Where's Stevie?

Being swept up in the middle of a raid wasn't the greatest feeling in the world, but I was increasingly confident that this whole thing wasn't about Viking, Chris and me. We clearly got caught in the middle of a much bigger situation, mostly because of the events of the last few days, and maybe a thousand or so little things before that.

That knowledge didn't take away from the fact that I was terrified and trying my best not to show it. Everyone has read the books and seen the movies about what you should do when you're arrested or put in jail. But all of it left my head when I was laying on the ground in handcuffs, with a rifle pointed at my head.

I would find out later that we had been scooped up in a massive investigation, a collaborative effort between various Canadian and American law enforcement agencies. Their goal was to diminish Jimmy's power in Niagara, and to prevent the RCR from invading Ontario. The operation had some cops working together on both sides of the bridge. When things started to spin out of control, even more agencies joined the effort. I heard later that Vince's murder was what brought the investigation to a close, that after that there was too much to do, too many other issues getting tied up in the initial investigation.

Of all the people arrested, they first showed a couple of full-patch members to the media. But I heard from about a thousand people that there was a big picture in the paper of me looking like a deer in headlights. When my Dad saw it on the news, he stormed out of the house. My mom immediately called Mac. She always like Mac, but she did not know that Mac was on the run or locked up at the time.

That was all stuff I wouldn't find out for days, though. After the arrests, the cops were in no rush to tell any of us what was going on; not that I was going to ask.

Booking took forever. It seemed like they had rounded up about 50 to 60 guys in Niagara alone. It also went down like that in Toronto, Vancouver, Cleveland, New York, Detroit and a whole bunch of other cities I couldn't remember. The media conferences would hit the same notes they all do — this is the biggest bust of all time, the main players are finished, crime doesn't pay, all that.

We were all dropped in one big room. Jimmy, Frenchie, his presidents, Chris, Viking, a whole bunch of Burnt and RCR members along with guys from the assorted lesser gangs.

No sign of Stevie. The guys, me included, started to agree on the idea that he had flipped. There was no other explanation as to why he wasn't in with us. We all saw how he was slapped around and perfunctorily dismissed. There was no way he escaped the dragnet of cops that descended upon us. It was obvious by the stares and glances around the room that this was the question was hanging heavily on all of us.

But no one said a word. They all just stared ahead, waiting their turn. Some of the low-ranking guys tried to play tough, telling the cops to go fuck themselves. Idiots. They were usually the ones who didn't have much to offer anyway. Or the first to look for a deal when they realized they were going away.

They would take five or six of us at a time and give each of us a quick once-over. They'd take our identification, and still ask us who we were. It was a time to sort everyone out. Once that was done, we were all thrown back in the same room to await hearing our names being called.

Of course, Jimmy and Frenchie were called in first. As the crowd thinned a little, I was surprised to hear my name being called out. On my way out of the room, I locked eyes with Chris for the first time. His look said: "Why the fuck are they taking you? I'm a bigger deal than you." That made me laugh out loud, which must have made me look like one of the guys trying to give the cops a tough time.

I was brought into a small conference room. Two cops, one who I didn't know but had seen in the area, and another big fat guy from out of town who looked kind of like Arnie.

No hellos, no offer of a Coke or anything. The local cop told me to sit down. When I didn't move fast enough, the out-of-towner practically shoved me in the chair. Okay, I understood their plan — they were playing Bad Cop and Worse Cop.

I reminded myself to shape up and not try to be funny or sarcastic. I was so nervous, I still can't believe I didn't puke. Worse Cop probably would've beaten me up for that.

"You got any ideas why you're here, boy?" drawled Worse Cop.

What could I say? Before I could think of anything a response, the photographs came out. There was Jimmy and me; Chris and me; Chris, me, and Stevie, even me eating at the Castle with Millie when Stevie was showing off his new patch, and Chris in the background scowling because he didn't have one yet.

"How does a nobody fucking strip-joint DJ nail a chick that hot, or hang out with these kind of guys?"

Niagara cop was up next. "I'll tell you how." He brought out more pictures. There was me and Mac unloading a truck, me on my bike dropping off a package, me unloading boxes into Millie's garage.

"You got your own shit going on, and when it went bad, you had your friend killed to cover your tracks."

We had a name for that kind of accusation. We called it throwing shit at a wall to see what would stick. They would insult me, my friends, my chick, all to see what I would say.

But a voice inside my head kept repeating: "They're working you. Keep your mouth shut. Still, I blurted: "Those boxes don't prove anything." I had to get it together. I had to shut my mouth. My brain reminded me that way smarter guys than me have gone down for way less.

"Lookee here, boy," Worse Cop took his turn. "You're a nobody, a fucking punk, but ya walked into some pretty weird stuff. International stuff, interstate commerce. Murder, even. You think these guys give a shit about a boy like you? God damn, your buddy the idiot giant is gonna rat you out for playing house with his sister."

Christ, did the whole world think I was sleeping with Bea? It sure seemed that way.

"You've done enough for us to lock you up," said Niagara cop, "but it's your lucky day. Your shit don't mean nothing stacked up against what these guys were gonna pull. You know you and your buddies were gonna get killed, right?"

Worse Cop picked it up. "See, as worthless as you are, you were fucking around where ya shouldn't have been, with people who shoulda known better."

Their technique had become bewildering. It seemed like their plan was to dump on me, give me some vague hints of a bigger situation, and then start insulting me. It kept me off guard, but not enough to bite. These guys, with their clichés and non-sequiturs, still know what they're doing. Just one wrong word, one wrong look in front of them and you've had it. It is always better to just shut up. Still, it was killing me not to be able to tell this cop it looked like he bought his tie at a gas station.

They eased up just a little. "You got a good family. Gonna put them through a long trial, embarrass their name? Think about something besides your dick, boy." Whether I liked it or not, he had a point. Chasing women was the beginning of all my problems. Queen Bea, Jenny, Millie, every fucking stripper I had ever been involved with.

Worse Cop had had enough: "Put him in a fucking cell."

I was yanked out of my seat and marched away. Walking past the other interrogation rooms, I could see Viking with his feet up on the table, charming the two cops questioning him. They must've thought he was a dumb hick that would crack. I knew he wouldn't say a word.

There would be no holding cell for me. Instead, they threw us all back in the same huge room. Someone had put cans of Pepsi and a few bags of pretzels on the table, which I guessed was dinner. I downed a can and was going to grab another when I thought it might put me in a bad light, so I just took a handful of pretzels.

Now that everyone was coming back to the same room, the cops let us sit wherever we wanted. I guess they wanted us to believe it was some kind of benevolent gesture. But I knew they really wanted us to talk, to start undermining each other, to start accusing.

Chris looked my way but didn't come near me. He was plunked down with his new RCR buddies. He looked over again and his insinuation was clear: I had to come to him now. So, I got up and walked over. "Frenchie told me to tell you to shut it. They ain't got shit on you, nothing important anyway. Just cool it." Clearly, Chris had found his deal with Frenchie.

Jimmy, on the other hand, sat alone, except for a few long-term ass-kissers. He was done, and he knew it. He would take the fall for everything and be blamed for the RCR coming to town. His empire was finished, all that was left were a few old-timers who weren't earning much anyway. You're only as good as your boys in this business, and Jimmy didn't have too many good ones left.

By the time I was finished listening to Chris's instructions, it was clear he had a new purpose. He had turned his back on the Burnt, and he was going to be part of Frenchie's cause. I didn't know how or why that happened, but I'm pretty sure it would come out in the next few days.

Almost everyone was back in the room. I was just thinking how I hadn't seen any heavy-handed moves. When Cody V got arrested, he played the tough guy and put up a fight. The cops beat him up pretty bad for that. They couldn't deny it either. His arrest photos on the front page of the Spectator showed his face busted open. Just when I thought that nobody would be dumb enough to try a move like that, four uniformed cops tossed Viking face-first into the room.

Viking got up without a word of complaint and sat back down. Taking a face plant in handcuffs has to hurt.

As soon as he sat down, I had to ask him: "What was that all about?"

"Well," he considered, "it was about my boots."

"Your boots?"

"Yeah, see, the cop got tired of me saying 'next question' over and over, so when he asked about my boots, I said I'd gladly stick them up his ass for all the other cops to see."

Classy. "So, what did they ask you?"

"The usual," he said, stretching back, "Why'd you do it, what's the deal, generic cop shit. They did ask about Stevie a few times. Where the fuck is he?"

That seemed to be the question on everybody's mind. It was impossible to think that he somehow slipped by all those fucking cops. I tried to look around for the two guys who walked him out. They might have been with us, but I couldn't see them.

We had plenty of time to talk, keeping it pretty simple because there was no doubt we were being recorded. It's amazing how many people get caught because they simply can't shut up. The need to impress or unburden themselves has sunk quite a few guys. The first thing you always hear is to keep your mouth shut. But guys just love to talk.

Of course, the cops know how to make you talk, and they can spot which guys will. Matching wits with them is pointless. But every single guy thinks they're fucking smarter and tries to debate with the investigators. That's why the deeper you get in, the more you rely on contacts. That's why these guys join. Whichever name you use — triad, mafia, biker club — it's all the same; there's power and influence in money. If you're in, lawyers take care of you so you're free to go out and break the law again.

As Frenchie reminded me earlier, Viking and I had no such protection. We were on our own, on the streets and in the courts. We couldn't afford the high-priced lawyers that members could. I could see and hear it even before it happened: Frenchie's slick lawyers telling the courts that he and his new friends wanted to expand their gentleman's riding club into Ontario. Viking and I would be depicted as some sort of two-man gang that killed at will all over Niagara, dampening their enthusiasm for motorcycling in the region. It would be plausible enough for court, I guess.

Even though I had little experience with the courts, Viking had been through it all, several times. Murder charges, bootlegging, stolen car parts, none of it seemed like a big deal to him. He had fought in court numerous times, and almost always beat the charges. It didn't hurt that some local lawyers knew he was going to be one of the richest guys in the area soon, so doing a little pro bono work was considered a decent investment. I took his expert advice to sit back and wait it out.

"They don't have fuck-all on you. They might try and give you some bullshit weed or steroid charge, and that'll only happen if you act like a total dick. Sit back, relax. Lenny will be here soon."

Lenny Behrens was the best-known criminal lawyer from here to Toronto.

"You were allowed to call him?"

Viking was trying to put together a makeshift cot out of two folding chairs. "He saw the news. He's probably representing half of the fucking guys here. I'll put in a good word for you with Lenny. I don't know who's gonna bankrupt me quicker. Your broke ass or my lawyer."

It was about 6 a.m. when Behrens made his first appearance. Most of the room had broken off into little factions, trading messages back and forth. Frenchie and his presidents were on one side, Chris and what seemed like his own little crew on another side. The biggest group seemed to be the lesser patches and their primary task was ferrying messages between Chris and Frenchie. Most of them sat there like puppies, waiting to be chosen.

Off in a corner was Jimmy and the few guys left loyal to him. No one paid them any attention.

And the last group was our little gang of two, Viking and me.

Behrens blew by us, only nodding in our direction to acknowledge Viking. Still, it was more than the bigwigs in the room received.

Later, Behrens sat across from us and started shuffling papers.

Viking attempted to speak, but Behrens pulled out his cell phone and answered it on the first ring. "This is it? You're sure?" Then he actually turned his back to us. We waited until his conversation was done. He resumed shuffling papers.

Viking finally broke our silence. "Lenny, get us the fuck out of here."

Behrens finally looked up. "It's not that simple. It's all bullshit, but you're about to formally be charged with being accessories to murder."

I couldn't speak. Viking finally croaked out the words. "For Vince?"

"No," replied Behrens "You're both about to be charged with accessories in the murder of Stephen George Inkster. I'll get you out if I can."

The cops immediately cuffed us and separated us from the rest of the guys.

Chapter 25
TG

Viking was legitimately stunned. "Who?" he asked.

The lawyer rifled through his papers, and clarified: "Stephen George Inkster, a.k.a. TG, a.k.a. Notorious, a.k.a. John Simon Ritchie."

Viking was in a fog or fucking around.

"He's talking about Stevie," I told him.

Viking just shrugged.

No one outside of his immediate family ever called Stevie TG. Notorious was his early '90s nickname, which he quickly abandoned. John Simon Ritchie was his favorite.

"What the fuck, Lenny?"

The lawyer just put up his hand. "You guys were at the clubhouse, during a major raid, when a member was killed. How could you think they were not going to charge you?"

Lenny looked at me. "Who are you anyway? I got nothing on you. Now these fucks want to charge you with trafficking ... and murder as well? That's a great way to introduce yourself, kid."

"Just work on getting us the fuck outta here, Lenny," Viking snapped at him "I'll foot his bill."

Lenny gave us a condescending look from over his glasses.

"Yeah, yeah, yeah, just get working on it. You're making enough here for another house." Viking clearly wasn't worried about money. Lenny would have a long night.

"I'll be back." Lenny then made his way over to Jimmy, who must have been happy to get some company. He had been more-or-less ignored, except for the two old nobodies who protected him. I wondered to myself if they had passed up on the RCR offer, or if they had been passed over.

The cops and investigators were in no hurry to take us out of the interrogation room. They were waiting for some scared kid to say the wrong fucking thing.

"What the fuck? What the fuck? What the fuck? What the fuck?" My brain kept repeating against my will.

"Relax," Viking offered, stretching out like he did in the holding room. "Did you kill Stevie? I sure didn't. We were surrounded by bikers and a fucking task force. They know we didn't kill him. They're trying to make you crack, Billy. You're the new kid in town. They figure you'll shit your pants, tell them everything, then run home to momma."

I stood up and stretched. "OK, OK, OK ... I'll trust you. How the fuck can you be so calm? They're charging us with murder!"

Viking didn't even look at me. "Billy, this is the kind of shit you read about in a book. I'm surprised you're not taking notes, to turn this into a story later."

"Yeah, well it's different when the charges are against you."

He was still trying to get comfortable. "They got nothing. It's all bullshit."

I wasn't convinced. "What do I tell my family? My grandmother is gonna read this shit."

Viking just grunted and tried to go to sleep.

Again, my theory that we were being watched proved right, because as soon as we got comfortable, we got thrown in the general room with all the boys.

Lawyers were coming in and out now, and there was activity all around. Lenny came back in and sat back down: "Don't ask why, but they want you bailed out one at a time."

Viking didn't even look up: "Bail him out first, I know the drill."

I wasn't about to argue.

I spoke too soon. Jimmy, Chris, Viking, one of the no-name bikers and I were called out by our full legal names and marched into a separate room.

Once we were all arranged, the charges were read to each of us. Viking and I were charged with conspiracy to commit murder and obstruction of justice.

I was trying to think my way out. From everything I've seen or read, they usually hit you with everything, then you're supposed to deal your way out. I figured that the obstruction charge would probably be tossed right away.

Both prosecution and defense could argue their own version of this story. The prosecution could say that I kept popping up everywhere because I was involved in all the events leading up to Stevie's murder. The defense could just as easily argue that I was stuck in a bunch of coincidental circumstances that can be easily explained. The prosecution would rebut with my last week of drugs and drinking — and being at the scene of a murder — was proof that I was a member of the gang, pure and simple.

As all the angles were playing out in my head, I couldn't stop thinking that having my name attached in any way to a murder probably wasn't good.

They read off a bunch of minor charges against No-Name, but I wasn't really paying attention. He was being an idiot, playing the tough guy, presumably to impress Jimmy. Like me, he clearly didn't know all the pieces of the story and didn't realize that Chris now held the power, at least in our little room.

I hate to resort to such a cliché, but they threw the book at Jimmy. They took their time reading his charges, which included proceeds of crime, weapons charges, being the head of a criminal organization and belonging to a criminal organization. Naming out both of those seemed a little redundant to me at first, but then I realized there was a significant distinction. Jimmy wasn't in the show, he had run the show for the better part of 25 years. When it came to the murder charges, they bumped it up. Jimmy was formally charged with Stevie's murder.

Chris seemed to get off pretty easy in comparison. His time as a prospect, and a lone-wolf criminal before that, worked in his favor. He was hit with conspiracy to murder and belonging to a criminal organization. His lawyers could easily tear that apart. The Burnt no longer existed, and he wasn't a member (yet) of the RCR. One of the lawyers would no doubt try to make a big show in court, asking exactly which organization Chris belonged to. That kind of stuff gets trotted out at every trial.

And every trial brings out an expert. There is one guy who has all the credentials of James Bond, is a "former member," and invariably proceeds to detail a life that is clearly intended to shock and appall. But the problem in most cases is that the witness is usually actually some low-level guy who doesn't really have much to offer, and just repeats stuff he's heard second-hand. The worst of the guys they use are the ones who just repeat the same shocking details, and don't really add to the narrative.

Sometimes it'll be an author that has written extensively on motorcycle gangs or criminals in general. Some are great, others are bags of wind. For me, they fall into two categories: the guys who glorify the biker lifestyle and just repeat the same ol', same ol' to sell their books. Then you get the ones that are just condescending, never adding to the story, just calling these guys punks and never showing us their true power in the world of crime.

As I thought about all of that, my name was called a second time. No one else, just me. I was led out of the room. With me were Lenny, a whole bunch of cops, and some other guys in suits. I was told to sit down. "You've made bail," Lenny started, "but you can't leave just yet. They haven't fully finished processing you." Lenny then explained the terms of my conditions. I couldn't consort with anyone with a patch if they had a record or not, and definitely no hanging out with anyone with a record, couldn't be out past 10, had to have a job, couldn't be caught drinking or using drugs, and I had to stay with the person who posted my bail.

Not having contact with the other guys was understood. No booze or drugs would probably be a nice little vacation for my body. I didn't think that I would ever turn into one of those guys who spoke of being on a "natural high," but the thought of cleaning myself out sounded good. I didn't know if I had a job anymore, but that could be sorted out.

"Uh, how am I not supposed to consort with any of the defendants if Viking is my guarantor?"

Lenny began shuffling papers. "Viking isn't your guarantor. He's paying your legal bill. No judge would ever agree to your guarantor being the co-accused in a murder charge."

"Well, can you tell me who my guarantor is?"

Lenny began shuffling papers again, which was getting on my nerves. There was this Spanish guy who used to deal for us at our card games. When he took too long, I would slap the cards out of his hands as a warning to move it. It pissed him off, but always got a laugh out of the players. While it was tempting to pull that on Lenny, it wouldn't have been viewed as amusing by anyone but me.

He finally stopped shuffling his papers and folded his hands in front of him. All the wait was killing me. "Your guarantor is Stephen Morgan Riordan, your father. As part of the arrangement, you are to stay with him and him only. I don't know your dad, kid; but he pulled a lot of strings for you. Good luck. He's waiting for you in the parking lot."

I felt like I was being picked up outside of the principal's office.

Chapter 26

Buick LeSabre

As the news hit me, Lenny was detailing the rest of my conditions. I couldn't consort with anyone who had been arrested in this whole deal, or anyone with a criminal record for that matter. There would be no drugs, no nightclubs, no booze, no being out after eleven. If I couldn't find a job immediately, I had better be looking. I was only allowed to stay at my parents' house. Any slip-up or infraction and I went straight to the Niagara Detention Centre in Thorold to hang out with most of my co-accused.

Still, I couldn't believe I was walking out of here. It made me feel like I was out of the story, just watching it like I was a character in a Camus novel, having no control over what had happened to me. Seeing my dad sitting in his Buick snapped any romantic ideas that I was in an existentialist book out of my head.

I got in the car and was greeted with total silence; no music, no small talk, just my father staring straight ahead. He loved to joke around, needle people, get them going. But none of that was happening. I didn't think that if I made a joke it would lighten the mood. We drove in silence all the way to Max's. He pulled into the driveway and still hadn't said a word.

"I'm staying here?" I asked him.

"Like fuck you are." Ah, his first words to me. "You got five minutes to grab what you need and come back. You're staying at our place, just like your bail conditions said."

I walked into the house and determined that no one was home. It was probably better that way; I didn't have the energy to talk or explain anything to anyone. I went downstairs to grab my clothes and some money. If you pushed back the panel in the ceiling above my TV, you'd find cash — there was always a couple of grand or so up there. Max knew where it was, but he never needed it. I took it down and decided to count it. Just over $2,800. You never know when you're going to need straight-up cash. I grabbed $400 and threw it in my bag. If I dug around enough at my parents' place, there was probably cash hidden in a book somewhere there too.

I made my way back to the car. I hopped in and we began to cruise down Drummond Road. No more words were exchanged. I thought we were heading home when my dad stopped at the Inn.

"We've got time for one."

Yeah, one. He wanted to hear everything I had to say before we got home. So much for the no alcohol rule — that would be the one bail condition my father would ignore.

We made our way inside and all the regulars moved out of our way. I guess being charged as an accessory to the murder of one of your best friends tends to make people shy away from you.

We stood at the bar instead of at a table, so he wasn't going to yell at me too much, not in front of the other guys. Dad had no problem putting you in your place, and he got loud when he did. But he was always respectful enough not to do it in front of others.

He ordered two beers and paid for four, so no one would disturb us. He drank most of his first beer before he spoke. "Murder No. 2? You're having quite a few days, aren't you?"

I didn't even want the beer that was already in front of me. "You know I had nothing to do with Vince's murder."

"So, you had something to do with Stevie's then? You've been friends since you were kids."

The only way I felt I could clear the air was to start from the conversation we had a few days earlier. I basically picked off from the point when I left him the other day.

"And don't leave anything out. You're up on murder charges, Ian, you have to be straight with me. You're my son, and I would do anything for you, but I'm not covering up a murder." I tried to speak, but he cut me off. "Just tell me the story. I'll let you speak. "

He kept to his word and didn't cut me off again. It took almost an hour, and by then we had plowed through our usual four beers, plus two more. I could see the reactions in his face as I brought Frenchie and Jimmy into the story. He laughed when Viking came up, and the strange things he did. My dad always liked him, although he would often say: "That boy isn't normal."

If being drunk was going to send me back to Thorold, then a police cruiser would have been waiting at the door for me. As he ordered our last beer, my dad called the bartenders John and Jay, the owner's sons, over. He asked them to drive us home in his car, then the other could jump back into the car with his brother. Even though my parents' house was only about twenty blocks from the Drummond, he gave them each twenty bucks. "No sense in all of us being in jail," he said as he threw John his car keys.

Settling down to finish my last beer, I was thoroughly drunk. Maybe the adrenaline of the last few days had finally shut down. I could tell it was definitely something to do with the lack of drugs in my system. But just being safe and with my dad was the biggest reason I relaxed.

"Tomorrow, you go see your lawyer. If there's any little detail you haven't told either of us, maybe it will come back to you after a good night's sleep. I'll drive you to the lawyer. We have to be there at ten."

He slammed down the rest of his beer and looked me in the eye. "I know you have to watch what you say, but you know your ass is on the line. You can still help your friends, but you have to cover yourself too. From everything you've told me, they messed with you at every turn, and wanted you to get caught in the middle of all of this."

"What am I gonna do? Help them put my friends away?"

"They're not your friends," dad's temper was rising. "The only one who helped you was Phil. I've told you before that he wasn't normal, but he stood by you this whole time. The charges might get dropped on you, but I have a feeling Phil isn't going to have such an easy time. He's only involved in this mess because you asked for his help. You have to think of him too."

Dad wasn't telling me to take a deal, or rat anyone out. He actually made the quotation marks sign with his hands to say he wasn't suggesting I "rat on anyone." But it was pretty clear that he wasn't above me cutting corners to get myself out of this problem.

"Talk to the lawyer tomorrow, then we proceed. C'mon, let's go." He waved John over to drive us home. Jay would follow. I didn't care for Jay. He had accidentally killed a guy in a fight in the bar years ago and was acquitted. He wore that distinction like a testament to his street cred. As always, the truth was a little tamer. Jay was a huge guy but not very tough. He began shoving the guy out the door and the guy fell and hit his head on the pool table. Million-to-one shot, total bad luck, whatever you want to call it. The guy died on the barroom floor, and Jay bragged about it every chance he got. Maybe he was nuts, maybe he was just a jerk. Either way, I stayed away from him.

We piled into dad's Buick LeSabre. Dad was a Buick man and a little pissed when he heard GM was ending production of his favorite model. Dad always did the driving, so for him to throw someone his keys meant he was really worried about something. Or drunk. Both was my guess this time. Either way, he was looking out for both of us.

The ride to their house took less than five minutes. I stumbled out of the car and saw my mom in the kitchen window. Dad thanked the brothers and sent them on their way.

I could smell the tea as soon as we walked into the kitchen. I sat at the table and waited for mom to turn around. She wouldn't talk too much to either of us when we had been drinking. She would wait until later to ask me anything that she thought Dad hadn't already told her.

She had made dinner, a hamburger casserole that I always loved. She told me to go lay down and we would eat shortly. I laid down on the leather couch downstairs. I was exhausted, drunk and a little bit in pain. I wouldn't realize until when I woke up the next morning that I slept straight through dinner.

When I finally got off the couch, dad was watching TV while mom was ironing. When dad saw me stir, I heard him say to my mom, "see, he's not dead."

I had slept for almost fifteen hours. I didn't wake up once; it was the most peaceful sleep I'd had in years. Being out for so long brought about an urgent need to pee, so I sprinted for the bathroom. They both probably thought I was going to be sick.

I went upstairs and saw the cereal boxes still on the counter. I thought, that won't do, and started to warm up the leftover casserole. I knew that a good chunk of beef and a can of Pepsi would kickstart me.

While it warmed up, I looked outside. A feeling of familiarity struck me looking out the window. Most of the families on this street had been here since the early '70s, but the complexion of the neighborhood was slowly changing. Everyone seemed relatively happy here, and only seemed to leave if someone died. Even as I became an adult, some of the same families were still here, a few had been even longer than my parents had.

Growing up here was pretty homogeneous. Everybody's dad worked the day shift, they were always home for dinner. Some of the moms were part-time professionals, nurses or teachers, but were usually at home. Everything seemed the same and pretty normal to us all. It was a scandal in the late '70s when the family down the street, the Tremonts, divorced. We saw nothing else out of the ordinary. When we were older, we heard stories about how things really were, but until then, we all grew up with a veneer of normalcy over everyone's lives.

I guess I should have followed suit and settled down, but that hadn't happened yet. I went to university, but I didn't work some regular job. I wrestled, worked as a bouncer, or helped Stevie and Chris sell whatever, collected debts a little bit here and there. Not exactly the resume of an up-and-coming professional, but I always thought it taught me to understand both sides of the street. I knew how to scare the shit out of some second-year university students who owed me money for weed, and I learned how to talk my way out of trouble with some bad-ass when I crossed the line. The problem was that I spent more time dealing with all that stuff then going to school, and that's why I was standing here, looking out a window at 7:30 in the morning and feeling nostalgic for the first time in my life.

I took the warmed-up casserole out of the oven and put it on the table. Then I looked for the newspaper. There was always a copy of The Toronto Star, sometimes The Globe and Mail in our house every day. I always liked reading the entertainment section first, then sports. I would pick up The Sun on the way to work, but that was mainly to find out which games were on TV, so I could make sure they were on in the bar. I couldn't remember the last time I sat down and just read the paper.

I was getting comfortable and thinking of heating up some more casserole when I was lightly whacked in the head with a newspaper. It was my mom. "Your father is out of the shower. Go get ready." She rubbed my hair and went back downstairs.

Chapter 27

The Sugar and Shit

Driving to Lenny's office was like going back in time. It was down on Victoria Avenue, past the bend after the casino. At one time, it seemed like there was a law office in every other building. Now there was five or six in all of downtown.

Back in the '30s, if you needed a loan you came to this end of town. The chief of police did all the money-lending back then. People got their cash, walked down to his lawyer and made the arrangements for their payments.

Most of the downtown businesses grew out of those two men, who practically ran this town until it just got too big for them.

I knew this area like the back of my hand at one time. My grandparents lived on what is now Fallsview Boulevard, and I roamed those streets as a kid. Even then, most of the families had been there for forty years or more, so it was safe for even little kids to be six or seven blocks from home without their parents. Everybody knew your dad, your mom or your grandparents, so everyone kept an eye out for you.

But it wasn't always so safe. In the 1930s, gang warfare broke out over the after-hours liquor business. My grandfather told me that everybody heard gunshots a couple of nights every week.

So, what I had gotten drawn into was nothing new, just part of a cycle — and on a bigger scale.

We parked right in front of Lenny's office.

This stretch of Victoria was my favorite. The left side looked like it had been frozen in time since the '80s. There was a 7-Eleven, a funeral home, a couple of restaurants, and a branch of the public library. I spent as much time in the library as I did at the karate dojo a block away.

Less than two days ago, I watched the RCR ride in a procession through a town that had long belonged to Jimmy and a B-team of assorted Italian gangsters. But everything had changed from those bootleggers in the '30s to Jimmy's boys to now. I had witnessed a lot; but now I would have to read it in the papers like everyone else.

It was nine a.m., and Dad and I were both already sweating out yesterday's beers. He insisted we both go to the lawyer with shirts and ties on. He was old fashioned, no showing up in shorts or a ball cap. If I had tried something like that, he would have slapped it off my head.

Lenny's secretary was a redhead, about 40 or so. Dad checked her out, although with a little more subtlety than I did. She informed us that Lenny would be with us shortly.

"Remember," Dad leaned in, while still checking out Red's legs, "You can't lie to your lawyer save that for all those women you're running around with. Besides, he has way more sources than you do. Let's figure out where you stand."

He casually leaned back and gave Red a friendly grin.

Lenny walked in at exactly 9:01 and waved us down the hall to his little office. He opened the office door and told us to sit down and relax.

He immediately took off his coat and tie and pulled a bottle of Scotch from his bottom desk drawer. He poured three shots into Styrofoam coffee cups. "Drink up, boys," he said. "I've got good news."

Dad and I shrugged at each other and downed our shots.

"I was just at the cop shop," Lenny put his feet up on the desk and poured us each another shot. "Except for the fact that they caught you in the clubhouse, there's not one single thing to tie you to Stevie's murder." He leaned back in his chair for effect.

My dad bit first. "And?" he asked.

"Well, there is a lot of circumstantial evidence to make you look like you had some sort of involvement." Lenny pulled out a folder and showed us the evidence photos — Vince and I in Toronto, Viking and me outside the Burnt clubhouse, me at Vince's funeral, me drinking outside the hotel with Chris and Viking. Except for the last batch, it occurred to me that these were all the same pictures that Frenchie had shown me. Probably just coincidence, I thought, but it also calmed me a bit — I hoped it indicated I had been caught up in a play where I was just a bit player.

"Of course," Lenny began to pour three more shots, "all these prove is that you've got a poor choice of friends, something I'm sure your father has told you before."

Dad accepted the shot and said nothing. He knew what I'd been up to all these years. No lectures, no reprimands. Dad had stayed out of my life, I think somehow finding it amusing, and figuring I'd pull it together eventually. I'm pretty sure it didn't take conspiracy to murder charges to make most people grow up.

Lenny was pouring us each our fourth shot of the day. Being with my lawyer was worse than being with the boys. It's wasn't even 10 a.m. and I was ready for bed. Lenny didn't even wait, he just downed his shot. I was beginning to think he needed it more than I did. I was also pretty sure there was a ball or two of Colombian bam-bam in that desk, but my dad wouldn't approve of such a thing. Shots at 9:30 were one thing, coke was another entirely.

Unfortunately, Lenny fell into the same trap I did. Line here, shot there, meet your "client" in the bathroom for a "meeting."

With any luck, I thought to myself, he was going to get to the point — otherwise I would need some of that coke just to finish this meeting.

Lenny straightened up in his chair and assumed his best lawyer pose. "Every cop I know has told me they're going to drop the conspiracy to murder charge."

I tried to show no emotion, but Dad was visibly relieved, or drunk, or both.

"So, when will the charges be dropped?" I asked.

Lenny stiffened a bit. "Well now it becomes a bit of a game of who blinks first."

My dad and I both leaned forward in an effort to get him to elaborate.

"You've been ensnared in a massive investigation; usually you get charged with everything under the sun, then you work your way out," he explained. "It's all a negotiation, they want to see what you will agree to be charged with."

"Agree to be charged with?" I asked. "Is this all some fucking game?"

Lenny looked out the window and then wrote down a few notes. "That's exactly what it is, young man. I can mount an aggressive defense that shows you had nothing to do with any of this," he looked at me, and said: But the problem is that you have to keep your mouth shut and play along."

My dad spoke for the first time in a while: "He'll play along." He gave me the look that told me to shut up and listen.

"It's going to take me a while to gather enough evidence that shows you just caught yourself in a bad scene," Lenny said, then looked over at my dad. "I know, it's every parent's nightmare."

My father pulled his checkbook out of his jacket pocket. "How much will this ..."

Lenny cut him off. "His defense is already being paid for, sir."

"But if there's anything that needs to be covered ..."

Again, Lenny cut him off: "It's all being taken care of, sir. Mr. Burns has seen to that."

My dad looked confused for a minute. Like most dads he didn't know too many of my friends' last names. I mouthed the word "Phil" to him.

"Go home, keep your mouth shut, and do not speak with anyone: media, friends, family," Lenny advised. "Mr. Burns is in the Thorold Detention Centre, and you do have the right to meet him to mount your defense. I would let a couple of days go by first. Phil knows the system and will be fine. He should be out by tomorrow morning."

"The charges against Viking are going to be dropped as well?" I asked.

"Maybe, you have some notorious friends, son." Lenny sighed. "His background will be searched a little more thoroughly than yours since he is ..." I could tell Lenny hated the cliché and even drew quotation marks in the air with his fingers, "... as they say, known to police ... take my advice: Relax, go home and take a few days to get yourself together. The media is going to paint all of you with the same brush. They won't make any distinction between members and those who were arrested. We have to show you were never a member."

It struck me as odd that my lawyer's advice was exactly what Frenchie had already told me. The media was going to make me a monster. My lawyer was going to make me look like an idiot who stumbled into a situation I knew nothing about. I was going to shut up, take it and hope that all of this never made it to trial.

Lenny then told us it would all work out and said he would be in touch. His entire presentation and summary did make sense — as the saying goes, I had enjoyed all the sugar up until this point, so now I had to eat some shit.

Dad and I stumbled out of the office and were standing beside the Buick. "I haven't drunk like that in the morning since I was in the army," he said, taking his key out of the door. "Let's walk down to Basell's for breakfast."

Chapter 28

Queen Bea and Viking

We sat in a booth at the back of Basell's. This place had been around forever, or at least as long as I can remember. It was nothing fancy, but different moments of my life had been spent in the back of this restaurant. Coming here occasionally with my grandparents for breakfast, then hanging out with my friends when we all belonged to the cadets, trying to pretend we enjoyed coffee. In my early twenties, I came here to study for exams, because the owner didn't care if I only ordered a glass of Coke and stayed all day. As recently as a few months ago, when Millie and I would go out for dinner, we'd go to Basell's because we wouldn't run into anyone we knew.

Dad and I sat near the back, my usual spot. It had become my habit to sit in the back, to get a view the whole place. If things got rough, I knew I could walk through the kitchen in the back, wind up in the alley that would bring me to Buckley Avenue and disappear into downtown Niagara Falls.

I knew every inch of these streets and alleys, just like I knew Niagara Falls, New York. My dad's parents lived on Buckley for years.

I definitely needed some grease in my system. I ordered four scrambled eggs, two sides of bacon, a Coke and a huge glass of orange juice. It's outrageous what they charge for a glass of orange these days — but I needed it.

Though mom wasn't around to make sure he didn't eat anything crazy, Dad got a bowl of shredded wheat and a tea. After half a dozen shots of scotch, that wouldn't quite have cut it for me. I almost ordered a steak, but I thought that would just make me sick.

"You're looking pretty good for a guy who just downed a half-dozen shots of Johnny Walker first thing in the morning." Dad said as he poured a ton of milk into his tea. "When you and your sister were little, I was working midnight in Buffalo on the loading dock. Unlike Ontario, in New York state you can order a beer at 8 a.m. I'm no stranger to having a quick beer in the morning. But scotch? Where did you find this lawyer?"

I started guzzling my orange juice. "He's been Viking's lawyer for years. And since he's paying the bill ..."

Dad just nodded and drank his tea. "From what I heard" he said, waiting for his tea to cool, "almost everybody is getting out on bail tomorrow."

"What do you mean, 'from what I heard?'" I asked.

Our food had just arrived. "I still know some people, and I made some calls to see if I could help you out."

Dad did know a lot of cops, although he never involved me in any conversation with them.

"Jimmy, Phil, what did you call him, Viking?"

I smiled and nodded.

"Well, Jimmy, Viking, Chris and a few names I didn't recognize are all getting out tomorrow."

I didn't like the sound of that. And I didn't really like being at mom and dad's house with all these guys back on the streets. People had already died, and coming after my family to threaten me wasn't out of the question.

"Fuck that, Dad, I will ..."

He raised his hand, chewed his shredded wheat, and took a big gulp of tea, seeming to enjoy making me wait. "Well, after talking with your lawyer, I learned that you're remanded into my custody; but you can be left on your own if I have a family emergency."

I had no idea where he was going with this.

"I think your Uncle Morris isn't doing too well, and your mom and I should leave to go see him this morning."

What was he telling me?

"Listen to me, Ian. When your mother and I get back, you're done with everything, and I mean everything you're involved with. If you have to stay with us and I pay your way to finish your teaching degree, I will. But I won't have any part of what's going on, or what you have to do to get out of it. I've talked to Beatrice (pretty sure Dad was the only person who called her that) and your lawyer has agreed she can stay with you until your mother and I come back."

"You talked to Queen Bea?"

"Yes, I have. And she loves you. Forget all this other garbage, son. I don't know how you're getting out of it, and I don't want to know. But call it quits, go your own way, and take Beatrice with you."

He paused pensively. "Phil as your brother-in-law ..." he drifted off and we both laughed.

Viking as my brother-in-law? It was funny and terrifying at the same time. I could just see the family get togethers.

"C'mon, let's go" Dad drank his tea and paid for everything. "Your mother is probably sitting in the kitchen waiting for us." Then he slipped me a couple of hundred dollars. "When this is all done, you should take Phil and Beatrice for dinner. Those two stood beside you this whole time when all your other friends did nothing to help, or made it worse."

He had no idea how true his words were. I created the problem, but many people used it to their advantage.

"If you want to stop at the bar and get anything, we should do it now."

I shook my head no. It would be a perfect time to go. Just before eleven, there would be next to no one there yet. But there was nothing in my locker I needed — a couple of CDs, maybe a bit of Coke. I'm sure that Cody had rifled through it by now.

Most lockers there had a shelf life of about a week. If you weren't coming back, or were fired, or we just wanted your stuff, I would take the bolt cutters to it. Mostly it was junk that was left behind, but I've lucked out a few times. You could find

$500 some dancer was hiding from her pimp. Once I found half a pound of weed, broke it in two, sold some, and spent the rest of the winter smoking with Mac. Usually it's just a box of condoms or underwear. Vince and I found over a thousand hits of ecstasy at Heart's once. I never bothered with that stuff; but it was a weird few months, watching everyone float around on it.

We made it back to the house and Mom was sitting outside on the picnic table, suitcases packed, having a coffee and reading the newspaper. Dad walked over to her and handed her the keys. She knew what this meant. He always drove unless he had been drinking.

She smiled a little. "Must have been quite the meeting."

Dad went inside to use the bathroom, leaving just the two of us outside. Mom slipped me a hundred dollars. "That is in case you need anything in the house. And I expect Bea to sleep in our room. Alone."

My parents were leaving the country, so I could break every condition of my bail and mom was worried about Queen Bea and I sleeping together.

Mom and Dad weren't much for goodbyes, so they were gone pretty fast.

Queen Bea showed up within the hour, in denim shorts and an orange tank top. She had brought a bag with a few things, I guess not realizing how long we might be here. She wasn't one of those people who showed up with a warehouse of clothing for a couple of days. She threw the bag on the couch and then sat down beside me.

"You're out of jail and Phiw isn't?" she was the only one who called him that, usually as a taunt, but also because she had trouble pronouncing l's as a little girl.

"His idea. I guess he figured I couldn't handle being in a cell."

"And you're both being charged with murder?"

"Conspiracy to murder," I corrected her. She spun her hand in the air, while she waved the other one toward herself, as if to say, yeah, yeah, yeah, get to the point. I had forgotten that most of the hand gestures I used in the club and with Vince — I had stolen from Queen Bea.

She was really pretty as a kid and everyone I know hit on her. She wouldn't respond; she'd would just gesture to let you know she wasn't really paying attention. She didn't even talk to me for the first couple of months I knew her.

"I guess there's a lot to tell you." I grabbed two cans of Pepsi from the fridge. I basically caught her up from the morning she attempted to be our decoy so Viking and I could get into town. I ended it by asking: "Did the cop hit on you?"

"Of course he did. But as soon as you guys drove by, he hesitated. He seemed undecided as to whether he should follow you guys or keep working on getting my number. And he definitely wasn't one of the local guys."

"What do you mean?"

"Well, he had a Niagara Police uniform on, but wasn't familiar to me at all."

I didn't say anything, but figured they were bringing in newer faces so there would be no bias in arresting all of us. The Niagara police had a reputation for being notoriously corrupt. As much as people don't want to talk about it, the big gangs can't function without legitimate help from citizens, mostly cops, or anyone with influence. The belief is that unfamiliar cops wouldn't be as tempted to cut anyone a break or look the other way. That isn't always the case, though. Some people sell their badges or their authority to the highest bidder.

I went through everything I knew about the case, about the cops, laying on the couch with my head in her lap. The funeral, Viking and Stevie, Frenchie, the motel, and all that happened with Chris, Jimmy and every other guy with a bike in Niagara.

She didn't judge, didn't even really comment all that much. "So, Chris is in charge now?"

"I don't know. But he's clearly headed in that direction. Jimmy is done, and they should have someone local here looking after their action."

We both just sat there for a bit.

"I'm going to pick up Phil when he's released today. I should get ready to go soon. I'll take him to the farm, then I guess he'll have to make his way here." She started to get ready.

"What's the hurry? You can be at the jail in ten minutes."

I got the look. "Ian, we're not fooling around in your mom's house."

"It's not that."

"Well then, what is it?"

I just shrugged.

"Ian, tell me."

"Nothing, forget it." I went out to the driveway and sat at the picnic table. Queen Bea followed me outside.

"You know, I know this hasn't been easy for you, but what about me? You could both be in jail, and Phil is still there for helping you."

I couldn't argue any of that.

She sat on the driveway and looked up at me. "You don't want to be by yourself, do you? You know I'm staying here, right? I'll be back soon, you big fucking baby."

With that she punched me in the arm and kissed the top of my head. "I'll be back soon."

I didn't really want to be alone, she was right. I didn't know if it was fear or if I was just being selfish. The last five or six years had been a non-stop party. The only time I was ever alone was when I would disappear for a break. I took it for granted there will always be someone around. Someone is always up for a good time, someone always wants to join in. It got suffocating, seeing the same people at work, at the gym, at my apartment. It was like the movie Groundhog Day, with strippers, coke, booze and money. And as great as that sounds, it was starting to wear a little thin.

As soon as Queen Bea picked up Viking, she would call the house from a payphone. I would let the machine get it. The message would be her tapping the phone twice with her fingernail. No code words, nothing for anyone to interpret. If there was no call, she hadn't picked him up yet.

I did what most guys do when there is nothing going on. I turned on the TV and flopped on the couch. Even with the fifteen-hour sleep the night before, I immediately nodded off. I felt like I would have to sleep for an entire week to catch up for all the late nights and double shifts.

By the time I woke up, the room was dark.

Queen Bea was curled up on the other couch watching Jeopardy. "Hey boy, 'bout time you lifted your head. There's pizza on the kitchen table."

I began to stretch and slowly wake up. "How come you didn't wake me?"

"I tried about four times, but you were out. I dropped Phil off at the farm, then drove around for about an hour in case anyone was watching."

I reminded her that she was legally allowed to be at the house with me, but she didn't answer. Instead, we went upstairs to grab the pizza. I could have eaten the entire thing, but I slowed down so Queen Bea could eat.

"So, what did he say?"

"Nothing really. Said he'd be by tonight."

I knew he wouldn't tell her anything, but I had to ask.

"He said no one bothered him."

I was not surprised. The last couple of days had definitely added to his reputation of not being a guy anyone would want to mess with.

Queen Bea said he seemed kind of relieved to be out — not that anyone wouldn't be.

We ate in silence for a while. There was nothing to do but watch TV, act like an old married couple and wait for Viking to show up.

I immediately fell asleep. It was even easier this time knowing Queen Bea was standing guard.

Chapter 29

You and Your Fucking Plans

I slept soundly until around 8:30. Queen Bea was watching some show on TV, I wasn't sure what it was. I no longer knew what shows were on TV unless they played at 4 a.m. And even then, it was always old kung fu movies, how to get rich quick infomercials, or Gilligan's Island.

We hadn't arranged for Viking to call ahead, he would just show up when he decided to. What was going to happen next, I wasn't sure. Viking had led the game this far, so maybe I should just stay back and keep my mouth shut.

I couldn't see myself walking away unscathed, regardless of what the lawyer was telling me. But, as strange as it sounds, the charges weren't even the top thing on my mind. I had involved my friends and family, and as bad as it was looking for me, no one had turned on me, no one that mattered, anyway.

Whether I wanted to admit it or not, I was done at the bar. That didn't bother me. I had stayed there too long anyway. It wasn't a job, it was a lifestyle, one I thought was great, but no longer wanted to live anymore. Arnie, Tyler, Cody, I didn't care about any of them. Any new bar, legal or otherwise, was going to fall under the RCR's sway, and they had already made it clear I was out. I wasn't really losing anything, except the money.

Phil and I had that conversation in Toronto. Unless I was willing to get involved in the drugs, enforcement, or the violent side of the "life," I had nowhere to go. My little side hustles of weed, gambling and steroids were already finished. Frenchie had told me as much, but that didn't seem to matter either.

Now every cop in town knew, and even with permission to continue under the RCR, they would take the bulk of the cash. No side business, no job, I was clearly being forced out.

Queen Bea brought me more pizza and a Pepsi. "You're pretty quiet," she said, almost as a question.

I said nothing.

"You know the charges will get dropped," she offered.

"I'm not so sure. The cops are gonna make it look like I was a willing participant," I disagreed. "And the fucking prosecutors, who are going to make it look like I'm gangster Number fucking 1."

We both ate in silence. Queen Bea shook her head. "So, leave. Your dad already said he would help. You can stay with Phil. He has a lot more money than you think he does."

I just shrugged. "How can I ask for anyone's help now, after all the shit I've caused? My parents basically ran out of town, I've got no job, and I'm waiting for a guy to show up that I legally shouldn't even be talking to, let alone hanging out with ..."

I could tell she wanted to explode, but her words weren't all that harsh. "Hey, listen. You fucked up. Bad. Really fucking bad. But you're not dead, or in jail, and you still have people who want to help you. I can't believe your dad showed up at my place."

I looked up at her and turned my head, our long agreed-upon sign for "what?"

"He showed up at my place at four in the morning. I started crying. I thought he was gonna tell me that you or Phil, or both of you, were dead."

Tears were welling up in her eyes. "They both left because they love you, but they know this shit isn't done yet." She put her hands in mine and lowered her voice. "Do what you have to do, and then walk away. I'll come with you."

Well, that was a nice little surprise.

I wanted to make a joke about how it was only after I was charged with murder that she would take me seriously, but it wasn't the time.

"So, I leave, become a square teacher, and you'll come along?"

"Yes, I will. I knew you long before you got involved in all of this. I remember when all you did was work out and read. I wouldn't mind having that guy back."

She put the dishes in the sink and started running the water. I got up to help her and just put my arms around her from behind and stood there.

"And all those other girls go, as of right now. Right?"

I was going to answer, but we heard the backdoor open. Viking stood in the doorway. "Well look, it's Ozzie and Harriet. Any pizza left in that box?"

There wasn't, so we ordered another pizza. It wouldn't look good if he answered the door if anyone was watching, so we stayed downstairs. As we waited, Viking ate the leftover crusts from the first pizza and caught me up with what happened at the jail. "Those RCR guys got pull everywhere. The place is fucking jammed, and half of them got their own cells. The guys who didn't, were all housed together, which they usually don't do."

"What about Jimmy?"

"Jimmy is done. He must be paying those guys who have been hanging by his side — no one else will talk to him."

I saw the pizza guy pull up, so Viking went downstairs, while Queen Bea and I stayed upstairs to make everything look all nice and normal.

We brought the pizza downstairs and put the TV on loud, so no one could hear us.

"Chris?" I asked.

Viking shook his head. "Chris is the man, or pretty close to it. Got his own cell, guys are running his errands, bringing him cigarettes. This could all work in your favor."

"How?" I asked.

"Well, you never treated him like an idiot, and he seems to blame all your shit on Stevie. Pretty easy to blame a fucking dead guy. Makes me wonder how much Chris had planned this all out and just let Stevie hang himself."

I began to run all the events of the last couple of days through my mind. Stevie seemed to have everything under control, while Chris sat back like he didn't care. And Stevie followed us over the river, not Chris. There didn't seem to be any repercussions from us getting away from Stevie and making him look like a fool. There were lots of other little things, but I couldn't process them all at that moment.

Queen Bea got up. "You two need to talk about a whole lotta stuff I shouldn't hear." She hugged Phil and kissed me on the forehead. "I'll be upstairs watching TV in your parents' room. We'll sleep in your old room when you're ready." Viking raised his eyebrows and smiled but said nothing.

We waited until she was all the way up the stairs and Viking cranked up the volume on the TV even more. "Playing fucking house with my sister again? When are you two gonna stop?"

It wasn't time to talk about it, so I let his jab pass. I started giving him more examples of how Chris had changed. He had originally been furious when Stevie became a full-patch member. He was constantly scowling, and then it suddenly stopped. He didn't seem to care about Vince or any of the other stuff going on. We had that heart-to-heart talk in the park; but he might just have been playing me. And his attitude changed for good when the RCR bodyguards took him into his house to get his Burnt gear. Maybe he was given a sign that he was in.

"It makes sense. But he couldn't have killed Stevie. He was with us the whole time."

Why he brought that up I had no idea. If he didn't kill Stevie himself, he must have known it was coming and left him on his own. All my theories about what was going on had been pointless. I spent so much time worrying about Stevie that Chris just sat back and watched. These guys double-crossed each other all the time, so why would I think they wouldn't do it to me?

"So, what's the plan?"

"Well, I heard that Jimmy, Frenchie and Chris were all supposed to be out — not long after I was released. Jimmy might not have anything to say, but I bet Chris has a lot on his fucking mind."

I looked down at the ground and then closed my eyes. "I'm going to break nearly all of my bail conditions to get myself out of this shit, aren't I?"

"Well ... not everyone; but here are your options. You do nothing and sit in your parents' house, or we figure out what the fuck happened and get us out of it. And where are your parents anyway?"

It was my turn to catch him up. My dad going to see and bring back Queen Bea, my parents' sudden "emergency" and their subsequent exit from town. He seemed genuinely impressed about all of what my dad had pulled off to let me take care of my own business.

"Well," Viking said, pulling weed out of his boot, "Let's break that last condition. We'll have to roll it, Big Daddy is at the farm, if the cops haven't already taken him."

The weed did settle me down, but also made me edgy. "So, the plan?"

Viking stretched out on the couch. "You and your fucking plans. We'll wait 'til the bars close, then we'll go looking around. The cops are so fucking lazy they call it a night after the booze is cut off. I guess they believe nothing bad happens late at night."

We both smiled. Viking always loved taking any shot he could at the cops. And I thought it was funny because I was going to miss the late-night ramblings, eating dinner at 4 a.m., then going to bed.

We both knew that Queen Bea wouldn't be thrilled about our late-night plans, so we were just going to go without telling her. If she woke up, I would deal with it later, but I was really hoping she would pass out watching TV and we would leave without her realizing it. An electric company right-of-way ran behind my parents' house, so I knew from experience that we would sneak out that way. I'm pretty sure that's how Viking got in here anyway. It led all the way to Drummond Road, and Dorchester Road in the other direction. If need be, I could disappear into those fields. It shouldn't come to that, but it was on my mind.

Viking slept while I watched The Simpsons. No plan yet, just a 3:45 a.m. wake up call for Viking.

Chapter 30
It's On

At exactly 3:50 a.m., Viking sprung awake. "Let's go," he announced.

"Hold on, don't you want a coffee or something?"

Viking stretched out, and shook his head no. "Go tell my sister we're leaving."

That was the first I had heard of that idea. I thought we were just going to sneak out, and deal with the fallout later. And I told him so.

"Nope, deal with it now. She's put herself on the line for you. After all these years, you wanna fuck this up now? Use your head, Billy."

He was right. I crept upstairs to tell her. She was lying face-down on the bed, fully dressed. I sat down on the edge of the bed to touch her back, and she immediately rolled over. "You guys are still here?" she asked.

"How did you know we were leaving?"

She rolled backed over on her stomach. "Well, why else was he coming over? And besides, even with the TV cranked, you guys still talk way too loud."

I smiled and tried to thank her for everything. She cut me off with a wave of her hand. "Just remember what I said earlier, no more girls, bars, coke, none of it. I can handle Big Daddy, but that's it. You're not gonna get a second chance, Ian. I've waited a long time for you to grow up, but this is it. Maybe we can talk about all this years from now, but I want it over. Little Ben needs a dad, and I need a husband."

She was right. There was nothing I could add. I just nodded my head yes. She sat up and took off her tank top and shorts, then just laid back on the bed. "I'll be here waiting."

"Well, I don't have to go right now."

She started laughing. "Yeah you do. You can wait a little longer." She kissed me good-bye and said: "I love you Doc." She had never called me by my nickname before. "And when you come back, Doc doesn't. You're just gonna be Ian."

We left all of our I.D., personal stuff and phones on the kitchen table. Our plan was to go to 7-Eleven and get ourselves a couple of throwaway phones, use them tonight, then dump them in the river. We locked the back door and made our way through my parents' backyard. The chain-link fence was about five feet high.

"Watch this, Billy." Viking took off running, put his hands on the top of the fence and swung over. Not an easy feat for someone his size.

I was impressed, but I wasn't interested in trying it myself. I walked to the far end of the fence and walked through the doorway my father had installed into the fence. "Why didn't you tell me there was a gate?" he said, punching me in the shoulder.

"You never asked, Billy."

It only took about 10 minutes to walk towards Dorchester Road. Drummond Road was even closer, but we considered it too well-lit and decided it had too much traffic — even at this time of night. There was a time that the area we were in was considered the limit of the City of Niagara Falls. Further down, it was considered the Village of Chippewa. But with all the new subdivisions going up in the area, it was much busier and distinctions between individual communities blurred. More people, more traffic, more sameness.

It wasn't at all busy when we passed by, though. Actually, it was pretty quiet. Dressed in jeans and T-shirts, we knew we were unlikely to attract any undue attention.

As soon as we exited the field and were under a street light, a white van appeared, running the curb, nearly swiping us with a side mirror and stopping inches from our faces.

I wish I could say that I was surprised when Chris emerged from the passenger-side door.

"Where the fuck are you two going?"

Viking and I both turned instinctively towards the field but didn't start running. Chris held a gun up close to Viking, but not close enough so that he could touch it. He wasn't making the rookie mistake the guys at the farm made.

No such precautions applied to me, though. Some prospect kicked in the back and hit me over the head with something that dropped me to the ground but did not quite knock me out.

Chris looked over at me quickly, then brought his attention back to Viking. "Make a run for it," he said. "I dare you."

Chris waved Viking into the back of the van with his gun. I was pulled off the ground and thrown in the back like a bag of laundry.

Chris sat in the front, while one of Frenchie's guys was driving and the other guarding their prisoners. Maybe they were two different guys than I had seen before, I couldn't tell anymore. The guys who kicked and hit me were new. It looked to me like Chris was putting together his own little crew.

Chris lit a smoke and then threw us the pack. "Just where the fuck were you two going?"

Viking lit a smoke and pocketed Chris's pack. "Out for a stroll."

Chris pulled the pack out of Viking's pocket. "Shut the fuck up, Phil," he commanded, spouting out Viking's name as sarcastically as he could. "You're gonna tell me what's going on. Now."

Viking just shrugged.

Chris turned to me.

I shrugged as well.

"Fuck you two idiots. We're going to the Tree."

The Tree was a booze can that Mac and I had opened across the street from Heart's Desire. It started out as just a place to drink and bring the girls. As sad as it sounds, I still lived at home when I started at Heart's Desire, so I couldn't exactly bring home two girls and tell my parents I'd be downstairs doing coke off their ass cheeks.

From there, it grew, and we started making some really good money. Enough money that I moved in with Max and bought a new car. When some locals tried to shake us down for protection, Jimmy told them to back off. I'm sure Mac had to throw something Jimmy's way, but it never affected my cut.

The combination of booze, drugs, girls and Mac's "anything goes as long as no one gets shot" policy made us pretty successful. It was only a matter of time before every wannabe tough guy in town showed up. And the cops weren't far behind.

So, after the pressure mounted, we ran it like a rave, with no fixed location. It was always "meet me by the Tree" in case someone was listening. Even when we moved it around, it was pretty easy to find. If you couldn't figure out where we moved for the night, you weren't trying hard enough.

Mac shut down the original location when the 15- and 16-year-old girls started showing up. "That shit is gonna put us all in jail," he declared even if some, if not most, of the older guys were all for it.

These days, the original Tree location served as a late-night office when Heart's Desire was closed, or a meeting place for Mac's various secret conversations and scams.

"How did you know we would go see Mac?" I asked Chris.

"I didn't know for sure, 'til now. Why didn't you just come talk to me?"

"How, Chris? We're not supposed to be meeting or talking, any of us."

He scrunched up his face and waved me off.

"I'm fucking serious, Chris. Maybe this shit isn't bugging you, but I'm terrified." I seemed to be the only one who was concerned that we all had a murder charge hanging over all of our heads.

"You wanna see Mac?" he asked, turning back towards me. "We'll go see Mac. He fuckin' works for me now."

Main Street in the Falls had seen better times, so there was a fair amount of police presence in the area. That wouldn't help us.

The bodyguard guy driving parked the van at the side entrance of the building, and we all walked in. The rule always was that if someone was standing outside, you kept driving. If no one was there, you went in. As soon as you made it through one door, you were standing in front of a huge sliding metal door with cameras on both sides.

I knew the door code, so we didn't need to knock.

Even after 4 a.m., Mac was still impeccably dressed. No throwing on sweats after work for him. I'd known him for 10 years, and I don't think I ever saw him in a pair of shorts.

He stood up as we walked in, and although he would usually greet me first, he nodded quickly, then turned to Chris and gave him the biker hug, a handshake with one arm and the other in half a hug. "Congratulations my friend, it all worked just like you said it would."

He shook hands with Viking, officially addressing him as Phil. Viking nodded back.

The bodyguards and others were assigned to a table behind us. It was now only Chris, Mac, Viking and me.

"These two are out" Chris started, "of everything. That's how I want it."

Mac nodded solemnly and turned to us. "Unfortunately, our association ends, my friends. Don't take it personally, it's just business."

Man, how many times had I heard that over the last few days. "Why?" I asked. "I'm no threat to you guys."

"You're out" Chris repeated. "This isn't for you. I'm doing you a fucking favor. Wanna wind up like Stevie?"

Viking put his feet up on the table. "Fuck you, Chris."

Chris immediately kicked over Vikings chair and was on top of him.

Mac moved in and pushed Chris back. "Not here, Chris, not now."

Viking regained his composure and immediately sat down and put his feet back on the table.

Mac asked Chris to leave for a moment, so he could talk to us alone. Once he had left, Mac shouted: "Get your feet off my table, you fucking hick." Mac didn't usually talk like that and I was trying to make eye contact with Viking to beg him to back off.

Chris was pacing in the room behind us. This wasn't going to turn out well for any of us.

Mac sat down beside me and seemed to relax. "This is your last chance, Ian. Get up, walk out of here and don't come back. You are not going to get another chance. We have had this conversation before. This isn't the life for you."

He then looked over at Viking and told me. "Don't worry about him. He'll always be able to handle himself. But you should distance yourself from him too."

"What about Queen Bea?"

"That's your personal life, and you should keep it that way. Don't pull her into this. That girl has everything going for her, and she's begging you to leave. Go."

Then his tone softened. "You were so worried about Stevie, you didn't pay attention to Chris" he said as he lit three cigarettes, handing the other two to Viking and me. "Stevie wasn't meant for this life either, although he put up a good front. That worked with Jimmy, but not in the big time. Stevie was all flash and didn't pay attention to the details."

"So, Chris set Stevie up?"

"Not really," Mac replied, absent-mindedly blowing smoke rings in the air. "He just sat back and let Stevie mess everything up. Chris is a gangster, make no mistake about it. He saw what was coming and took care of himself. You know you're only alive because of Chris, right?"

He then stared at Viking. "How you're still here ..." he began, before his voice trailed off.

"So, I should kiss Chris's ass now that he's the king? Fuck that," Viking spat out.

Mac ignored him. He looked at me again. "Get up and leave. Don't come back."

No handshakes, no big blow-up, no teary farewell. I got up slowly from the table, trying to take notice of every single person in the room. For the first time since I began playing this little game, I truly feared for my life.

I looked at Chris, but he was already finished with me. As I kept walking, Chris began whispering something to his new crew. They immediately fell into line behind me. I was being separated from Viking.

While I was terrified, Viking showed no emotion, almost like he knew how this would all end. He looked down, then looked back at me and smiled. "Relax. wait for it." I had no idea what he meant.

As they separated us, I was being pushed out the door. All four surrounded me, while five or six more surrounded Viking, who was still smiling.

As they all pulled guns out one by one and pushed us toward the van, light shone everywhere. Suddenly, it was all yelling, uniforms, lots more guns pointed at me, complete hysteria. All I could do was laugh at the realization that I wasn't dead.

Instead, I was caught up in another raid. Viking was being beat down by the cops for refusing to get on his knees, laughing at them the whole time. Not as impressive as the last raid we had been caught in, but pretty cool nonetheless.

Chapter 31

The Beginning of the End

The suit who had thrown me the Coke was in charge, and he tried to make that fact look obvious. When he stopped to speak to me for the first time, the entire room, which was filled with lawyers and cops talking, papers shuffling, people mixing cream and sugar into their coffees, fell absolutely silent. It stayed that way until he leaned back in his chair and nodded his head. The nod of his head seemed to be the cue for everyone to get back to work, and they did. Immediately, the room buzzed with three or four separate conversations, presumably all about me.

Everything about this guy said: "I'm in charge." From the way he walked in to the room, to the way it went silent when he spoke, to the way everyone in the room would defer to his judgement spoke louder than anything he could say. He didn't look like the kind of hip lawyer they show on TV these days, more of a classic-style lawyer they used to. He wore a three-piece suit, and his shoes were shined to a deep gloss. He even wore a pocket watch, which he took out and played with to emphasize when he was thinking. My dad would have liked this guy right from the start. If he was trying to impress me, it was working.

Even Viking knocked off his constant stream of one-liners and insults. "Where do you think we stand here, sir?" he asked.

"Sir?" Nice fucking touch, Phil, I thought to myself.

Suit played with his watch, checked the time, closed it and let it slide down his hand into his vest pocket with ease. Definitely a practiced move. The little conversations in the room ground to a halt when the watch slid into his pocket. Everyone awaited his words. His command of the room made Frenchie look like a simple schoolyard bully.

"You have a long history with most of the men who were arrested." His measured, almost friendly tone reminded me of Tom Hagen, Robert Duvall's character in the Godfather. "The deceased was a friend of yours?"

I nodded yes.

"And Chris Parkinson? I assume it wouldn't be hard for any detective or lawyer to find pictures of the three of you together?"

Again, I nodded yes.

"What about Luc Moreault?"

That name didn't mean anything but I'm pretty sure he was speaking about Frenchie. Suit took a picture out and placed it on the table. We were definitely talking about Frenchie.

"There is some question as to how Mr. Moreault made his way into the country." More photos followed, capped off with Frenchie (who I then knew as Luc Moreault) and I sitting in front of city hall, making me tell him what the deal was between Jimmy and me.

"Before this meeting, you had no idea who Mr. Moreault was?"

The room fell silent again. I felt I should answer out loud instead of just shaking my head.

"No, we never met before that day."

"Did you know who he was?"

"I assumed he was a big shot with the RCR."

Suit got up, lifted an office window, and pulled out a pack of smokes. He offered them to me and Viking, but no one else. Viking took one, but I shook my head no.

Suit lit his and seemed to smoke half of it in the first drag." Mr. Moreault was born in Sept-Îles, Quebec. He made his way through a bunch of local gangs, but never hit the big time. Somehow, he wound up in the States, Indiana to be specific, and worked his way through the ranks of the RCR. He's been their point man in their concerted effort to take over Canada. When the province of Ontario resisted, he decided to look over the operation personally."

Suit immediately lit a second cigarette. "He's ruthless, been a suspect in a dozen homicides, and seems to prefer killing over negotiation. He's never failed in securing a territory for the RCR." He paused. "So, I guess the big question is ..." he sat back down as the room became quiet again, "... why didn't he kill you when you turned out to be so problematic?" Suit then sat down in his chair and waited for a response.

I sat back and thought before I spoke. "Look, I was never a member. Stevie, Chris, they were my friends since I was a kid. Jimmy, well Jimmy helped me out with ..."

Suit put up his hand. "I don't need to know any of that. And it's irrelevant to the case. Stick to the question, son. Don't ever offer up any information that isn't asked of you."

That made me pause to rethink my answer. "I guess there was just no point in killing me. It wouldn't have changed anything like it did with Vince."

Suit began shuffling papers. "Yes, your friend. This is where your story gets a little problematic." Again, the room went silent. If this was all rehearsed, it was still impressive. And intimidating.

"Your friend's father basically ran all of the gambling in Niagara Falls, New York, back when that actually meant something. Because of that, he had contacts and the backing of people in Buffalo, New York City, Florida and Pittsburgh. On this side, his influence drifted into Toronto, but not much further. Still, it was an impressive little empire for an eighth-grade drop-out who worked as a day laborer."

Vince never played up his old man and I never asked. Vince was supposed to go on to play ball with the New Orleans Saints. When that didn't pan out, he went into the family business, so to speak.

"And that was the beginning of your problems," Suit said, grabbing his smokes. "Gambling isn't what it used to be, with all the casinos popping up all over, OTBs, lotteries that sort of thing. So, your friend kept up the gambling, but also started to sell marijuana and steroids. He kept it small, but you joined in, too. So, there's no doubt in my mind there was some type of contraband crossing the bridge. Even though you've never been charged, you are going to get pulled over and searched by the customs authorities every time you cross for a very long time." That seemed to be the least of my concerns.

Suit lit another smoke and tossed Viking what was left of the pack. "You. You aren't walking away without any charges. The enormous amount of paraphernalia found on your premises looks like it came from a movie set. Your lawyer seems ready to fight any charges we bring against you due to the search of the farm. You've already stated through your legal counsel that you would look at a short sentence if your friend here walked away."

Viking nodded in agreement.

Suit looked over at Lenny. "Please ask your client to respond verbally for the record."

Viking finally spoke. "I've already agreed to that."

"Agreed to what?" I asked.

Suit grabbed his smokes and stood up. "You two need to talk privately. You can do it here." With that, Suit, Lenny, and everyone else filed out of the room, leaving Viking and me alone.

Once we were alone, I started in on him. "Wanna tell me what the fuck is going on. A deal? We're gonna start ratting guys out?"

"We're not ratting anyone out." Viking lit a smoke and sat back down. "The murder charges are gonna get dropped against us. If they could prove any of that other shit, there wouldn't be a deal on the table."

"And the deal is?"

"The deal is I do some time for weapons charges and running that still. Doesn't matter to me. They were gonna hit me with something anyway. No one rats, and you don't do any jail time."

"So how long has this all been in place?"

"Look, you gotta take the fucking deal now. Walk away, look after Beth, my kid, and Bea. We'll discuss all the details later."

I didn't know what to think anymore.

"You're not getting out so easy," he continued. "It's gonna be a long time 'til all this stuff dies down. Take the deal and walk away. You got no choice. Chris was gonna kill you, dude. I know you don't think so, but you just kept pushing. Going out that last fucking time was stupid."

"So, why did we?"

"We don't have fucking time for this, Ian. I wanted you to see how much you pissed everyone off. I can't go into all the details, but I had things in place."

"What things? What was in place?"

Viking looked up at the ceiling. "Your parents leaving. Bea at your place. The cops showing up. I can't tell you everything right now. Trust me, there will be plenty of time for that when you're visiting me in here. They promised me two years less a day, so I'll wind up in Thorold. Trust me. It's the only way out. You're a good guy, and probably my only friend, but you can't do time, you're too fucking soft. Look after my shit and my family, and it'll all work out. That's all I can tell you now. If not, we go to trial and they bring up every stripper you ever fucked, all the drugs, every bottle of Deca-Durabolin you ever sold. It's gonna destroy you and your family."

"So, you just go to jail? All fucking happy?"

"I ain't happy about it. Thorold is Thorold, but it's still jail. I'll be out in just over a year. None of these other guys will get such a short sentence, so I'll more-or-less be left alone. Enough yapping. You in or not? I gotta know. No more fucking talk. Fuck you talk way too much sometimes." With that I got the crooked Viking grin that scared the fuck outta people, but still got him phone numbers like that little salesgirl in the suit shop.

"Deal, Billy, deal."

Viking let out a huge whoo! that brought all the suits back into the room.

Lead Suit sat back down at the head of the table. "So, we have a working deal?"

Now it was Lenny's turn to do the lawyer shit. It wasn't over yet, but it was looking a lot better. A little more than a week ago, I was complaining about losing my DJ shifts, thinking of chucking it all and going back to school. Now, I would be walking away from murder charges.

It was a couple of weeks I would never forget, that would shape everything that would come after.

Viking and I were put back in the general room. That meant it was Chris's turn to be grilled. He wouldn't even look at us when he walked by.

"It's nice this is coming to an end," I said to Viking, as we watched Chris go into the room.

"Oh, this is far from being over, Billy. It's not the end, it's just the beginning of the end. Let's enjoy the fucking ride!"

Chapter 32

A Potential Goldmine

Being put back into the general area felt like home. It also helped me realize that I was a bit player in this drama, and I had just been given the break of a lifetime. My lack of foresight into exactly how vicious my old and new friends could be had nearly cost me my life, and the life of what now seemed to be my only real friend (I realized that Viking had genuinely looked after me out of concern and not what it could do for him). All I could do was sit and grin.

Frenchie had been removed from our little area almost immediately upon arrival. There was no doubt he was the big prize in the room for the cops. As I learned more about him, I realized that Frenchie was both the thinker and the doer for the RCR. He wasn't the Supreme leader, but definitely in the upper echelons. One of those guys who dictated policy and guided not only the day-to-day operations of the club, but their overall strategy and philosophy as well.

On paper, at least, Niagara should have been a simple acquisition for the RCR. There's a method to these takeovers that I had learned. To think that a "club" just decided to ride into town and take it over is pure fiction. Years of planning, negotiations, intimidation and promises are put into the process well before anyone shows up in force.

It starts with the reason why they want to be there. An existing club will only take over an area if there is something in it for them. The boys weren't coming to Niagara to hang out at the casino or enjoy the sights. Niagara Falls isn't simply the falls, Clifton Hill and Lundy's Lane. This town actually had two casinos, four strip clubs right within the city limits alone (thirteen if you counted the local region stretching from Fort Erie to Saint Catharines), a vibrant underground with a lot of drugs and a border crossing. These kinds of activities didn't make it into the tourist brochures, but they employed scores of people, legally and illegally. The local Italians had it all wrapped up for years and kept it pretty quiet.

Most of the old timers in the mob didn't make it to see the 1980s. They were probably the last era of Mafiosi that had the luxury of dying in bed. The next generation wouldn't enjoy that. They were ill-prepared to take over and got out-muscled and pushed aside pretty quickly. Law enforcement was also hammering relentlessly at traditional organized crime. The Italians who survived left the life.

And into that void stepped guys like Jimmy.

Jimmy got his start with the old timers, running errands and providing muscle. But he came to prominence when the less skilled (and less ferocious) new generation tried to take over. Jimmy still worked for them but began chipping away at their scams until he was on nearly equal footing with the bosses.

Next came a complex game of alliances — through divide and conquer, not to mention betrayal — that Jimmy played out in Niagara over the next fifteen years. The only thing that Jimmy used as a barometer in any situation was how it would benefit him. He got rid of guys who weren't cutting it, until he surrounded himself with a crew that were not only capable, but also absolutely loyal to him. They eventually became the only game in town. And that's what Jimmy wanted. It all changed when Frenchie showed up.

When Frenchie came calling, Jimmy followed the rules, letting Frenchie talk, but never agreeing to anything. Jimmy didn't want to be part of a bigger club, especially after spending years building his own little fiefdom. He had his connections, and he knew who owed him favors. Joining a bigger club and giving up control wouldn't work for Jimmy. "They will never figure out how it works here," Jimmy told me on numerous occasions.

And it looked like he was right. The RCR weren't above killing and taking new territory by force, but they had developed other methods. Simple in theory, and brutally effective. They'd figure out who's in charge and work their way from there. Competing gangs in the area? Make them fight each other and deal with the winner. The RCR had the backup and connections to make it work. Some alliances, a little prodding, and if that didn't work just start eliminating those who stood in your way.

It looked like Jimmy was right. This Niagara blunder had made Frenchie and his boys look like amateurs, held back by a bunch of locals who had destroyed their plans. Two murders, a ton of bad publicity and two arrests. To make it worse, Frenchie had never even made it to our meeting. But to be honest, I had no idea why Frenchie would be there anyway.

At the time, all of these things were running through my head.

Every time I tried to bring up the subject of our "deal," Viking would just smile and clam up. It was funny and annoying at the same time.

As soon as we sat down, Chris was ushered into the conference room with the Suit. It was pretty clear that Chris wouldn't tell them anything, because his meeting lasted less than five minutes. He was ushered back into the common area and just glared at the two of us.

Chris still had to show that Niagara was his now, or at least that's what he was trying to do. He sat down across from Viking and said nothing. All of his bodyguards stood up and began to move towards us. When Chris looked at them, he shook his head no. They seemed confused and just kind of stood there. Chris's annoyance boiled over and he told them to "sit the fuck down." They kind of all stood around, not understanding what they should do. One by one, they eventually all sat down, staring at us the whole time as if that would protect Chris.

Viking had the upper hand – and he knew it. He wasn't going to disrespect Chris, but he wasn't going to be spoken down to, either. As far as he was concerned, he was Chris's equal, and the RCR could go fuck themselves. Viking slowly locked eyes with Chris and asked: "What?"

Chris asked: "What did you tell them?"

Viking smiled and looked away.

Chris's rage boiled over and he tried to knock Viking to the ground. Viking simply side stepped him, letting Chris fall to the ground, but being careful not to touch him or act at all aggressively. Chris hitting the floor, of course, brought in all the bodyguards as well as the cops, and a major shoving match ensued. Chris was yanked from the ground, while Viking simply sat down and kept on going with that inscrutable grin.

That was the end of everyone in the same room. Chris was walked out, and his bodyguards just sat there, looking like little kids who had lost their parents in a department store.

All we could do was wait. It wasn't long before one for the Suit's boys came to bring us back into the conference room. The stress was killing me, and the Suit knew it. He put his hand on my shoulder and told me: "Son, relax, we just have to cross the I's and dot the T's. It takes time."

After a lengthy wait, Suit let one of his guys do the talking for the first time. "We see no direct evidence that either one of you knew about any plan to kill Stephen Inkster. Those charges against you will be dropped."

It didn't sound real. Were we cooperating? I wanted to know what was expected of us.

Suit read my mind. "You won't be asked to testify, you will be cut from this case. There is no deal. You will be released sometime in the next few days."

Those words couldn't be real. Suit threw me his smokes and sat on the edge of the table. "Son, your loyalty to your friends nearly cost you your life. Were it not for some planning by your family and friend here, you would have been murdered last night." He let that sink in for effect. "Your friend here won't get off so easy, though. He's looking at weapons charges and a few other things. I think the two of you should talk about the events of the last few days and what should happen next."

Suit grabbed his smokes and left the room, followed by his boys.

It was just the two of us. Viking gave up on the grinning Cheshire Cat act and told me to sit down. I did and had no idea where to start. A few days ago, I was a strip joint DJ, and even though I was tiring of the life, I always viewed it as a temporary thing. I saw myself as a mini, Canadian version of Goodfellas. I was making money, I had contacts, the party never ended. A continuous party, with broads, drugs and booze. I don't even know why I shared a house with Max, I never slept there. Between all the fucking around, I slept in my own bed a few times a month. Max knew that, and I found the occasional stray girl in my bed when I would come home. That didn't bother me. If she was up for playing, she could spend the night in my room. If she wasn't, she was downgraded to the couch.

That all came crashing down with Vince's murder. Nothing brings you back to the Earth like a murder can. From there, it just kept rolling. And it landed me here, walking away from murder charges. Some people will go to trial and take their chances, but I had no frame of reference that made me confident I could beat a prosecutor at his own game, on his home court.

I could probably go back to the bar, but that was pointless. Arnie would get off on telling everyone: "don't fuck with Doc, he walked away from murder charges." If the old cliché about perception being reality was true, Al would use it to his advantage, and I would be portrayed as some kind of stone-cold killer — hardly the image I wanted to cultivate.

Viking sat there just staring at me for a while before he spoke. "So, do you believe me now? We were supposed to die last night."

My only reply was to blurt out: "Well then, how come we're not dead, and why did we even bother to go see Chris?"

Viking shook his head and then went into serious mode. He spoke in a softer tone than I had ever heard from him. "Because you had to see how bad you fucked up, Ian," he told me. "That was the only way to convince you it was over."

Again, all I could offer was "how?"

"How what, Billy? How did we get out of it, or how are we not dead? Ya gotta choose."

I sighed as I realize that it didn't take him long to return to acting like a dick. My face must have flashed annoyance and a lack of understanding of what happened, because he began talking.

"After the raid at the clubhouse, I knew it was over, but you just couldn't see it. Jimmy was cutting you loose. He wasn't going to help you or Vince, and he told you that you were on your own."

I began to replay the meeting in my head. Viking paused because he wanted me to piece it together. I guess I took too long because he filled in the blanks. "There were no warm handshakes, it was all business. He was telling you that he wouldn't help you, and whatever happened next wasn't his problem."

After he paused to let that sink in, Viking continued. "Your father didn't want his boy to die, so he started talking to Queen Bea. Your parents didn't want to be directly involved but they thought you would listen to her."

I was trying to piece it all together. Queen Bea looking after me made sense at the time, but I didn't see any type of plan. "So ... the second raid? All that shit?"

Viking leaned back. "You can thank my sister. That was all her. She knew everyone was gonna fuck you over and she was right."

Viking wasn't big on details, but he was filling in the blanks. My dad thought I would listen to Queen Bea, and it only made sense to have her brother watch my back. "I thought we could trust Mac. That was a fucking mistake. Didn't take long for him to team up with Chris."

I just sat there, trying to process his information with how I remembered things going down. "Queen Bea decided to call the cops the minute we left your parents' place. She didn't trust anyone to help you."

"So, you knew we would get fucked?"

"Nah, but after what happened, could it have turned out any better? We owe her our lives. That was all her."

It was all too much to think about. "Getting arrested that last time just proved to all these cops and lawyers you're no gangster. You made too many dumb mistakes. Charging you over little shit now is pointless. And I'll take the blame for my own shit."

A lot of people had helped me get this far, and some luck didn't hurt either. I felt helpless, the footnote in what I thought was a story all about me. There was nothing to do now but see how it played out.

Chapter 33

All Publicity's Good Publicity, Right?

The trial put Niagara Falls on every Canadian and many American TVs and computer screens for months.

I was cut loose and tossed aside almost immediately; which, of course, I did not mind at all. Viking was almost immediately separated from the main case and charged with weapons infractions and running an illegal still. After looking at murder charges, he shut his mouth and took a sentence of two years, minus a day, mainly so he could stay in Thorold and not be taken far from his family. He offered no testimony and since his charges were not part of what the press dubbed the "Honeymoon Biker Trial," his own trial flew under almost everyone's radar.

You certainly couldn't say that about the RCR. At the cost of widespread bad publicity, they got what they wanted, Niagara. All they had to do was lay low in the area until the shouting dissipated to whispers.

The RCR were notorious for running heroin, which they couldn't do with so many eyes on them, which was good for the area. But when it inevitably happened, I had a feeling it would come with a vengeance and destroy a lot of lives. I could drink with anyone, and have snorted enough coke to stun a moose, but heroin, that's where I draw the line. Never saw the appeal in a drug that can kill you the first time out. Besides, I was terrified of needles.

I had actually gone almost six months without anything stronger than coffee. Until last night. When Queen Bea found out that her brother would be released in the next couple of weeks, we went out to celebrate. It was a pretty tame affair compared to what we would have done a year earlier. We settled for Pizza Hut, with a couple of beers beforehand. And quite a few after.

We had dropped Little Ben off at my parents' house, so it was just the two of us. Three beers in and I was bombed. "Let's get the pizza to go," I suggested. "We can go home, and I'll be the delivery boy. You can be the chick who answers the door naked and has a special tip for me."

Queen Bea rolled her eyes, laughed and kissed me on the forehead. "We have plenty of time for that later tonight. Your mom said we could leave Ben there 'til lunch. We're not going to have too many nights to ourselves soon," then her tone changed, but only slightly. "I can't believe my brother is getting out soon."

It did seem unreal. Between time served and Viking behaving himself in jail, he was going to be released in less than two weeks. He sat for a total of eight months, and it agreed with him. He started working out in the yard, and with a little chemical help, he had become absolutely huge.

He didn't take any chances in Thorold, though. His first day in the yard, he beat the shit out of a couple of RCR hangarounds he thought might give him trouble. "This ain't sports," he always told me, "hit them first, hit them hard, and a good kick to the face on the way down always helps." After that, he was given the jailhouse sign of respect. The others didn't walk beside him, or even dare walk behind him. They walked around him, usually avoiding him if they could. Other than that first fight, which the guards pretended they didn't see, he was left alone. It got so boring for him, he asked me to bring him a couple of books. Now, that was a shock. If it wasn't a car manual or something with a centerfold in it, I had never before seen Viking read.

Not that everything was all rainbows and puppies in those days. I had trouble adjusting to my new life. After being able to do whatever I wanted and always having the money to do it, staying home was something new. Staying in the house with Queen Bea, her son, Beth and Viking's daughter was fine, but I had to wrestle my baser urges.

School started soon. I had been accepted into the master's program at Buffalo State. I could have gone to Brock in Saint Catharines, but I figured no one would know me in Buffalo. I had already gone to the orientation. It was a nice, academic setting, full of a bunch of young kids who thought they were going to change the world. I could do the work, but I had nothing in common with these people. There were a few older ladies who had gone back to school after their spouses had died, but in general it was all kids. Not that much younger than me actually, but I felt a lifetime removed. All I could think was, I would burn down this whole campus for a bottle of Corona, a cigarette and a line of coke. It's strange what you think you need to keep you happy.

The itch was definitely there, though. I didn't go through withdrawal, but Queen Bea was adamant: no booze and no drugs. She would let me smoke, because she smoked, but without the beer and the drugs, cigarettes tasted like shit. So, I wound up cutting out all three, until tonight anyway. I did get a little cranky, but mainly it was just sleepless nights. You can't sleep after a little bit of partying? When it goes on for two days, you'll fall asleep at every traffic light. But now it was just two beers before the pizza, and my head was spinning. Times had changed.

I knew I could do the school thing, but I began to think of Viking. I began to wonder if it was really all over. The RCR weren't the mafia. They wouldn't wait for years letting someone get comfortable. Revenge would be swift and brutal. Queen Bea? my parents? Viking's kid?

Nothing too sophisticated. Gunshot, burn the house down, make sure it received attention. Jenny and her daughter, Millie? Arnie? All these people meant nothing to the RCR. I began to wonder who was going to pay for my stupidity. I had to live with that. There was only one thing that would clear my head.

First thing the next morning, I went to the Niagara Detention Centre in Thorold to see Viking. I had only been by a few times because Viking had told me not to bother. "Just put some money in my canteen fund and come back and get me when I'm done," he said. "Don't waste your time visiting." I had gone once or twice, but it weighed on my conscience that he was in jail for helping me. But he was surprisingly philosophical about the whole deal. I don't think I would have been if our roles were reversed. He would just shrug. "I was going to jail eventually anyway. You just sped the process up being so fucking useless."

Visitors couldn't enter the jail before 8 a.m. I parked and was immediately met by security. Two guards. First, they check the car, then they check you. Not too intrusive, but it's not a great feeling. I was escorted to the prison doors. I was told to take my shoes off and turn all my pockets inside out. I was checked thoroughly. Under the tongue, under the arms, crotch. I then made our way through double doors and was told to stand and wait. The doors buzzed open. I was escorted through the metal doors and told to sit at a long table. It wasn't like the movies. We weren't separated by glass, and I didn't have to pick up a phone. There wouldn't be any dramatic banging on the glass.

When they brought Viking in, he looked huge. He had told me earlier on the phone that he pounded out two guys on his first day and then retreated to his cell. The only time he came out was to lift weights or eat. He was never a little guy, but now he was a mountain. "Fuck that bodybuilding faggot shit," he always used to say, but now he was doing five sets of benches, five sets of deadlifts and five sets of squats, three times a week, running three other days, and taking one day off. It sounded suspiciously like our old workout from before our lives became overtaken with drugs, and murder.

Viking simply towered over his two guards, easily outweighing both of them together. The guy looked terrified, although the female guard kind of looked like she was in love. It always amazed me how many cops and prison guards ruined their careers sleeping with the wrong person. I guess I wasn't one to talk. Went right through a few girls at the bar until Queen Bea said it was her and her alone. Most dancers were pretty horrible in bed, simply because there was nothing you could do to them that hasn't been done a thousand times before. Then there were those who were so disgusted by men that they barely let you touch them. It was like having a Maserati and never taking it out of the garage.

Viking greeted me with a big smile, something that looked weird on his face. Not quite his familiar crooked, leering grin, but an actual smile. He sat down and immediately propped his feet up on the table, revealing his jail-issue flip-flops. For some reason that made me break out laughing. I had never seen him in anything but high tops or cowboy boots. "These," he lifted one leg, "are the most comfortable things I've ever worn. 'Cept for working on the still or in the garage, I'm gonna wear these all the time." We both laughed.

The skinny stick of a guard joined in the laughter, which changed Viking's disposition. "What you waiting for? A fucking tip? Go wait by the door." He did as he was told. He made eye contact with the female guard, who didn't go to the door, but gave us space.

"So future bro-in-law, I get pulled away from my breakfast to get told you're coming. No notice, and you've only been here, what, twice?"

"Hey," I shot back, "you told me not to come so much."

He rolled his eyes and leaned back. "Get to the point ... today?"

I didn't know precisely how to word it, but he understood.

"You wanna know if it's over?"

I nodded yeah.

"For you it is."

"How can you be so sure?"

"I'm in fucking jail, ain't I? I paid for your sins motherfucker."

I had no reply to that. He was being funny, profane and threatening all at once. He was the only reason I made it this far.

"Besides," he leaned over the table, "you're almost family now. If they come back, I just might have to get pissed off and start killing those fuckers. It's over." No trace of a laugh, or a joke.

There was so much more to talk about, but this wasn't the place. I had seen enough movies to know to limit my words. This wasn't the time for loose lips.

"So, what's going on out there anyway? You been doing more than nailing my sister?"

Now it was my turn to be the asshole. "Well, trust me, there's been plenty of that, but to keep myself busy, I turned your place into a brothel. Problem is, it turned gay pretty fucking quick."

Viking rolled his eyes again. "Yeah, turned gay. Like I haven't heard the rumors about you smoking pole." We both laughed. He got up and tipped an imaginary hat towards me. "Get the fuck outta here, go look after my kid, my old lady, my sister and your brothel."

I tipped an imaginary hat back at him.

As he walked away, he turned back toward me. "Hey man, thanks."

I had no reply, right away anyway. "Yeah, yeah, shut the fuck up before you start running your gate. We made it this far because of both of us." He motioned towards the little guard. "C'mon, Barney Fife, get me outta here."

As he walked out, I yelled out hey! He turned to look at me. We both looked at the female guard. He nodded his head and said: "I think I got a date for your wedding. If not I'll have to settle for that old wop's daughter at the dress shop."

I sat back down for a minute to collect my thoughts. How we pulled through was still a mystery to me. Apart, we would have failed. Together we practically rewrote biker history in the Falls. And fucked with a whole bunch of cops, wops, dealers and strippers along the way.

Just as I was getting ready to leave, two guards entered the room, easily Viking's size. I was pretty sure the one was even bigger. As a got up, I got the nod. The sweet old doorman nod. It was almost like our secret handshake. Anytime I wanted someone's attention without making it too obvious, or wanted to make a contact without touching them, I used the nod. Every cop, biker, wrestler, and wannabe I ever met used it. It was a way of saving face. If the nod wasn't returned, you moved on. Or you came back with ten of your friends and beat the guy through the floor for not responding. It got me out of a few jams and started a few others. It was pretty simple. You lifted your chin and looked to the left.

I lifted my chin and returned the nod. I didn't have any reason not to. Maybe he was someone from the gym, an old buddy I didn't remember.

The smaller of the two, who wasn't small at all, spoke up. "You're not done yet. Grab a seat." I sat back down but wasn't sure why. Maybe Viking had forgotten something. I sat back down, while another guard secured the door. I began to look around the room, not really paying attention, then for some reason stared down at my shoes. I rarely wore anything besides a pair of Doc Martens. I had worn this particular pair since university. One was actually held together with tape.

As I looked up, Jimmy was standing in front of me, with two hangarounds, trying to look as tough as they could. I sprang up in surprise.

Jimmy didn't stop walking. He motioned for me to sit down, and then did the same. He looked good. Back in the holding center, he looked like he had aged twenty years, a broken man, watching his life's work being torn apart. Criminal or not, Jimmy worked at it. There were no toy giveaways or P.R. stunts with Jimmy's version of the Burnt. People knew who he was and what would happen if you crossed him. He looked relaxed and fit. Jimmy hated lifting weights, but the thousand pushups and thousand sit ups a day must have still been in effect.

"Doc, I heard you were coming in today. A little disappointed you didn't swing by and not say hello." Swing by, like he was staying at the Hilton and wanted to catch up on old times. He had obviously gained some influence or contacts in the jail to find out so quickly that I was coming. I was on Viking's list, but had never just decided to show up like I did. The jail in Thorold was limited to sentences of two years less a day or shorter and didn't operate like a big lockup such as Kingston, but it was still a jail. The guards could have refused entry, but they had been cool. Now I began to wonder what Jimmy was up to. Maybe he played a role in me getting in here so easily after hearing about it from one of the guards. Jimmy didn't give a fuck about Viking. He was being pretty coy at best, although it was leaning towards being irritating.

"So, what can I do for you, Jimmy?" That came out wrong, but Jimmy let it slide.

"I need you to get a hold of a few people."

"Yeah, like who?"

"The one who's not dead."

It took a minute for my brain to let that sink in. Chris? That's the only one he could be talking about. I knew better than to ask why. "How am I gonna do that, Jimmy?"

Jimmy couldn't even bother looking at me. "You'll figure it out, kid. That's why you're so smart."

"I start school in a couple of weeks, why would I...."

"School, school, you've been saying that for years. I need your help kid. And you're gonna do it. I ain't asking again."

"Jimmy, listen to me. I got accepted. I start in less than a month. I'm done with the club, the bars, everything."

Jimmy scoffed, and spit on the floor. "Yeah, yeah, you're gonna play house with that retard's sister. You're not fooling anybody, you're one of us. You have been for a long time."

I had nothing.

"And if you go running to that giant goon and tell him what I said, they're gonna find him in his cell with his balls in his mouth."

The hangarounds got up and stood on either side of me. The guard looked up from his paper but didn't interfere.

I chose my words and my actions very carefully. "Jimmy, I know I owe you and all, but I can't do this."

For the first time in years, Jimmy looked at me like we had no history. He was scanning his brain. "You owe me?" I couldn't believe he couldn't remember. He didn't ask, but I blurted out the words "for Brian."

He legitimately looked puzzled, as a smile broke out across his face. He got up and had a look of bemusement and disgust on his face. "Brian? You think this is all about Brian. Fuck, kid, grow up. Be here tomorrow at the same time, we got some things to go over." He got up and started to walk out, leaving the threat on the table. "Do what I need you to do, kid, and it'll all be nice and easy for everyone, no bullshit. Try and run ..." he didn't even look back at me. He didn't need to. The hangarounds and the guards let me know in no uncertain terms that he was serious.

Just like that, I had the last ten years of my life erased, and the next ten fucked.

Chapter 34

Heated or Unheated?

"So, you want to drive to the jail to talk to Chris?"

"You're not going, Ian."

"That's not what I asked. And lower your voice."

Queen Bea was getting pissed, and I was trying to avoid an argument at my parent's house. We were sitting on the picnic table in their driveway. They had a long, L-shaped driveway. Before the garage and patio were built, we always ate outside on the driveway picnic table. There was another in the backyard, but this where we sat to eat and drink.

My mom was sitting at the one in the backyard, helping Phillip color. I'm pretty sure she heard every word, but unlike Dad who would have stormed over and interrupted, Mom would wait until later.

Queen Bea lit a cigarette without offering me one. The sight of someone smoking would usually bring my dad outside to sneak a drag or too. He had quit dozens of times but had officially quit a few years back.

As if on cue, the smell of the smoke brought him outside. "Where's your mother?" he asked.

We pointed towards the other picnic table and he walked over to sit beside Ben. Didn't even try to sneak a puff. Maybe he had really quit this time.

Queen Bea on the other hand, butt hers out and frustratedly lit another. “School starts soon, you going to tell your teacher you have to bow out early because you need to drop off some coke?”

I waved her away and grabbed the cigarettes. “It’s not like that. Jimmy is asking for a favor.”

She looked over at Ben and my parents. She lowered her voice, and her words were anything but happy. “They’re always looking for favors. How long before you’re running some club again? What did I tell you?” She began to get up and walk towards Phillip and my parents.

“I mentioned Brian.”

She stopped and came back to the table. “Why would you mention Brian?” I didn’t answer right away, so she sat down beside me and rested her head on my shoulder.

“Remember when I told you I had an in with Jimmy, a reason he always returned my calls?”

Queen Bea got up and sat across from me. “Jimmy didn’t care about Brian, or you, anybody, Ian. When are you going to see that? And why is Tyler calling your parents’ house looking for you?”

That was new. I hadn’t really talked to anyone at the bar since Viking shoved a gun in Tyler’s mouth. He had no choice but to call my parents. I had thrown the cellphone Arnie had given me out the window of the car when my dad had picked me up in the Thorold jail. Less than a handful of people had my real cellphone number, and Tyler certainly wasn’t one of them. No way he was calling on his own. I was almost positive Arnie put him up to it. “Queen Bea, I haven’t talked to any of those guys. That’s done.”

That was true. No matter which way my story went, going back to the bar wasn’t going to happen. I didn’t want to call the bar from my parents’ phone.

“C’mon let’s walk up to the 7-Eleven.” It had two payphones outside, so I could call that idiot back to prove to Queen Bea that I was never going back.

We told mom and dad we were going and invited Ben, but he wasn't interested.

As soon as we hit the sidewalk, Queen Bea hit me with it. "After all these years, why would you bring Brian up? You still feel bad, don't you?"

That was good question. I had never really discussed the issue with anyone, except having to tell Frenchie under duress, I guess. "I don't know. Jimmy looked at me like I was an idiot. I guess it doesn't mean shit to him."

Queen Bea grabbed my hand and kept walking. "Because none of it meant shit to him. You keep holding on to this idea that Jimmy owed you, and his guys did too. You have to see that now."

I didn't really respond. "Fuck," was all I had to say. I was a little more concerned about why Tyler was calling. No doubt it was for Arnie. Tyler and I weren't friends, especially after I punched him out in the kitchen and Viking smashed out his teeth the last time I was in the bar.

It was time to assure Bea I was never going back to work in a bar. As far as not talking to Jimmy again, I wasn't as sure, but I didn't tell her that. We made it to the 7-Eleven, and I didn't need to ask for any privacy. She swung the door open and asked over her shoulder if I wanted a rib sandwich.

Man, I realized that I've eaten a lot of those over the years. "Yes please, unheated."

That made her turn around. "Those things aren't disgusting enough, and you don't even want it heated? Ugh ..."

I just smiled and picked up the phone receiver. The number was tattooed on my brain. I was hoping it would get picked up by their voicemail, so I could say something like"I called you back, don't call again," but the new guy answered. Full of enthusiasm, I guess. What was his name again? Larry? Luttrell? No, Sean. That was it. "Hey, it's Ian."

Before I could finish, he was off and running. "Ian! Holy shit! Where you been? The last time I saw you was at Mints."

He was full bore into his conversation. But I can't honestly say I was really paying attention.

Queen Bea had just come out of the 7-Eleven, threw my sub at me, then sat on the bench by the payphone and lit a cigarette. She looked absolutely perfect; and she made listening to this guy go on about how he couldn't get into Heart's without me pretty uninteresting, so I finally cut him off. "Look, dude, I need to talk to Tyler or Cody." I knew Arnie wouldn't come to the phone. He was always afraid that any call might be from a creditor, or the police, or the mother of the last dancer who turned out to be 15. He treated that office of his like a bunker. His line of defense had been Vince keeping the outside world at bay. Now it was him calling the shots, protected by Tyler and Cody. That self-absorbed trio would destroy this place, I thought to myself. But I shouldn't care about them or the club. I wouldn't be around for it.

As the DJ babbled on, I thought it would be about Vince, or the arrests, or why I was gone. But this guy's biggest worry was actually how hard it was getting into Heart's without me holding his hand.

Maybe he was all right after all.

"Dude, listen, just tell Cody I called, and whatever it is, I'm not interested."

That got Tyler on the phone right away, all smooth, like we were old pals. "Duuuuuuuude, where you been. I've been looking all over for you."

"Tyler, whatever it is, I'm not interested. And I'm only going to say this once: Don't call my parents' house or show up there." That was Tyler's style. Everyone time he got fired, he would make it look like he was being begged to come back. The truth was a little less glamorous. He would call people in the middle of the night and go through his own version of a 12-Step program, although this one had fewer, simpler steps: Beg, threaten, harass, then beg some more to get his job back.

Then his story would change about how the place couldn't run without him. It must have been killing him that Arnie made him reach out to me. No one ever begged him to come back, and he had always been the better DJ, or so he thought.

I thought it might be fun to fuck with him a bit; but, before I could say anything, he started in again.

"Duuuuuuuuude, you got it all wrong, things aren't the same without you."

Yeah. The same. Tyler and Cody had to work now that I wasn't in the fold, and it became obvious after years of drug and alcohol abuse, they could barely function anymore.

It was time for me to twist the knife. "What's the matter, you fucking retard? No one smash out your teeth lately?" Losing a fight was always a sore spot for Tyler the tough guy. Long before Viking shoved a gun in his mouth and loosened a few teeth for him, I had knocked a few of them out one night in Heart's.

Arnie, or Cody, or both must have been in the room, because I could just hear Tyler's irritation, but he didn't bite. "Fuck ... yeah ... whatever ... listen, what's going on with Port Colborne?"

"How the fuck would I know? That offer is off the table. Don't matter anyway, I'm not coming back, and you can't DJ with no teeth."

That did the trick. "Fuck you, goof!" he shouted. That was Tyler's go to: goof. Supposedly, no self-respecting biker or anyone who had done time would let themselves be called a goof. Since I was neither, the word never bothered me.

"Hey, hey, we're all friends here." The phone had been taken away from Tyler, and now I was speaking with Cody.

I might as well keep it going, I thought. "Hey, it's the star of the show, the old has-been, still trying to cash in on the old glory days. You're fucking pathetic."

"What's that all about? Were just sitting here with Arnie, figuring out how to bring you back."

Christ, this guy's brain was shot. "Bring me back? For what? To do all the work so you can blow Arnie the Hutt to keep your job, old-timer? Retirement is around the corner, if I were you, I'd be saving my nuts."

This last crack made Queen Bea look over. She shook her head and muttered "here we go."

"You fucking idiots need me. That's the only reason you're calling. Stay away from me or my family." Whatever deals were made in the old days were done. These guys thought it was business as usual. They were in for a surprise. I thought I should keep going so I could get Arnie on the phone and take a shot at all Three Stooges, but Arnie wouldn't get on the phone. He was a step above these two, not a big step, but he wouldn't lower himself to screaming on the phone. He liked to do that in person, so he could play the tough guy.

I don't think they had any idea if how things were to change. It might look the same for a while, but things were to proceed differently. "Gotta go, Cody, don't call and try not to break a hip blowing Arnie." I figured he needed a nice low blow to go on. Then I hung up.

Queen Bea walked over and grabbed my hand. "That sounded like fun. You feel better?"

"Heh, heh, I do, actually. There was much more that could have been said, but I made my point. I'm done."

She looked up and smiled, just for a second. "Are you ready to have the same conversation with Jimmy?" She wasn't leaving me an out. I definitely couldn't talk to Jimmy the way I talked to those two, but her point was made. I would say the same thing, but maybe with a little more tact.

About the Author

Paul Lafferty was born on Staten Island, New York, and grew up in Niagara Falls, Ontario. He left university in 1995 with a bachelor's degree in political science. Like most political scientists, he spent the next 20 years working as a bouncer, bartender, manager and DJ, gathering ideas and stories for this book. He returned to university in 2006 to acquire a master's degree in education. He is currently working as a French teacher and trainer in basic self-defense techniques and weightlifting.

About the Publisher

Contact the Meager Press at themeagerpress@gmail.com.